TOM SEIGEL

CAUGHT ON FILM

CAUGHT ON FILM

a novel

Tom Seigel

Woodhall Press
Norwalk, CT

woodhall press

Woodhall Press, 81 Old Saugatuck Road, Norwalk, CT 06855
WoodhallPress.com

Cover design: Jessica Dionne Wright
Layout artist: LJ Mucci

Library of Congress Cataloging-in-Publication Data available

ISBN: 978-1-949116-42-7 (paperback)
ISBN: 978-1-949116-43-4 (electronic)

First Edition

Distributed by Independent Publishers Group
(800) 888-4741

Printed in the United States of America

Caught on Film is a work of fiction. Names, characters, places, incidents,
and dialogue are products of the author's imagination or are used ficti-
tiously. Where actual institutions or locations and real-life historical or
public figures appear, the situations, incidents, and dialogues concerning those entities, places, and persons are entirely fictional and are not
intended to describe actual events. In all other respects, any resemblance
to actual events, locales, or persons, living or dead, is entirely coincidental.

For Helene, Taryn & Carly

The plaintiff J.D. Salinger is a highly regarded American novelist and short-story writer, best known for his novel, *The Catcher in the Rye*. He has not published since 1965 and has chosen to shun all publicity and inquiry concerning his private life.

—*Salinger v. Random House*, 811 F.2d 90 (2d Cir. 1987)

An object at rest stays at rest and an object in motion stays in motion with the same speed and in the same direction unless acted upon by an unbalanced force.

—Newton's First Law of Motion

September 2015

"You mentioned the *Titanic*, didn't you? Don't tell me you forgot. Airtight my ass. I'm not paying $900 an hour for some glorified ambulance chaser. I want a goddamned, custom-made loophole. I'll be twenty-five in three months. You think I can play that part in my fifties? Let 'em try to toss me in jail. I dare them. I double dare them. I swear to Christ I am making that movie. You know what it means to me. I *will* be Holden Caulfield."

Brandon Newman slung his phone to the floor where it landed face up with a cushioned thud against a yoga mat. Its wallpaper flashed a paparazzi shot from the red carpet at the Golden Globes—Brandon, spray-tanned and tuxedoed, frozen in a gunfight pose with Harrison Ford. He yanked a five-pound kettlebell from a weight rack and smashed the glowing screen until it shattered and went dark.

"When did you stop?"

"When it hit the floor." Just beyond the scatter of shards, Luis Valladolid sat on an exercise bike, resting a professional-grade video camera on his lap. A muted Yankees game played on a wall-mounted flat-screen. Above the penthouse gym's glass ceiling, two enormous ceramic falcons, standing watch against marauding pigeons, cast long late-day shadows toward the East River.

Brandon slammed the kettlebell back to the rack and stepped over the fallout zone to snatch a caffeinated energy drink from the mini-fridge. "Did you at least get the money shot? The way I popped the heavy bag when I said 'loophole'?" In a mirrored wall, he checked the flush in his cheeks. "I was perfect." He toweled his head, spiking his sweaty, blond hair. "I bet you missed it. You should've set up on my terrace. Through the door frame, I said. Twice I said that."

"Sure, Brando, you told me, but the street noise, the shadows—"

"What are you talking about? I'm sky-high, twenty-third floor. Nobody ever . . . they don't listen to me. What the hell does USC stand for? University of Shitty Cinematography?" Brandon bugged out his eyes and tossed the oversize can to the trash after two sips. "Maybe I should've picked some pube-faced hipster from NYU instead." He ripped off a drenched Kawasaki t-shirt and flexed to inspect the reflection of his lean biceps. The fading track marks were barely visible. "You know I'm gonna make you famous."

Luis, bird-boned and man-bunned, with feral eyes, like Lin-Manuel Miranda, slid off the bike and reached for a dish of shelled pistachios next to a silver tray of chilled face towels. "I might have something to do with that, Brand."

Brandon tossed his wadded t-shirt toward Luis, who batted it to the ground. "Three months ago, you were squatting over a bodega in Washington Heights. Now you're crashing my loft and pimping my cred to sashay your ass past every velvet rope in the City." He wiped his face with a frosty cloth. "The favors I do for people, honest to God. You are not screwing this up."

"You want some pistachios, Brando? Or are you gonna fire me again?"

Brandon squinted like Luis had been speaking Spanish. "I *want* you to show it to me."

Luis adjusted the view screen and held the camera at arm's length. "It's good, Brando, tight on your face, the intensity, the singularity of focus. It's all right there."

"No, it's not. I told you. You see that?" Brandon's fingertips smudged the screen. "Even Hendrix over there could've done better." His rescue pit bull lay between elliptical machines, engrossed in the methodical destruction of a flip-flop. "My fist isn't even in the frame. We got to reshoot."

Luis pointed to the iPhone debris field.

"Get her on yours."

Luis spoke with his agent's assistant. "She's transferring."

"Put it on speaker, on the stool." Brandon threw a flurry of punches. "Working the bag, both hands."

"What now, Brandon?"

"Shari, *bubelah*." A trio of snap jabs. "Tell those stuffed shirts I'm about to shitcan their poison Ivy League asses." A forearm thrust to swing the heavy bag. "I'm beginning to understand why Plato wanted to have them all killed." Luis looked into his own armpit but kept the camera steady.

"First of all, number one, stop hanging up on me. We can't keep doing this. You think I won't walk? Who do you think I am? Broadway Danny

Rose? Second, number two, it was Shakespeare. Plato hated poets, not lawyers. Fourth of all, number four—"

"What about three?" Left jab, right cross.

"I'm getting to that. Fourth, I told you the law firm gave us a legal opinion, a very freaking expensive legal opinion. There's no way to break it. The Cornish Perpetual Literary Trust has got an ironclad ban against making *Catcher* into a movie. The CPLT and its briefcase brigade would slap an infringement injunction on us before you could say *Palme d'Or*. And they've got a war chest overflowing with royalty checks. Fool's errand, Brando. Nobody can touch that book until the copyright runs out in 2046."

Right cross, left hook, right cross. "What's number three?"

"Number three, don't *'bubelah'* me, tough guy. Your white-bread *tuchus* never heard of pumpernickel until we hosed that thick Oklahoma clay out of those corn-fed ears."

Brandon circled a weight bench, taped fingers locked behind his head, elbows out wide, like he was about to be frisked. "Why do I keep getting scripts then? Two more this morning. And not just zombie-eyed coverage twerps. Big names, Oscar winners, dying to work with me." He chased a double left jab with a right hook.

"You get those scripts, Brandon, because you plastered your pipe dream all over social media. That doesn't make them legal. In fact, if you'll recall, your unfortunate tweet got us an ever-so-polite cease-and-desist letter from esteemed counsel to the CPLT, brass knuckles inside a velvet glove. Remember what I told you. Kazan wanted it on Broadway. Billy Wilder, Harvey Weinstein, and Spielberg—*Spielberg*—begged Salinger for permission. All they got was a door slam in the face. You understand what I'm saying to you? You think *those* guys are used to losing?"

"I was born to play that boy." Brandon leaned against a treadmill, ripping boxing tape from his hands. "Let's duke it out in court. I could explain everything. A jury, that would be . . . I could make them understand. Remember *Mock Trial Club*? Three seasons, thirty-nine episodes, never lost a case. Holden Caulfield belongs to the world, not in the death grip of some rotting carcass."

Shari lowered her voice. "Brand, don't I always give it to you straight? Trust me. Even the miracle child can't pull this one off."

"People used to polish my head like it was a holy relic plucked straight off of Calvary. They won't stop me. They can't."

Brandon Newman's life, as he always told the story, had been saved by a drug overdose. His father, Chuck, a DEA agent, was running late for work. He turned his black Chevy Impala into a strip mall parking lot after receiving a "911" page from an informant. The snitch, a fellow Desert Storm veteran, had relapsed on crystal meth and rode a chopper through a storefront window. He had sent the red-alert code from an emergency room, terrified the local cops would arrest him. Chuck promised to be there as soon as he dropped his son at day care. After he shifted into gear, a thunderous explosion rocked the car. Toy dinosaurs flew out of Brandon's four-year-old hands. Chuck rushed him into a Walmart, flashed his badge, and left his son with an elderly greeter. The man with a blue vest and Santa Claus beard plopped him in front of a monitor in the electronics section and popped an animated version of *The Wizard of Oz* into a VCR. Shoppers and employees began to gather around the big screens, some slack-jawed, others crying. In the spaces between them, Brandon glimpsed images of dust clouds and smoke billowing into the sky, mimicking the dark swirl of the furious twister uprooting Dorothy's home. The DEA regional office had been in the Alfred P. Murrah Federal Building in Oklahoma City. A few of Chuck's coworkers—and all of Brandon's playmates from the federal day care center—were dead, victims of the worst incident of domestic terrorism in American history. On April 19, 1995, Brandon Newman had become a miracle.

"Brando, are you even listening? We got copyright laws for a reason. You know how much we lose on all those black-market copies of *Zombie Brigade*? If anybody could get permission, you're the only one. No question. Eastwood cheekbones, Presley sneer, Fisher Island blue eyes. Total package. But Salinger sealed up that book's fate inside of his coffin. No, it's worse than that, inside of a two-ton Egyptian sarcophagus. Forget it. Finish the *Megiddo Island* reshoots and take some time off."

Brandon swished the balled-up tape from across the room, his frozen follow-through like a long-necked crane. "I'm done with all that bull crap. I want to make *my* movies, *my* ideas. I'm through with all the product placements and the merch-ploitation." He spit into a laundry hamper draped with used towels. "I'm not gonna be shrunk down into an action figure anymore. Forget the next sequel. I don't care what they offer. Don't even call me."

"There's this house, Brando. Lake Como. It's primo. I'm telling you. The absolute best. I know a guy. Better than Clooney's. Late September—no crowds, private dock, indoor pool, full staff, high walls. You can do a couple of liquor ads meanwhile, limoncello or some other syrupy Euro shit. Easy money. Say the word and you'll be on a Gulfstream out of Teterboro next week."

Brandon pointed a finger at the phone as if Shari could see it. "Don't even mention George. You're the one who talked me out of reading for *The Descendants*. I would've been perfect for Shailene's sidekick. Instead, what do you do to me? You dumped my ass into that souped-up ATV chasing little green men all over Mars." He looked up through the glass roof at a darkening sky before letting his chin drop to his chest. "Nobody took me seriously after that." He lifted his head to stare straight into the lens and whispered, "This is not over. I swear it's not." He took the phone from the stool and held it flat in his palm, the microphone close to his lips. In a resolute baritone, his words flowed slow and hot like magma. "Get me a meeting, tomorrow, with the lawyers. This is not over until the fat lady sings, or until Jesus H. Christ comes back to tell me it's time to go. And *that* ain't happening."

2

Brandon stepped off the elevator and into the law firm's reception area. He wore a three-piece, charcoal gray suit, vermillion tie, and matching pocket square. "Fighting fire with fire," he had told Luis, who trailed him in ripped jeans and a *Barça* jersey. The quiet, airy space looked like a modern art gallery, or an ultra-chic spa—immaculate, curated, shiny surfaces everywhere—high-sheen hardwood planks, black lacquered cabinets with gleaming brass hardware, muted recessed lighting. Soothing silk paintings—water birds with toothpick legs, foggy mountain peaks, empty canoes on still waters—hung on a backdrop of beige linen wallpaper. Squat African statues perched on an array of white marble pedestals.

"Don't buy into this antiseptic feng shui bullshit." He waved his arm around like a game show model. "Spoils of blood sport." He patted the scalp of a stone-faced warrior clutching a spear.

The firm's office manager, a middle-aged woman with a bushel of brittle, bottle-black hair and a droopy navy pantsuit, met them at the receptionist's desk. She appeared dismayed by the camera but forced a smile. "Is this gentleman with you, Mr. Newman?"

"I'm filming a documentary about my movie."

"I see," she said, despite a blank stare.

"*The Catcher in the Rye.* You know, Holden Caulfield."

Her eyes brightened. "Yes, the one who shot Ronald Reagan. I recall that."

Brandon sucked in his cheeks like he'd eaten a sourball and drew his words out like a copacetic stoner. "Yeah, you nailed it all right. That there's the one." Two girls leaning over the back of a white leather couch burst at the deadpan remark. "What's so funny, ladies?" The pair, fifteen at most, snapped around, burrowing their faces into the safety of their smartphones. Brandon approached, pouncing on an opposing wingback. "You two must be in some deep shit to need this kind of firepower." The girls looked at each other wide-eyed, their faces contorting in failed efforts to suppress nervous laughter. "Seriously, I'm planted until you let me in on all the big yuks." The office manager hovered over Brandon, holding open hands at her waist, apparently unable to determine their next move. Luis stood behind the girls, using their heads to frame Brandon's face.

The freckle-faced girl sat up taller and rolled her pressed lips in and out, as if to reset and purge the giggles. "Holden Caulfield was all talk. He never shot anybody. John Hinckley shot Reagan in 1981. The police found a copy of *The Catcher in the Rye* in his hotel room. Mark David Chapman had a copy in his pocket when he killed John Lennon. He even started reading from it as soon as he dropped the gun." As she spoke, her thin lips revealed a mouthful of metal. Her straight strawberry-blonde hair tickled the back of a sleeveless lime green dress.

Brandon pulled a silver cigarette case from his jacket and a lighter from his pants pocket. Luis made a slow semicircle around the scene. The office manager tapped Brandon's shoulder. "I'm very sorry, Mr. Newman. There's absolutely no smoking in the building. City ordinances."

"Sure thing, chief." He lit a cigarette and jabbed it at the girl. "You don't sound like a juvenile delinquent. What's your name?"

"Alda. My father's your lawyer, Douglas Blackburn. This is my friend, Charlotte." Her companion—possibly Korean, short copper-colored hair, black-and-white polka-dotted jumper—dug an elbow into her thigh and smashed a palm into her face. She wouldn't raise her head to meet Brandon's eyes, remaining hunched over as if she wanted to slip down between the cushions.

"What are you two doing here, really?"

"Prep schools start late. We're roommates. Dad said we could come as long as we didn't bother you."

Brandon blew smoke at the ceiling. "Well, that plan went to shit." The office manager fanned with convulsing arms, warning of the imminent arrival of the authorities, as if making a statement for the record.

"Please don't tell my father." She tilted her head toward Luis. "He wouldn't approve."

Brandon snapped a dismissive hand, flicking ash into a dish of peppermint candies. "You've read it?"

"*Catcher*? Three times."

"But you're just a kid."

"No, I'm not." She glanced at the camera as if surprised by the bite in her voice. "I mean, I'm a junior. I skipped sixth grade. My mom teaches literary theory at Columbia." Alda tapped her foot as she spoke, jangling a tennis racket charm along a silver anklet chain. "He's not crazy, you know."

"Your dad? I know that, just obscenely expensive."

"No, not him. Holden. He was traumatized. He was trying to heal. Hinckley didn't understand it. None of them did."

Brandon snuffed out his cigarette on the September cover of *The Atlantic*, right between the eyes of a shriveling Henry Kissinger. "Exactly. That's what I've been saying all along." His voice softened. "They never got it. That he hadn't given up."

"Totally," Alda said.

The office manager cleared her throat. "The attorneys are waiting in the conference center, Mr. Newman."

Without moving his head, Brandon raised his index finger in response. "You're what Grandma Ruthie would call 'back-row smart,' aren't you, Alda?"

She shrugged. "I get good grades, if that's what you mean."

"Nope. Granny taught fifth grade at McKinley Elementary in Norman, forty years. Said the front row never coughed up anything but pure textbook, chapter and verse. The back-row brains, she said, always had something more interesting to say."

Charlotte, her head still down, gripped Alda's wrist and whispered, "That's totally you."

"Thanks," Alda said. "I hope you get to make your movie."

"Your old man says it'll never happen." Brandon sat up and checked the time.

"I think somehow you'll figure it out."

"Right on." He punched a defiant fist in the air. "Keep the faith, Back-row." He stood and swept a hand forward, asking the relieved office manager to lead the way.

"I've got some other ideas, if you're interested. About Holden, I mean."

"On the clock with pops . . . but why don't you text me later?" He offered his new phone. Alda's eyes fixed on the device as if it might explode. "Go ahead. Take it." She typed a number. A muffled two-note chime from her purse confirmed the connection. "Promise you won't sell that to *TMZ*?"

Alda clutched the bag against her stomach. "I promise."

Brandon winked at the office manager, turned to Luis, and pretended to slit his own throat.

Long-dead lawyers and judges stared at each other from the walls of the conference room. A retractable whiteboard hung at the far end of a banquet-size mahogany table. A firm employee in an unconstructed green jacket and soft-soled shoes rolled in a cart loaded with pastries and hot and cold drinks. Douglas Blackburn—early fifties, round pasty face, light gray herringbone suit, tortoiseshell glasses, and a Dartmouth class ring—extended his hand. "So glad you could make it today. This is my associate, Ernest Wong." A young man in a boxy, navy pinstripe stood two steps behind. Brandon offered a bro-shake followed by a fist pound finish.

"*Superheroes Under Siege* is, like, my favorite movie. I saw it three times opening weekend. Your superpowers and the effects, they were—"

Brandon shot out stiff, splayed fingers, like an angry sorcerer. "Yeah, I wish to hell I could've used those radioactive hands to vaporize the critics."

"I warned Ernest. Be ready for anything with this guy. He's no reinsurance actuary here to talk about misstated loss ratios." Douglas elbowed his apprentice, apparently to trigger a synchronized laugh at the unfathomable inside joke. "In all seriousness, we're genuinely pleased to have the opportunity to flesh out the opinion we've provided to Ms. Mishkin."

Brandon grabbed a bottle of sparkling water from the cart and sat at the head of the table. "You want to see the dailies?" Luis had remained in the doorway.

"I'm sorry, Brandon. Your cameraman can't be in our meeting. Aside from any filming being against firm policy—and your little *mens rea* documentary being a very bad idea, legally speaking—having anyone else in our meetings is not in your best interest. Our conversations are protected by the attorney-client privilege—secret. If a third party is present, the privilege is vitiated, broken. In that case, any of us could be forced to testify one day as to what we've said. You never want to be in that situation. Trust me."

Brandon told Luis to leave the driver and take the subway. Once the door had closed, he sprawled his arms on the table and lolled his head against a shoulder. "All I want is a sit-down with the trustees. Can't we at least do *that*?" He sighed. "No lawyers. If I could only explain." Douglas leaned forward, mouth half open, as if about to speak. Brandon held up a hand to muzzle him. "I want to tell them about me, about why, about what I've been through." He jumped to his feet and buttoned his jacket. His voice crescendoed as he paced. "They would listen. I could make them see it." Ernest kept his head down, typing notes on his laptop. "I know all about the big shots who tried to get permission, but I'm different. You know what happened, the thing when I was a kid. And the rehab. And there's other stuff, my parents. I could change their minds, no doubt."

"We can't imagine what it must've been like."

"Exactly. You can't. My whole life has been preparing me to play that role— the bombing, the con-artist preacher Momma shacked up with after my daddy left, the creeps at the talent contests, the wonderful world of Disney, and the drugs—all of it. I know that kid better than my own moronic chiropractic brother. Thinks he can cure cancer by cracking your neck."

Douglas flipped through a legal pad filled with red ink scribbles. "Your agent says you get blockbuster scripts on a daily basis. Pick of the litter. Why, then, choose a costly, lengthy, and ultimately, in our view, futile legal fight over an unquestionably good mid-century book whose pages are nonetheless beginning to yellow?"

Brandon stood nose-to-nose with a pen-and-ink portrait of an elegantly wigged English jurist. "I read *Catcher* practically every day for three months after Shari checked me into Elysian Prairies." He continued to speak to the richly robed judge as if no one else were present. "Holden calls BS on all the fakers and cock-yankers." He stroked his hair with both hands, pretending to try on a powdered wig. "You think I don't know what that's like? Televangelists, studio execs, the kiss-ass entourages. If he could've been right next to me so many times, I swear to God I wouldn't have had to say a peep, just looked at each other and laughed our asses off. And especially about what my momma turned into. He wouldn't have been fooled by none of her holy ghost smoke screens for a New York nanosecond. Holden saw through it all, bastard had x-ray vision for that crap. And he nailed it about Hollywood, dead right, what it does to you." Brandon spun around. "Whenever I picked up that book," he exhaled and pushed down palms like he was calming a troubled sea, "it was like putting on a pair of glasses I didn't know I needed. All of a sudden, the blur and the haze disappeared." He extended his arms like a slow-motion umpire. "I was safe." He braced himself on the table, his gaze fixed on Douglas. "People need to see what I've seen through those eyes."

"And perhaps to see you in a new light," Douglas said.

"Two birds with one stone, Doug, weaning myself off all that green screen crack money. Might even do this one in black and white."

"I'm afraid, Brandon, even if a trustee were sympathetic, that couldn't make any difference."

"Why not, Doug?" Brandon dropped to his seat.

Ernest's head popped up from the keyboard. "Douglas, if I may."

"Please," Douglas said with a be-my-guest wave.

Ernest dimmed the lights and cued a PowerPoint presentation on the whiteboard. "I've conducted a comprehensive review of the trust documentation." The first slide showed *Catcher*'s carousel horse cover next to a photograph of an aging J.D. Salinger in blue coveralls raking leaves at his secluded compound in Cornish, New Hampshire. He looked like an inmate on work detail.

Below the images was a quotation from an affidavit filed by trust attorneys to stop a writer from publishing an unauthorized novel about Holden Caulfield's adult life: "Mr. Salinger made it pellucid during his lifetime that *The Catcher in the Rye* should never have a sequel or be made into a movie. The trust posthumously memorializes this unwavering position in clear and explicit terms. Accordingly, for the foregoing reasons, we respectfully submit that this Court should grant the plaintiff's request for a permanent injunction and order the defendants to pay the trust's attorneys' fees and costs." Douglas noted that the would-be publisher lost the case and had to pay in excess of $200,000.

"Salinger," Ernest continued, "gave unambiguous directions to stop anyone from trying to make a film of *The Catcher in the Rye*." The next slide included bullet points with excerpts from relevant provisions. "The corporate trustees have no discretion to depart from these express mandates. If they were to try to give you consent, they could be removed and replaced, ordered to pay damages, and conceivably even held in contempt of court. Your pitch could be perfect, Mr. Newman, but it unfortunately could never persuade." Douglas smiled as if his protégé had provided irrefutable proof of the preeminence of his firm.

Brandon's phone, face up on the table, vibrated with a text. "Sorry, boys." He hunched over the screen. It was from Alda.

`"Wong's a first-rate party pooper, right?"`

Brandon's cheeks inflated like an airplane life jacket. He slapped a hand over his mouth and let his breath escape with a forced cough. "Hold on a minute, counselors." He answered her with a "thumbs up" emoji followed by a winking face. "Ok, Ernie boy, keep going."

Ernest displayed a table outlining the history of the trustees' zealous protection of *Catcher*—the lawsuits, injunctions, and attorneys' fees awarded. Douglas said that if the trust had not been so "ferociously litigious," there might have been a way to get around the prohibitions. He explained the doctrines of laches and estoppel, common law principles that forfeit property rights not regularly and uniformly asserted by the owner. "If the CPLT had allowed fan fiction, sequels, or prequels to be published without objection, we'd have at least an argument that they 'sat on their hands' so to speak and therefore couldn't stop you. But they've been like a thousand-eyed Argus. They'd get a restraining order just to stop you from publishing Salinger's old grocery lists."

Brandon's phone buzzed again. `"Dreamers don't follow rules or build prisons. Charlotte wants to know if you'll go to the back-to-school mixer on Friday? [heart eyes]"` Brandon strained to keep a poker face. He slipped the phone into a pocket and bounced to a chair next to Ernest. He shook the young man's forearm as if to wake him. "You sat in the front row at law school, didn't you?"

"Usually."

"You think if Jobs and Zuckerberg had listened to lawyers, you'd have an iPhone, or all those friends on Facebook? You do have friends, don't you, Ernie boy?" Brandon turned to Douglas. "You know what the great J.D. Salinger would say, don't you? Because I sure as hell do." He hopped to his feet, moving in front of the screen still coated with trust victories. "You lawyers are the biggest drips since Moses. Try to have a little fun in the freaking desert—sing, dance, be creative, just do something to distract yourself from the sand in your crotch, the miserable heat, the starvation and all—and then this sourpuss cop, I mean a real killjoy, tramps down the mountain to break up the party. That burns me up. Stone tablets or handcuffs. No fucking thank you. Dreamers never build prisons."

Douglas bounced his palm on the table like a gentle gavel. "Brandon, we understand. Completely. We would love to see you do the movie. So would my fifteen-year-old, Alda. She's a huge fan. I let her sit in the lobby today to get a glimpse."

"I didn't notice."

Douglas rose and waved his hand around the room. "Conference rooms and courthouses have never been mistaken for Parisian garrets or Silicon Valley garages. We get that." With glasses at the tip of his nose and hands on his hips, he looked like he was sizing up his latest opponent. "We're not afraid of a good, long fight—in fact, my last *Jarndyce v. Jarndyce* bought me a lovely summer place in Sag Harbor—but it's our professional obligation to tell you when a mission would be *kamikaze*."

"What about Roman Polanski?" Brandon asked.

Douglas glanced at Ernest, whose shoulders pinched at the puzzling reference. "I'm sorry, we don't follow. As a potential director?"

Brandon grabbed a dry-erase marker from a supply tray and ordered Ernest to clear the slide from the whiteboard. "Polanski's been on the run from a statutory rape charge for like thirty years, right?" As he spoke, he drew a rough outline of the lower forty-eight and marked it with a giant "X." The lawyers nodded in unison. "Right, so he stays out of the country, makes his movies in Europe." Brandon sketched a barely recognizable Great Britain, France, and the Iberian Peninsula, and with a swashbuckler's flourish, drew a clockwise circle around them. "I could make mine here, there, anywhere." He punched dots on each of the countries. "They couldn't touch me. You know what . . . of course, that's so perfect, why the hell not, he *could* be the director. Roman and old J.D. had similar tastes, after all, didn't they?"

"*Kinder* spirits you might say," Douglas let slip through a smirk. Ernest wagged a finger as if to scold him for the edgy German pun.

Brandon snapped on the cap and rolled the marker across the tabletop. "Exactly. I rest my case."

"Bring up the next slide." Douglas took a seat, and Brandon returned to the head of the table. Ernest superimposed a multicolored world map over the sketch. The different colors, a legend explained, indicated nations that had been a signatory to one or more international treaties on copyright protection. "Your agent asked us to scour the Earth. Extra-territorial production won't work in any of these countries."

"But a few of them are blank."

Ernest rattled off a list of rogue states and tiny island nations like Turkmenistan, Kiribati, Palau, and Somalia.

"They're not ideal, but so what?"

"It's not only logistics," Douglas said. "A United States District Court, and courts in most other treaty countries, could enjoin, stop, that is, any part of the process—casting, pre- or post-production, publicity, distribution, *et cetera*—from happening within their jurisdictions, even if you were to shoot the movie in some fringe state that would allow you to film, the only benefit being you couldn't be stopped while on location. You would, nonetheless, confront significant obstacles in ever reaching an audience or reaping any profit."

"Maybe I'll give it away for free."

Ernest raised a hand as if he were back in school. "Even then you would arguably be diluting the value of the copyright. The trust could probably stop you, and perhaps get damages, despite the fact a movie might actually cause a brief surge in book sales. You would still be looking at a potential injunction and a punishing award of legal fees and costs."

"And years of litigation if you want to fight through appeals," Douglas said. "But if you want to make it in Eritrea, which doesn't exactly resemble Pennsylvania or Park Avenue, pay for it all out of your own pocket, and put it online for free global consumption, you could reach the world, at least for a few days, until the trust obtains an injunction requiring all of the ISPs to take it down." Douglas stood and approached the copyright map. He tapped a spot in the Mediterranean, south of Spain. "Always wanted a villa in Majorca. You don't really want to do that for me, do you, Brandon? A short-lived victory, which in our considered judgment is the best-case scenario, would come at a huge personal and professional cost. Remember how the RIAA went after Napster? You'd end up being blackballed and broke."

Alda snuck back into the room through Brandon's pocket. "Make it and they will come. [baseball diamond, applause, moneybag, trophy]"

He put the phone face down and stood to remove his jacket. "What about those copycat skin flicks, Ernie, like *A Clockwork Orgy*? How do the guys in Van Nuys get away with it?"

Ernest looked to Douglas, who'd just taken a bite of scone. "Let me explain that." He wiped crumbs from his lips. "There are surprisingly few cases in which movie studios have tried to sue pornographers. The prevailing defense argument is that adult films are a form of parody—the First Amendment right to comment on, or ridicule, another's original creation. *Saturday Night Live* skits are a good example."

"Remember last year, when you hosted?" Ernest had interrupted without raising his hand. "That skit you did in drag as Clare Danes in *Gnomeland*, and that miniaturized Mandy Patinkin with the Papa Smurf voice? Something like that, which was awesome by the way."

Brandon, hands on top of his head and eyes to the ceiling, began to pace. "So, Doug, you're telling me I could make a porno version of *Catcher,* and they couldn't touch me?"

"The corporate trustees have a clear mandate to be aggressive. Therefore, I can't rule out a lawsuit, despite the parody exception, but yes, you would be on relatively safer ground doing an adult version—and the bluer and cheesier the better, I'm afraid."

Brandon stretched his hands high and wide like he was framing a theatre marquee. "You could be in it, Ernie. Picture your name up there in big letters and bright lights. 'Ernest Wong stars as *Holdon Cockwell*.'"

Douglas took a coffee mug from a credenza and patted his associate on the shoulder as he passed. "And you thought Sigma Nu hazing was bad." Ernest's fake laugh sounded like a car engine that wouldn't turn over. Douglas's icy stare silenced him. "Why don't you review the legislative angle for us?"

Brandon leaned against a wall, one leg up, flamingo style, his arms crossed. Ernest lowered his laptop's screen. "It would be impossible to reduce the current copyright protection period for at least two reasons, one legal, the other practical. Shortening the period could be deemed an unconstitutional taking of intellectual property. Even without the constitutional obstacle, however, the entertainment industry would launch a furious effort to thwart any proposed legislation, assuming you could ever find a congressional sponsor."

"In fact," Douglas said, "it's quite possible that Congress will actually extend the copyright period in the next few years."

"Why? Jerry's trustees got some senators in their hip pockets?"

"No, they don't have that kind of money, or directive, but some people do."

On the whiteboard, Ernest played a clip from Mickey Mouse's first cartoon, *Steamboat Willie*. While Mickey bounced and whistled down river, he described two occasions, in 1976 and 1998, when Congress, as a result of Disney's dogged lobbying, had extended the term of copyright protection so that the world's most famous mouse wouldn't enter the public domain. "The Copyright Term Extension Act of 1998, also known as the Sonny Bono Act, after the late congressman and entertainer, gives them a Mickey Mouse monopoly for eight more years, until January 1, 2024."

Brandon checked his phone for new texts. "None of this congressional, political crap even matters. If I can't make my movie in the next two years, it'll be too damn late." He pressed his hands against his cheeks and slid them toward his ears. "There's got to be another way. I have to do it now. I can't wait. I won't."

"I know you wanted us to be thorough. I wish we had better news."

"Let me see your glasses, Doug, for a second." Brandon slipped them on. "These specs might help you see me now," he squinted and shook his head before taking them off, "but they're for shit when it comes to seeing the future. It's like in *Field of Dreams*. Nobody else could see a thing in that cornfield until the very end." He put an arm around Douglas and brushed spread fingers across a distant horizon. "It was there all along. You just had to believe."

3

Brandon balanced an acoustic guitar on his lap in the backroom at Handel, a gastro-pseudo-dive in Bushwick, the frontlines of Brooklyn gentrification. Junkyard handlebars from rusty trikes, Japanese dirt bikes, and Harley choppers dangled at staggered heights from greasy chains. Amy Winehouse burbled bass clef runs from dark, vaulted rafters. Repurposed headlights and safety reflectors bounced low, uneven light. Sepia-toned photographs of mustachioed baseball players, barbershop quartets, and turn-of-the-century firefighters decorated the walls. Brandon had poured himself into distressed jeans and a strategically ripped vintage Motorhead t-shirt. He held a martini glass half-filled with a Messiah, a house special, fortified wine with a splash of myrrh. A cigarette bobbed in his lips as he spoke.

The club's owner, Josh Fiumara, perched on the edge of pool table, its faded red felt rails pockmarked by butt burns. He kept the private room for VIPs. An unmarked alley entrance provided inconspicuous access. Two years earlier, they had met at Elysian Prairies, a rehabilitation center outside Park City, Utah. A mutual love of motocross sparked their friendship. Though drug-free since rehab, Josh's long face was still overdrawn beneath Johnny Depp hair curtains, his Adam's apple ripe for the picking, his belt always cinched to the last hole. A trust fund baby from Short Hills, he left Bowdoin in his junior year to move to New York and open the club. In rehab, he had recommended *Catcher* to Brandon. "If misery loves company," he said, "you're not gonna find a better soulmate."

Josh snatched an eight ball from a side pocket and played one-handed catch while he sipped a club soda. "Believe me, buckaroo, the one thing I know is prep schools. Please. That's exactly how they are. Bull's-eye." His staccato voice had the driving tempo and certain cadence of an infomercial announcer.

"Everybody keeps telling me it's a wild-goose chase with a blindfold on." Brandon covered his eyes with one hand and flared it away. "Well, I'm not giving up. Why should I? Momma's got her savior, and I got mine." He strummed the foreboding notes before the lead vocal of "Wanted Dead or Alive." "Fucking lawyers, all they know is censorship."

A young woman, latex-tight black dress and snow-white cheeks like alpine cliffs, jumped from a circle of chairs in a near corner. "Bon Jovi," she shouted, drawing out the last syllable, her hands held high, her accent Russian. The young men surrounding her, shiny suits and slick-backed hair, demanded more Cristal between bursts of laughter and tipsy high-fives.

Brandon flicked a half-wave, acknowledging them like a performer beginning a familiar encore. "How'd they get in here?"

Josh checked to see if anyone was listening. "The *boychiks* from Brighton Beach? Doing something huge with credit cards. Please. I make them pay cash. They know better than to bother you." He pointed to a stocky male with a blond crew cut. "See the one with the giant crucifix?" Biceps bulged beneath the man's tight-fitting blazer. Christ dangled in the vee of his unbuttoned shirt, bouncing against a waxed chest. "That thing chipped a tooth last week." Josh thrust out his chin and smiled, using his tongue to indicate a jagged canine. "I should have made him take it off."

"Is it serious?"

"Nope. Dentist will cap it on Monday." Brandon let his head drop toward his knees. "I know what you mean, Brando. I'm not a moron." Josh flipped to an exaggerated Spanish accent. "He's a good kid, but no more *ménages con Jesus* unless he's Dominican, *papi.*"

"*Olé,*" Brandon said, punctuating the remark with a *presto* Flamenco progression. Two Russians broke from their circle and mimed a bull and matador.

"You're not jealous?" Josh winked.

Brandon shot up, his back stiff, his head cocked, watching his friend with one eye squeezed shut. "Dude, that was rehab. Whatever happened—"

"I know, Brando. Sit down. I'll stop it, all right? You're the original Fast Eddie Felson. Straight pool only."

"Tommy Cruise was in the sequel," Brandon said, returning to his seat.

"Is that a question or a statement?"

"I don't know. Could go either way." Brandon's knuckles rapped a rim shot on the guitar.

Josh flew off the rail like a jumping spider, his spindly arms and legs flailing, and plucked a cue from the wall rack. "So, which is it? Can't make the flick, or can't show it? What if you're only shooting it for yourself?" He rolled the stick on the table to check for warp.

Brandon played the opening lick from "Purple Haze." "This ain't about making a grainy Super 8 for granny's rumpus room. It would be ironic as hell, though. Salinger said he wrote a bunch of books in that concrete bunker that he never intended to publish. 'Oh, I want you to know about my other books, but only so I can tell you they're off limits, forever.' How could such a hypocrite write the greatest novel about a kid who hates hypocrites?" Brandon put down the guitar and grabbed his phone from a purple velvet footstool to reread a text Alda had sent him earlier that afternoon.

`"dad says you'd make a good lawyer. salinger's dad was a Jew who sold ham. cognitive dissonance from the crib KWIM?"`

Josh rolled the eight ball into a corner pocket. "How long are you gonna stare at that screen? Is it that Brazilian chic from the perfume ad? Dude, her straddling that elephant's trunk. Please."

"I broke it off last week. All she ate was microwaved lettuce." He looked at Alda's message. "What the hell is cognitive dissonance?"

"Definitely not the Brazilian. It's when your melon splits from trying to make sense of two things that shouldn't go together. Like, say, your mom or pop used to smack you around sometimes. Love 'em or hate 'em? What the fuck are you supposed to do? It's like that."

Brandon gulped down the rest of his drink and lit another cigarette. "And Jerry was the worst. Leave me alone, come closer. Read me, don't read me. Which is it? That shit would've driven Holden crazy."

"Even crazier, you mean." Josh took aim at Brandon with the butt of his cue stick pressed against an eye socket. "You want to get this movie done? My advice, dog-pound the legal beagles. Rules are booby traps for genius. If you can't fight city hall, you make your own detour. Find the guys with the shortcuts, the hookups." He put down the cue and thumped his own chest. "If I'd gone by the book, I'd still be boxed in by scaffolding, trapped inside a municipal regulation jail cell." He made parallel vertical fists and pretended to shake prison bars. "Work permits plastered all over the front door. Please. Get the ball rolling. Know what I mean? Inertia, Brando. Get up enough speed, they won't be able to stop you. Pi-choo." He blasted the cue ball into the railing, watching it carom at forty-five-degree angles.

Brandon took a drag and blew smoke through his nose. "I swear to God it burns my ass to think that of all people *Salinger* decides no movies, not ever. That hermit freaking loved the movies. I mean, who else keeps stacks and stacks of black-and-white reels? And he actually watched them all the time. That creepy shut-in probably made his teenage groupies curl up on his lap and sit through all that cornball shit from the Forties."

Josh cranked back his cue stick, holding it choked up like a baseball bat, scrunched a Popeye cheek, and did his best Jimmy Cagney. 'Say, what gives, doll face?' Brandon, smiling, pointed at his friend and tapped his own nose. Josh modulated to the bone-dry vocal fry of a millennial hipster. "Nice dialogue, Mr. Mayer." He stopped a server to order another club soda and a plate of chocolate-dipped bacon. "And what about what Salinger made Holden say about hating movies? Total scam, right? That boy is always pretending to be a movie actor—some spazzy tap-dancer, dude going blind, or getting shot and bleeding to death."

Brandon stared into the bottom of his empty glass. "Who's the two-face now, Jerome? Put Holden in a looney bin and tie up his story as long as you can in legal straitjackets." He replied to Alda. "Tell pops he could pick up some pointers from me in MTC. I'll send the boxset. school started yet? u should b [zzz's]"

Brandon picked up the guitar and, in a whisper, sang the slow opening lines of "American Pie," strumming on the beat. He snapped a chord mid-verse and stood the guitar between his legs, hands tight around its neck. "All Jerome managed to do by chasing after all those miniskirts was to turn himself into the same dirty old man, Chaplin, who stole his first girl."

Josh snatched his bacon order from the server's tray. "Please, I bet Jerry watched *Vertigo* all the time. Trying to get a do-over. Maybe that's why he went Hindu."

Brandon stood up to put the guitar in its case and backhanded Josh's bicep. "You hear the one about how Holden Caulfield starved to death in a five-star restaurant?"

"No, how?"

"They only served pheasant under glass, and he wouldn't touch it."

Josh pushed Brandon away with a two-handed shove. "That two-bit recluse couldn't even get bunkers right." Bacon dangled from the corner of his mouth like a flattened cigar. "They're supposed to be belowground, buried, like mine." Josh had become a fervent doomsday prepper after reading *The Road*. For months, he had been building an elaborate subterranean shelter on family land deep in the Pine Barrens of southern New Jersey. Brandon kept his dirt bikes there and would sleep over whenever they rode backwoods trails. "You want to come out for a few days? Kawasakis, bow-hunting, and all the canned goods you can carry." Josh stockpiled shrink-wrapped cases of freeze-dried meals, cartons of Mexican antibiotics, and a small arsenal of firearms for the impending apocalypse. He incessantly reminded Brandon that the Yellowstone Caldera was fifty thousand years overdue for a massive, cataclysmic eruption. "Don't forget Old *Fateful*," he'd say.

"Shari says I should go to Lake Como, kick back. She's got the Count of Monte Cristo's shack all lined up. What do you say?"

"That's a hard pass, Brando. Sicilianos don't go north of Rome. Come out to Jersey, bag your first deer. Dirt biking and brainstorming. I guarantee we'll find you a back door to the theater that's unlocked."

Brandon sat down to check messages.

`"don't worry Dad [winking face] friday night = NO school mañana [tears of joy] u should c campus. Totally Pencey. Plus there's a surprise you won't want to miss, if you want to know the truth"`

Brandon responded with a thinking face emoji and wedged the phone into a tight front pocket. "You know what? Give me a week. Pickups and a couple of reshoots in LA. Mind if I bring Luis?"

"Stay away from those so-called La La Land *amigos*. Remember what happened last time. Wait, is he Dominican?"

"Colombian, you moron. And he's not—"

"Bicoastal, I know. And no filming on the way in. I don't want people being able to track me down."

"I'll blindfold him."

"You can save that for later." Josh pulsed his tongue in a cheek.

Brandon leaped from the chair, wrapped Josh in a headlock, and dusted his nose with red cue chalk. "Better watch out, Rudolph. I've got an arrow with your name on it."

4

A week later, Josh roused his guests at dawn with the sadistic glee of a leather-throated drill sergeant on the first day of boot camp. Barking orders, he slapped their faces with riding gloves reeking of dried sweat. "Get up, ladies. Let's move. Let's move. Drop your socks and grab your cocks. Oops. Sorry, boys. Reverse that. Must've been thinking of last weekend. Time to motor." He sputtered a frantic drum roll. "Let's go. Let's go." He insisted they try a new spot before breakfast. "Pineys just built this tandem. Legit epic. Please. Locals only. Early birds, know what I mean?" Blasting an air horn at their backs, he chased them—disheveled, half-dressed, their mouths filled with morning breath—down fluorescent hallways made narrow by floor-to-ceiling gray metal shelving stacked three-rows deep with Costco-size cans and shiny metallic packages of "just add water" meals, past a wall of well-stocked gun racks, up a narrow flight of stairs, through a double-curtained decontamination chamber, and out the sham ramshackle cottage covering the bunker entrance.

After a night of hit-and-run thunderstorms, a cleansing wind scrubbed through the Pines. Puffy cotton balls dappled a piercing blue sky. With a GoPro strapped to his helmet, Luis followed Brandon and Josh, capturing their wheelies through straightaway puddles and air caught over trail bumps. After a bone-rattling squeeze down a long, single-file path stitched with knobby roots, they came to a broad, oval clearing. Josh inspected the side-by-side earthen ramps for traction and flipped a double thumbs-up. Luis raced past to get in position. He wiped the mud splatter from his lens and signaled the wannabe stuntmen, who sat revving their engines at the forest edge. Their bikes screamed like chainsaws until launch. They cranked their front wheels to the left in unison at the height of their jumps, right hands flung high like rodeo riders, and skidded to a stop for an extreme close-up.

Brandon ripped off his helmet and thrust his contorted, mud-speckled face toward the camera. His Neanderthal scream radiated like a shockwave. Josh stiff-armed Brandon out of the shot. "Evel Knievel, baby, back from the dead. I told you. Didn't I tell you? You want some, Louie? Switch helmets. I'll take the camera."

"No thanks. I better keep my feet on the ground. Nobody's covering these freelance bones."

"Cut," Brandon said. "Put that jump on my Instagram, but don't say where I was." He clucked his tongue and finger-shot Josh. "One hundred thousand likes within the first hour, easy."

Josh offered jerky from a Ziploc. "Gonna use it for the doc?"

Brandon bit a strip in half. "Nah, not very Caulfield." He sat on a sawed-off tree stump and unbuckled his muddy boots. "That boy sure as hell would never ride."

"That's not it, Brando." Josh hopped on his bike, grooved two furious circles, and stopped short, spraying more mud onto Brandon's caked feet. "Opening montage. Going for it. *You*. Kinetic physics." Josh's outstretched palms shook with emphasis. He stared right past Brandon, like Dennis Hopper brain-fried in *Apocalypse Now*, babbling at breakneck speed. "The outlaw with his pedal to the fucking metal. Blast off. Full steam ahead. You're like the Juggernaut, some unstoppable bullet train." He hopped off his bike and stood over Brandon, his hands flailing. "Remember: Inertia. Inertia. Iner—"

"Stop it, please." Luis palmed the side of his head.

Josh spun around. "That's the whole point, Lu. You *can't* stop it."

Brandon pushed off the tree stump to meet Josh eye-to-eye. "Make it and they will come."

Josh shook Brandon by the shoulders. "Now that's your rebel yell. No doubt, zilch, absolute zero. Holden wouldn't make a movie about himself, but that ain't *you*. Get what I mean? He's not man enough to grab a sword and charge into battle."

Brandon pulled a red bandana out of a back pocket and sat down to wipe dirt from his face. "But Salinger sure as hell would take out a ballpoint pen and poison all of his enemies with it."

Luis, still straddling his bike, cocked his helmet back to pop a handful of Advil and lit a cigarette. "Left all the swords behind—not even his own sword, other people's swords." He drooled smoke through pursed lips. "Holden Caulfield was one impotent *pendejo* from page *número uno*." He spit on the ground. "And we're supposed to pity the poor little rich boy, *pobrecillo*? This is exactly what I've been talking about. Enough with the precious Upper East Side malaise. Some punk lifted his fur-lined gloves? Give me a break. It's more like baloney on rye. Let that stick-up-his-ass Whit Stillman make the movie." He pretended to cough. "Dry as day-old toast."

Josh handed him a water bottle. "Must be one bitch of a hangover, Lulu bird. Pissing that unfiltered battery acid again."

"Yeah, his little brother died of cancer, and that sucked. In my neighborhood, back in the day, you know what we would've called Holden? *Chimbero.* Lucky." Luis yanked down the neck of his hooded sweatshirt to flash an R.I.P. tattoo. "My best friend, Oscar, got smoked buying his mom some Rolaids. Caught a bullet for the checkout lady." He took a long drag and used the toe of his boot to grind the unfinished cigarette. "Meanwhile, cashmere Caulfield's crying about picayune bullshit like it's just as bad as losing his kid brother. Trivializes everything."

Brandon re-fastened his bootstraps. "Jawboning yourself out of a job again?"

"Thought you hired me because I was the only one with the *cojones* to tell you to your face that most of your movies suck. And I'm telling you that moldy Holdy needs a major rewrite. That book is not as timeless as you think."

"Lucy, you may not like little lord silver spoon," Josh smacked his lips as he popped an invisible spoon out of his mouth, "but you can't unread him. That's the whole enchilada. And it's not some social manifesto. Okay, *Ché?* It's personal, down deep on the insides. Right here." He pressed two hands against a pancake-flat abdomen. "All bad books are forgettable in exactly the same way, but all the good ones, like *Catcher,* leave this permanent mark, like a branding iron." Josh sucked in air, eyes wide, like he'd solved a puzzle. He slapped Brandon on the back. "Now *that's* one helluva porn name, 'Brandon Iron.' Get yourself one of those Burt Reynolds 1970s 'staches and you'd be the triple-X G.O.A.T."

Brandon, hands on hips, struck a superhero pose. "Beats the hell out of Jim Steele."

Luis bent down to smear his hands in soft ground. "All I'm saying is if you want to write a war novel . . ." He rose to flash filthy palms. "Get your goddamned hands dirty. Don't hide inside private school walls and drown your preppie sorrows in midtown bars. But that's just like Salinger, isn't it? Talking about the war from behind the lines."

Brandon grabbed a Red Bull from a fender bag and returned to the stump. "You still don't get it, Lu." With no warning and a quick unzip, Josh pulled himself out and puddled onto the ground right in front of them. "What the hell?"

"Settle down, sailors. At least you know where not to step." Josh stretched his free hand high to make a roof. "*Catcher* goes one bigger than a world war. It's operating on this higher plane. J.D.'s not working from behind the lines; he's working *in between* them." Josh lowered the makeshift ceiling to flick his tip dry. "We are, every one of us, were at one time, at least, teenaged Holdens just learning to fuck, that we *gotta* fuck, or get fucked, and we come to find out that most people aren't just fuckers, they're—"

"Motherfuckers is what they are," Brandon said. "That's why Holden breaks your goddamned heart." He cocked his head, eyes closed, and held up a hand as if to freeze the scene. He replayed the dialogue in his head. "The stuff about *Catcher* being bigger than a war, about what people really are, and then I'll cut it off like I just did." He took a huge gulp of souped-up sugar. "We need to roll that. Josh'll borrow some of your smart-ass shit, Lu, and then I'll blast it out of the sky." They got it in three takes.

"I'm not paying you for screen time," Brandon said.

"Please. Don't do me any favors. Not even gonna charge you rent."

"What rent?"

"My place. Listen, and don't fucking laugh. Lu, crank her up." Luis waited for Brandon's okay. "Hit me last night during the storm. Swear to God, I'm not kidding. My shower room, the bunks. We're gonna *Blair Witch* this picture right here in the Pines." Josh screamed "total privacy" so loudly the sound seemed to bounce off the clouds. "I could hook you up with Piney coffee shops and fleabag motels. Out here is *the* place for guerrilla shoots. We'll start at one end, like *Ché* and Fidel, gathering steam all along the way, and plow Hollywood into the fucking ocean, like that fascist lecher, Batista, before it's over."

"Cut. Maybe you'll get scale, but out here," Brandon inflated his lungs, "it's way too Hallmark Christmas." He held up his hand like a witness. "I am through playing that shy neighbor kid who stutters and limps his way into your heart just in time for the holidays." He pulled out his phone and continued to ignore a two-day string of increasingly frantic texts from Shari about the press junket for *Megiddo Island*. Each new message had more capital letters than the last. He texted Alda instead.

"Backrow, can u show me school? TOTAL DL. [finger over lips]"

Undaunted by the location veto, Josh offered a contemporary treatment about a part-time postal worker. Brandon rejected it as too cliché. Luis countered with a job at an IT help desk. Josh laughed so hard he had to Heimlich himself to clear a wad of jerky from his throat. Once he could breathe again, he hopped up on the tree stump and held up his hands for silence. "You know who he'd be today? I tell you exactly who. He'd be that four-eyed, dickless snake in the grass who stole all the secret squirrel shit from the NSA and gift-wrapped it for the fucking Ruskies."

"Shari sent me a script about that guy. Dude's name even sounded something like Holden. Molden, Scolden, what the hell was it?"

"Snowden," Luis said. "Snowden Caulfield."

Josh jumped off the stump and snapped his fingers midair. "Bingo. Dude probably had his only little Jodie Foster crush, like Hinckley. And some slow-witted goon who used to take his lunch money." Josh pretended to seize a shorter man by the lapels. "So now little Eddie Snowden gets to snow them all, plus a lifetime supply of vodka, caviar, and all the Slavic ass he wants, compliments of the Kremlin." He thrust his fists forward as if tossing an imaginary Snowden to the ground. "I wish to God he would've had the balls to stay here and fight. Where the fuck are all the Snowdens of yesteryear?"

"He could've run to Bernie Sanders," Luis said.

Josh swung an arm around Luis's shoulders and pulled him close. "Snowden Snowflake was a real leftist all right. Soon as he could, that's exactly what he did—he up and *left us*. Please, he'd rather run to *Colonel* Sanders." Josh pushed Luis away and flapped his elbows, clucking like a nervous hen.

Brandon mounted his bike. "No way we can make a twenty-first-century *Catcher*. Nobody remakes without an original. I don't owe J.D. nothing, but this time, this one—*mine*—has got to be the classic."

Josh flung a rock into the woods, thumping it against a pine tree streaked chalky white with bird droppings. "Fun to dream, though. Caulfield the air traffic controller? You gotta admit that would be priceless. Pilots? Stewardesses? Please."

Brandon crushed his empty can under a heel. "When we're strutting down the red carpet, you'll know who was right."

Luis offered to staff a skeleton cast and crew with out-of-work friends from film school—discreet, cheap, idealistic, non-union. Josh volunteered laborers for set construction who would "one hundred percent keep their mouths shut." He had used a Mormon company based in Idaho that specialized in constructing doomsday bunkers. "Just let them think they've got a chance of converting you. Or I could round up some preppers. They love your movies, especially all the post-apocalyptic shit-shows. And we're pretty resourceful, good at building stuff and being inconspicuous when it counts."

Luis ducked behind a maple tree to spray its bark with the dregs of last night's IPA. "What about the trust?"

Josh put his hand up to silence Brandon. "What I said before. Freaking revolution, *Ché*. It's year zero, understand?" His eyes glazed over with a crazed glare. "From now on, CPLT stands for 'Crap out of Luck Trust.' *Ars gratia artis* and any other reasons we can throw up against the goddamned wall. A thing in motion stays in motion."

Brandon snapped off a robotic salute. "Aye, aye, captain."

Josh hopped on his bike to lead them back to the bunker.

Brandon reached into his pocket for a quick phone check.

```
"Away [football] game next Sat. campus empty
Darlingbrooke Hall in CT. c u at chapel 4pm wear
[sunglasses and hat]"
  "[Thumbs up]"
```

5

The next morning, while Luis slept in, Josh outfitted Brandon in camouflaged rain gear and dragged him on a three-mile, daybreak hike in a cold, stinging shower to prime deer hunting grounds. The Pines seemed abandoned, silent except for the persistent patter of raindrops on Gor-Tex. They followed hatchet notches rough cut into tree trunks. Despite Josh's preference to dress "full commando," Brandon insisted on wearing a neon orange trapper hat. "*Southern Comfort* is one of my all-time favorites. I'm not about to end up in some trigger-happy Piney's deep freezer."

Josh sang the first notes of "Dueling Banjos" in a nasally scat. "True enough. Whenever I see one of those top-loaders in the back of a garage, I always think there's a hacked-up body inside."

Around seven a.m., they hunkered down in a thicket of berry bushes bordering a meadow, its tall grass a seasonal beige, the blades tilting from the slant of a steady shower. Camo paint covered Josh's face. He poked at his eyes with two fingers, like a Navy SEAL, and pointed to a murky pond skirted on one side by a semicircle of low shrubs. "They come right through there." A strip of trampled vegetation cut through to the water's edge. A trio of mallards kept near the center, circling in tight formation.

Brandon, on one knee, inched closer to Josh. "Something about this spot. I don't like it."

"Don't worry. The inbreds don't get up this early. You're safe."

Brandon knew what bothered him. It was the ducks. They looked just like the mallards in his mother's watercolors. Sheila used to make him sit front-and-center with her pop-up displays after innumerable tent revivals. "Kids get more customers," she had said.

"Shouldn't those ducks be heading south?" Brandon asked.

Josh jabbed a cigarette into his mouth and roofed it with a cupped hand while he flicked a lighter. "Late migrants. Fucking common water rats. Never know when to leave."

Brandon wiped raindrops from his face and scanned for movement among trees on the far side of the pond. After the bombing, Sheila had given her son no choice but to live his life front-and-center. From Oklahoma fundamentalists to midwestern megachurches to national televangelists, she had charted a one-way path to his stardom. She became his manager, publicist, chauffeur, homeschool tutor, and vocal coach. A year after his father had left, she invited an itinerant evangelical minister with good connections to go on the road with them. The Reverend Holyfield (a stage name) trotted little Brandon, the "miracle child," up to the pulpit right before collection to chirp for their supper. He brought down the house every time with an *a capella* "Amazing Grace," striking a stiff pose when he got to the final "was lost but now am found," his gaze to the heavens, an outstretched hand showing the way to salvation and soliciting donations. His brother, Brock, three years older, was made to walk the aisles with a wicker basket until Sheila caught him skimming from the pot.

Brandon unconsciously popped up as he recalled the choreography of the old hustle. Josh hooked a beltloop and yanked him back to a crouch. "This ain't target practice, Brando. This is stealth bombing, *comprende?*" Josh braced himself against a boulder, using a small pair of binoculars for reconnaissance. "Salinger marched through a slaughterhouse in a forest like this. Belgium I think, or maybe France. He might not have been frontline infantry, but Louie's got it dead wrong. Jerome was in the legit shit, up close, fucking freshly chopped salad of arms and legs."

Brandon straddled a deadfall trunk crusted with orange lichen to inspect his bow. He drew back on the string, aiming at the oblivious ducks. "Salinger. It even sounds like a gun, like the heat you pack when you're not fucking around. 'Look out. He's got a Salinger.' It's like Salinger, Dillinger, know what I mean?"

"Derringer," Josh said.

"Exactly."

Brandon dismounted the fallen tree and sat on a wet carpet of greenish-white moss, his legs crossed. His father had seen young men and women die in Iraq but never had to kill anyone. At least that was what he'd said. Chuck worked in logistics, troop support. It finally happened in civilian life and much closer to home. He had to shoot a man tripping on PCP and waving a MAC-10 in the middle of a street. Brandon was two years old. Sheila blamed the eventual breakup of their marriage on untreated PTSD. She had said he seemed fine after the war, even after the shooting, but after the Murrah building, he had finally cracked. His supervisor and two close friends were among the dead. There was a picture of Chuck in the *Oklahoman*, the day after, carrying the lifeless body of a young girl.

The perpetrator, Timothy McVeigh, a name never spoken in the Newman household, had been a decorated Desert Storm veteran, like Brandon's father, before becoming radicalized. Within weeks of the blast, Chuck started drinking, staying out late, and smashing alarm clocks when he had to get up for work. He left the DEA within a year and took a job with a security contractor providing protection to oil company executives in Middle East hot spots. "Went Arab on us," Sheila used to say. Other times she said he wanted to be reunited with his flashbacks.

Brandon stood up slowly this time. He remained stooped over, pressing a finger to his lips to show Josh he hadn't forgotten the objective of their covert mission. He surveyed the shallow pond, too small to hold any fish, tadpoles at best. Josh, his hand flat, palm down, looked like he was slow-dribbling a basketball. Brandon complied, returning to a squat. "I've never even been fishing either. Must be the only kid from Oklahoma who knows shit about fish and game."

"When did your dad leave? You were five?"

"Six. Mom was too busy making me into a fisher of men. Turns out all she really wanted was a slick pickpocket." When Sheila wasn't pimping out Brandon at the pulpit, she was dragging him to immersions up and down the North Canadian River. Accounts of his pop-up appearances at open-air baptisms later became stock material for the talk show circuit. "I swear to God I should've grown gills," he'd say as he swiveled the backs of cupped hands by his ears, always getting laughs. "Back in the day, if you went noodling for flatheads anywhere in Central Oklahoma, you'd more than likely have pulled my ball-peen ass out of a mud hole in some god-forsaken riverbank." He must've used that line at least a half-dozen times.

"Is your dad still coming for Christmas?"

"Far as I know."

"How long's it been?"

"Couple years ago, when I was in Dubai. He loves it over there. Works for like three different security firms. He's got more stamps in his passport than the Dalai Lama. I offered him a job as a technical advisor on a Jackstone sequel, thought it might break the ice. Instead, he acts all offended, like he didn't need some handout from his rich, famous son. We ran out of things to say to each other in about ten minutes."

The recent birth of Brock's first child was the reason for Chuck's return, Christmas with the new grandson. Brock's relationship with Chuck had been as bitter and distant as Brandon's, but since becoming a father, his brother had been trying to reconnect. He invited Brandon to join them. Sheila, however, remained in exile. She couldn't have come anyway. A multistory billboard in Times Square announced to the world that she would be hosting a nationwide simulcast of the Fort Lauderdale Christmas Pageant. Brock had never forgiven her for treating Brandon like an only child. "At least Dad left us both," he'd once said. His brother used a personal shopping service to ship a crate of presents to Brock's new baby, but he had no intention of visiting.

"Saw your mom flipping past that 'Jesus Saves' network a couple weeks back."

"How long were the falsies?"

"Dude, it was bad, like she'd stuck a pair of daddy longlegs in her eyeballs before she went on camera."

By the time Brandon was twelve, Sheila had dumped Reverend Holyfield at the state line—too much dead weight for the shiny new Cadillac. A year later, before permanently relocating to Los Angeles, she had deposited Brock with her sister to finish high school. Even in the Caddy's ample backseat, there was no room for the less talented brother. As Brandon's fame grew, Sheila managed to collect her own stardust. She became a frequent guest on Christian talk radio and had a family cooking show called *The Daily Bread*. Her hair became bigger and blonder, her teeth whiter, her eyeliner darker, and her lips and politics redder. In 2008, weeks before the presidential election, a fundamentalist PAC featured her in a pro-life, school prayer ad. "I know a thing or two about miracles," she said, posing in front of the gargantuan "praying hands" sculpture at Oral Roberts University in Tulsa.

Brandon sat against a pine trunk and lit a cigarette. "When you saw her, she was doing that prodigal son bit again?"

Josh bowed his head. "Yep. Praying for your return and all."

"Can't believe there's still milk in that teat."

"You ever think about reaching out?"

Brandon used the inside of his hat to dry his face. "I never looked back." Months before turning eighteen, he had been planning his escape, discreetly enlisting the help of an executive producer at Nickelodeon to line up an attorney, an accountant, and Shari Mishkin to take over his management. On the morning of his birthday, he got up before dawn, left a fat envelope from his lawyer outside Sheila's bedroom door, and tiptoed to the garage.

Brandon pulled an arrow from his quiver and scraped an "X" in the ground, retracing it as he spoke. "She'd better hope I don't return to the fold. Me coming out as an unbeliever has kept her botoxed, powder-caked, self-beatified face all over the gospel channels. Fact is, she ought to send me a thank you card."

"Don't hold your breath for a bouquet of roses on opening night, Brando. You playing that snot-nosed, blaspheming Park Avenue atheist is gonna give her enough ammunition for a month of Sunday sermons."

Brandon scooted closer to Josh, who was still pressed against the boulder. "She'd make it all about her, as usual, me playing that godless grump out of spite."

"You have to admit, Brando, your movie would be a helluva potshot in her direction."

Brandon shook off the suggestion. "It's all about getting better, not getting even." He took aim at the lone drake. "Why doesn't this thing come with a laser sight? My props always got them. What if I want to red dot Osama bin Bambi right between his beady brown eyes before he gets wasted? Convert that bastard to a Hindu before the kill shot." He started to laugh, but Josh's hand slapped over his mouth.

"Keep your voice down, rook. Remember how we practiced. Steady draw. Slow breath. Focus. Broadside, double-lung shot." He thumbed a line across his own chest. "Got it?" Brandon snapped a salute. Josh opened a thermos and offered the first sip. "Coffee and schnapps, breakfast of champions."

Brandon took a whiff and spoke in a husky voice, like an elderly Robert Duvall reprising his role as Colonel Kilgore in *Apocalypse Now.* "Smells like, smells like . . . hell, I'm too goddamned old. Can't smell a freaking thing anymore. Maalox? Pepto? Who the fuck knows?"

"Sounds like it's safe to make other plans for Oscar night, Brando."

"I'll get my Oscar. You'll see. *Argo* won and that shit wasn't even good." Brandon used a stick to scrape black mud off the bottom of his boots. "Why'd it win? I'll tell you why. Because old has-Ben Affleck puckered up and planted a big, fat, wet kiss on Hollywood's ass. Told them exactly what they wanted to hear—moviemaking can save the world, free the hostages. Well, I'm gonna rescue *the* American character, the ultimate misfit who's been held hostage for sixty years. Now tell me who in the Academy ain't voting for *that.*"

They finished the thermos and took turns napping. No signs of deer for two hours. Brandon used Josh's backpack as a pillow and dozed on a bed of dry needles under a sprawling pine. He awoke to the feeling of a hand on his foot. "Sorry, Sleeping Beauty. That snoring, Jesus Christ. We're not calling moose over here." Josh held a trowel in his other hand.

"Keep watch. I got to go find a nice, quiet spot to pipe some fertilizer."
He headed back the way they came and veered over a low ridge.

Brandon scanned the water's edge. Nothing. The rain had petered to
a lingering mist. He checked his phone again, still no service, lit another
cigarette, and turned back to the water. A deer—no antlers, knobby
knees, wobbly gait—crept toward the pond. He crushed the cigarette
against a rock. The animal's eyes seemed to swell as it emerged from the
bushes. He nocked an arrow and drew back on the bow like Josh had
taught him. The deer lowered its head to the water and began to flick its
tiny tongue, a final kiss shattering its reflection in the glassy surface. He
aimed for the rib cage but didn't let go. His arms began to shake. The
strain on his shoulder was twofold, the tension of the bowstring and the
weight of his father, sitting there, exhorting him to finish her off already.
Chuck surely could have done it. He had enough guts to kill a man, but
Brandon had only killed extras with blanks. Stuntmen had fought all
of his battles, threw all the punches, took all the hits. His only swords
were made of foam rubber. His blood had never been spilled in battle,
only extruded from a tube. The arm tremors became more violent, the
strain unsustainable. He peeked over his shoulder to make sure he was
alone and surrendered, releasing the arrow into the pond. The low-angled
shot skipped off the surface without losing speed. Water sprayed along
its track. The mallards quacked in alarm, their wings beating a frantic
escape. The arrow ricocheted off a rock at the water's edge and sunk.
The startled deer leaped toward the brush and vanished into the woods.

When Josh returned, Brandon explained the lost arrow as a near miss,
inflating the size of his prey and shrinking the window of opportunity.
He shielded the feelings he'd experienced—guilt, frustration, shame,
inadequacy—behind a façade of quickly confessed impatience and resulting inaccuracy. After hearing the fudged account, Josh insisted they give
it one more hour. As they waited silently, fruitlessly, Brandon couldn't
stop himself from making the inevitable comparison. Would *he* have
been able to do it? Skewer the unsuspecting, blameless doe innocently
trying to quench her thirst? Not a chance. Holden talked a good game,
the best, saw all the angles, especially the ones most people missed, but
he wasn't much of a player. He'd scream at the umpires from the stands,
but would he ever grab a bat and step up to the plate?

Brandon took comfort in Josh's declaration that the two were not
the same. Play him, of course. Love him, absolutely. Commiserate with
him, even better. Recognize parts of him in the mirror, perfect. It was
never Brandon's ambition to *be* him. Outwitting Salinger and his lawyers,

succeeding where all the Hollywood moguls had failed, being the one to finally make the most famously forbidden film, that would require a completely different makeup—determination, fearlessness, ingenuity, execution. Envisioning the success of his against-all-odds project felt liberating, as if the production itself would be a kind of exorcism. To be Holden, ultimately, would be to overcome him.

On the return hike, they resumed a running game of dropping hapless Caulfield lookalikes into situations meant to drive them nuts—working the counter at the DMV or auditing tax returns for the IRS. "Brando, you know he'd be one bitchy Jimmy Olsen. Insane jealousy of that smug, self-righteous stiff of steel and secretly in love with that sassy tart, Lois Lane. What he wouldn't do for a chunk of kryptonite."

"Can you imagine a Holden in the military?" Brandon asked. "Making his bed with hospital corners, marching in formation. That kid couldn't even take the Boy Scouts."

"That would be the sequel, Brando."

Brandon clutched Josh's arms at the elbows. "That's genius. We'll do that, next. Definitely. He gets off the funny farm and decides to start a new life in the army, right before the Vietnam War."

"Korean, you mean."

"Whatever. Picture the boot camp scenes—knucklehead recruits, psychotic NCOs, tons of stupid rules."

"And lots and lots of live ammo," Josh said. "You could call it *Full Metal Straitjacket*. All the indigestion bubbling down in that boy's gut. Somebody's definitely gonna get plugged before it's over."

6

The afternoon ride to Darlingbrooke Hall lasted a little over two hours. Luis drove most of the way. Thick swaths of maple trees, their leaves woven like red-and-gold quilts, lined the Connecticut parkway. Supersize houses—three garage bays and at least as many chimneys—floated like mega-yachts on an open sea of wavy hills. Luis pointed to a marble mansion with a first-floor arcade and second-floor balcony that belonged on the *Piazza San Marco*. "It's like they're beating their chests for attention."

"Look at me. Look at me," Brandon said in the taunting singsong of an elementary school playground.

Luis thrust his head out the window and copied Brandon's rhythm. "*Épater la bourgeoisie.*"

Brandon got a text from Alda. **"Access Hollywood just set up satellite truck by front gate-JK don't b late [alarm clock]"**

He responded with the blood orange angry face. "I bet it's all lawyers and fucking radiologists around here."

"What you got against x-ray docs?"

"Antisocial twerps sit alone in the dark and tell you what's wrong but don't fix a goddamned thing. Film critics of medicine."

Brandon took the wheel of the black Range Rover for short stretches of road trip rants, a rehearsed litany of grievances about Hollywood's rampant incest and its epidemic of test-marketed sequels and overwrought remakes. He was burning bridges as fast as he could light them, convinced it meant freedom from the "tyranny of profit-driven mediocrity" and not career-ending self-exile. The lights and siren of a state patrol cruiser interrupted a naming-names gripe about the shameless sham of Auto-Tune. He got off with an autograph, as usual.

His longest monologue was about *Catcher*—about his dream of turning the most important American novel of the twentieth century into a movie, about how Holden would have hated being banned from movie theaters by an "overprotective Geppetto unwilling to cut the puppet strings" and held captive for another thirty-one years "behind the bars of some lawyer's paper-made cage." He cited as proof Salinger's reference to the Book of Mark: "In all of the New Testament, the one guy Holden Caulfield says he loves the most is that wild man who keeps breaking the shackles on his arms and legs, refusing to ever be bound again."

At the guard hut, Luis flashed a parking permit that Alda had sent. They passed through a mammoth wrought-iron gate hanging between weathered stone columns. Evenly spaced trees edged the gently serpentine path. Beyond a border of towering oaks, manicured grounds, blown free of fallen leaves, glowed an unearthly green beneath the late-day sun. A quartet of female students in their fall weekend uniforms, oversize sweatshirts and black leggings, played Frisbee on the lawn. Their wild flings traced opposing fishhooks in the air. Luis parked at the base of a broad red granite staircase leading to an imposing stone and mortar building with a roof line like a row of identical jigsaw puzzle pieces.

Brandon held up a hand to shade his eyes, surveying the soaring Gothic architecture. "Why are all these fancy-pants schools always like castles, or old-time prisons?"

"Keeping the right kids in class, Brando, and the wrong classes definitely out."

"Give it a rest, Vladimir." Brandon bounded up the first flight of stairs and waited for his close-up. He wore dark blue jeans with matching knee holes, Adidas Yeezy Boost 750s, and a white long-sleeve with a crimson "OU" (Oklahoma Sooners) logo. He swept his hand back toward an arch capped with a lion's head and twisted around to shout over his shoulder. "The barbarians are storming the gate." He turned back to the camera for a mischievous wink.

Passing beneath the archway, they entered a deserted quadrangle. A crisscross of flagstone paths sliced the lawn into triangles. Mature maples with clusters of stubborn leaves fluttering in the breeze anchored each corner of the quad like giant stakes on a picnic blanket. Brandon leaped onto the lip of a catch basin surrounding an empty fountain and did a front flip, landing with his arms out and one knee bent like a tightrope walker. He held the balance pose for dramatic effect then started for a building with a colonnade spanning its façade. "Don't forget to post that flip."

Brandon had received acrobatic training during his one season as Billy, the troubled teenaged lion tamer, on *Circus Freaks*. He'd thought that line in his resume made him a shoo-in to play Philippe Petit, a role he coveted in 2014, as soon as he had heard about the Robert Zemeckis project and watched YouTube newsclips of the French aerialist's 1974 spellbinding and illegal tightrope walk between the Twin Towers. "Bob loves you," Shari had assured him. When Brandon found out that the part went to Joseph Gordon-Levitt, he showed up at Shari's apartment at three a.m., drunk, vomited into a Lalique vase, and passed out on her couch. In the morning, she consoled him with coffee and a mix of sour grapes and sweet lemons. "He's all wrong for it," she said. "Too old, for one, and doesn't even look like the guy. So what if he speaks fluent French? Besides, it's strictly a tri-state draw, got no legs in Peoria." The movie's opening weekend coincided with his furtive trip to Alda's school. Brandon's advance screener of *The Walk* sat unopened in a box of DVDs at his apartment.

Beneath an ornate stone crest, the name "Blackburn Hall" in raised block letters peeked out from a tangle of green ivy with red highlights. "Shoot me from the other side." Brandon waited for Luis to set up at the end of the arcade then jogged toward the camera, picking up speed as he got closer. He extended his arms, airplane wing style, dipping from side to side, singing fragments from Pink Floyd's *The Wall* as he ran. He stopped short for a close-up and slapped a flat palm against the building. "Thought control." He plopped on a stone bench, slightly out of breath, and waved off the camera.

Luis sat next to him to check the shot. "Brando, what about adding a high-octane fantasy sequence at Pencey?"

Brandon peaked a doubter's eyebrow and pressed a finger against Luis's lips, keeping it there while he stood, to shut down the proposal. As he shook a bowed head with emphatic rejection, he felt a stream of saliva spilling out. He yanked back his finger and dried it on Luis's shoulder. "Fuck you, that's disgusting."

"*Quieres otro dedo?*" Luis held a down-flipped center digit toward Brandon's face, threatening to turn it up. "Even if it's the holy grail, you got to get rid of the dust and rust before you take a sip."

Brandon slouched against a column and swung up an impatient but obliging hand. "Give it your best shot, Fellini."

Luis put the camera aside. "That scene where Holden leaves Pencey for good, he's giving the school a giant middle finger, right? He's walking down a hallway in the dorm when he decides to bolt. While he's alone, right there, mind made up to bug out, you quick-cut to what he could be imagining—he's trashing a library, or a locker room. He TPs the john, maybe busts up a classroom skeleton." Brandon let his head drop. "Brando, stay with me." Luis stood to mime a demonstration. "You could use a plastic femur to smash a globe on a teacher's desk, like Kubrick's apes. Total silence, or maybe something like the *Hallelujah Chorus* in the background, or Jim Morrison, like when Martin Sheen kung-fus that mirror in *Apocalypse*. A few cutaways, that's all you'd need to crank up the volume on his 'kiss my ass' farewell."

Brandon locked fingers and pressed out palms to crack his knuckles. "The classic, Lu. Too far off script."

Luis sat down and pulled a rubber band from the breast pocket of his lumberjack flannel to make a ponytail. "The greats always add their own spice, Brando. Kubrick, Buñuel. Textual fidelity is its own kind of straitjacket. Not for nothing, it would be like a rage echo of when Holden breaks the garage windows the night his little brother dies. You got to flash to that too, mix them together. Bro, we've got to see *your* vision of him," Luis tapped a finger below his eye, "and that boy ain't shy about fantasy. It's all violence, escape, and messiah. Millennials would totally connect. It could have this first-person shooter game feel with a speed metal soundtrack. That book needs an amplifier, I'm telling you."

Brandon extended an open hand. "Hit me with a stick." Luis handed him a cigarette pack. After a few puffs in silence, he spun around. "Holden's not some flash-bang in a crowded theater." He held up the end of his cigarette to show the flickering orange in its ash. "That boy burns like a slow fuse."

Luis picked up the camera. "You want to shoot that line, right?"

"Not here. Strawberry Fields, Central Park, where Lennon got whacked. The Dakota in the background. See why I won't let you direct? When you read *Catcher*, you're always returning to the scene of the crime."

A campus security guard approached them on a golf cart. The young man—early twenties, premature dad bod, rusty brown hair, and puffy cheeks—wore a loaded-down equipment belt—a ring of keys, thin metal flashlight, pepper spray, old-fashioned billy club. "Can I help you fellas?" As he got out of the cart, "DUNBAR" (the name engraved on an ID badge) took a step back and exclaimed, "Holy shit. I know you. Sure I do. Jesus." He shook Brandon's hand like it was electrified. "Are you serious? Come on, now. My sister, she's gonna flip out when I tell her. She's got this huge poster, you in that wetsuit with the surfboard. Remember? *Mega-Tsunami: Last Ride on the Last Tide.*" Brandon accompanied Dunbar's familiar starstruck patter with a bobbing, indulgent nod while Luis, eyes fixed on his Doc Martens, muffled snickers. "What the heck are you doing here at DH? Geez, could I get an autograph? Or a selfie maybe?"

"Love to, but the thing is my cousin goes to school here, total hush-hush." Brandon lowered his voice. "Don't want to draw any unwanted attention. You understand, of course." He put his hand on Dunbar's shoulder.

"Yeah, sure I do. I had no idea. Really? Who is it?"

"Alda Blackburn."

Dunbar rubbed his chin. "Yeah, I know her. Pretty. Plays soccer. Red hair like Cathy's, my sister. Hey, you gonna make a sequel of that surfer movie?"

"Not unless they can dredge me up from the bottom of the sea. Yep, she's the one. Supposed to meet her at the chapel. We try to get together when the coast is clear, undercover, spy-like."

"I get it, Brandon, sure I do. What if maybe a whale gulped you up and spit you out onto the shore, Jonah-style?" He palmed his face. "I'm sorry. That's so stupid. Never mind. Geez, I called you Brandon." Dunbar held up his hands as if he were about to turn himself in. "It's like I know you. Must get that all the time. Gosh, I'm really sorry. You and your friend want a lift? I could take you."

Brandon bounced into the passenger seat and grabbed an unopened water bottle from an open glove box. Luis sat in the back.

"What's the camera for?"

Brandon took a drink before answering. "Home movie. A surprise for my aunt and uncle, their twenty-fifth anniversary. Need some shots with Alda. Her mom will cry her eyes out, a real waterworks for that kind of thing."

"You look just like you do on TV. So much better now than, you know, that other stuff a few years back. The *National* whatever-you-call-it sure raked you over good about that hotel suite in Maui and the rehab."

"What's your first name, Dunbar?"

"Rudy, you know, after the kid in that Notre Dame movie. My dad loves it, tears right up, just like your aunt, at the end, every time."

Luis slipped a stick of gum in his mouth. "Everybody loves the movies." He held out the pack to Brandon, who took two. "Almost everybody."

"These kids up here could really use a talking-to from somebody like you. Scared straight style, if you know what I mean. Twenty-four-seven pharmacy—pot, coke, X, you name it. Even crystal meth once. Confiscated a backpack stuffed with Oxy last week. What the heck these spoiled sports need painkillers for?" Rudy hit the brakes at a fork in the path. "You two got a couple of minutes for some serious fun? For real, I mean."

"Luis?"

"Quarter to, Brando."

"What kind of fun, Rudster?"

Rudy veered down a gentle slope toward the athletic fields. "You'll see. Trust me. You guys got to meet my buddy, Monty. He's the firearms instructor. Huge fan. The biggest. He's gonna freak out. Guaranteed. He's probably taking target practice. He'll totally let you squeeze off a few rounds. Taught me everything I know." Rudy took a hand from the wheel to pantomime a pistol.

Brandon had faint, fragmented memories of the waiting room at the Point-Blank Firing Range where Chuck used to go for firearms qualification. A teenaged girl in braces watched the kids who'd come along with their dads. She could shoot dental rubber bands with her tongue. Brandon and Brock would accompany their father whenever Sheila went out hawking Amway. There was a wooden crate filled with toy guns, a fire truck, a handful of army men, a few Barbies missing an arm or a leg, some scribbled up G.I. Joe coloring books, and broken crayons. When Brandon pretended to fire, he didn't have to make the "bang bang" noise. He timed his shots to match the pops behind the door.

He texted Chuck. "Going to a shooting range. Like at Point Blank. Remember?" He stretched his neck to examine Rudy's holster-less belt.

"Nope, not allowed on school grounds. Got a permit, though, for everywhere else."

Luis leaned into the front row. "You really teach kids how to shoot here?"

Brandon palmed Luis's face to push him back. "Fencing is so last century."

Chuck responded, "It's 23:00 over here. Just got off a double. Don't kill yourself."

"DH's got this big donor. I'm talking huge. Made it a condition or something. Place used to be a military academy, way back. Teach the kids about firearms, lots of safety, of course, and we get umpteen millions. The air rifle team wins a bunch of tournaments every year. Tops in the nation."

"The limousine liberals haven't lost their sustainably farmed organic shit over this?" Luis asked. "Or maybe it's because they got bulletproof windows in all those stretches."

"Heck, it's all safer than the Oval Office. We got the latest smart-gun technology, a hundred percent fail-safe. Nothing more than souped-up BB guns anyhow. Kids have to get an okay from the school shrink. They can always drop out. Do arts or crafts instead."

Rudy kept his foot glued to the floorboard, showing no concern for the frantic squirrels scampering across his route. He slowed down only when they passed a girl working a horse on a show jumping course. "Brats go ape-shit if we spook their pets. Some of them cost about a gazillion dollars. Monty went to school here too, but he's not uppity-like, not a bit. He's awesome. Benedict A. Montimbanco, but don't ever call him that. Monty got a bronze medal in the '96 Olympics."

An upright gray granite slab, flanked by a pair of black cannons, each plugged with concrete, marked the entrance to the "Reddington Family Instructional Range," a gleaming, glass-and-steel geodesic dome that looked like a lunar research outpost. Brandon jerked his head toward the engraved stone. "How'd Mr. Big Shot make bank?"

"Chemicals, I think, or pesticides. We call it the 'ReFire' for short. Get it?"

Inside, Rudy led Brandon and Luis, who had begun filming, past a row of deactivated metal detectors and a trophy case packed with little gold marksmen, to the shooting range—a dozen narrow lanes with concentric circle paper targets mounted on overhead trolleys at staggered distances. Stacks of gun lockers lined the back of the gallery. A sign prohibiting "ALL video or still photography" hung above a wall-mounted first-aid kit. In the far lane, Monty, tight camo tee and loose cargo khakis, stood sideways, his back to the trio, heavy earmuffs clamped over a shaved head. His erect left arm formed a perfect ninety-degree angle with his body. His shot ripped a hole through an outer ring. "Fuck," he shouted. He slammed the pistol down on a side table and turned toward the approaching men.

Rudy's face could barely contain its grin. "Not every day you get a visit from Lance Corporal Axel Jackstone, live and in the flesh."

"What the—Brandon Newman?" Monty ripped off his muffs. "No shit. For real?" He reached for Brandon's outstretched hand. "What the hell are you doing here? I gotta tell you. *Black Ops Battalion* was like . . . I've seen it, I don't know how many times." Monty, swiveling his upper body, mimed a spray of machine-gun fire with vibrating hands. "'C-I-and-A-men, sleep tight motherfuckers.'" He blew across the muzzle of an imaginary barrel. "Not bad, huh?"

"Brandon's visiting a student, relative of his. We got to keep that quiet, though. Right?" Rudy nudged Brandon.

Monty's head shook in disbelief, eyeballs still bulging. "Roger that. I was just telling somebody about that scene where you tossed a terrorist off the top of a mosque. That was some iconic shit." He reached out to shake Brandon's hand again. "You got family here? Thought you came from working stock. Must be the white sheep, I suppose. Buck or Doe?

"Doe."

"Yeah, Jane Doe." Rudy smiled and snapped his head back as if to say that witty banter was not beyond the reach of his stubby arms.

Brandon checked his phone. Alda had just texted. "c u in 5? paparazzi out front no worries come in backdoor [crying eyes out]"

"Monty, should we introduce our new friend here to the assistant principal? I was thinking they might get along."

"Absolutely." Monty moved closer to Brandon and lowered his voice. "Air guns are for jerk-offs. You ever get to train with some serious heat? Got one helluva of buzz saw, brand spanking new, if you want to let her rip."

"Josh would die of jealousy. I think I can spare five minutes for that."

Luis stared at Monty as if the man had told him that Mother Teresa was secretly in command of the Taliban. "You *actually* let teenagers shoot assault rifles?"

"What's the camera for?" With stars still in his eyes, Monty apparently hadn't noticed it. "Am I on *Punk'd*, or like one of those *Candid Camera* shows? Now I get it." He scanned the rest of the gallery.

"Don't worry, Montino. No pranks. He's my student, you know, the apprentice." Brandon aimed two finger pistols at Luis. "You're fired." He let the mock weapons drop. "Teaching him basic cinematography. Practice is all. Believe me he needs it. I swear I should make him stick his thumb up his ass just so it stays out of the frame."

Monty and Rudy laughed like they'd never heard a joke before. "I got you. No, the assistant principal is only for me. Not really supposed to keep him here, but he's always double locked. Only bring him out on weekends, real quiet, like this one." Monty scurried to a nearby office and emerged with the shiny weapon strapped over his shoulder and two new targets in his hands—ink-blot black featureless torsos. He bumped shoulders with Brandon. "More realistic this way. Matter of fact, I like to name them, sharpens the aim. Still using 'Osama' and 'Saddam' after all these years. The classics, they never get old." After hanging the targets,

Monty gave Brandon the rifle. "Hold it like you did in that scene when you rescued those hostages in Yemen." He adjusted Brandon's hands. "Relax your shoulders. There, like that, the trigger's easy and the recoil's light. It's like riding a tricycle."

Brandon made sure Luis was filming and spit out his gum. He took aim and swiss-cheesed a faceless man with twenty rounds. Paper kills he could handle. He made a snap pivot to the camera, rifle at his waist, chest heaving. "In a world where corporations own the rights to your imagination comes the epic story of one man's quest for freedom. Brandon Newman stars as a courageous young dreamer, an unlikely hero yearning to tell the truth, to show the world something new. The establishment doesn't want him to speak out, but he'll stop at nothing to let his unique voice be heard. Coming this fall to a theatre near you, *Kill All the Lawyers*. They won't be chasing ambulances. They'll be in them." Brandon whipped the barrel toward his second target and fired a fatal burst.

Rudy and Monty clapped their hands like groupies, high-fiving and whistling with fingers shoved in their mouths. "You just make that up?" Rudy asked.

"It comes sometimes, like speaking in tongues." Brandon twisted the rifle in his hands, examining it like a prospective buyer. "Hinckley could've done a little better with one of these."

Monty flicked on the safety. "Damn right. Saturday night special is a piece of shit for assassination. You get hit with this baby, you know you've been fucked."

Luis lowered the camera. "Brando, I think it's about time we go. You've shot enough unarmed black dudes for one day."

Brandon remained silent as they left even though he was tempted to correct Luis by reveling the identity of his imaginary victims, Timothy McVeigh and his accomplice, both of whom were undeniably and militantly white.

7

On the ride to the chapel, Brandon got a text from Shari. "MTV presenter. best new artist, next wk. UR in? told them ok already. Don't snub free pub. New togs from [Italian flag] coming soon. REMEMBER 2X tagged posts per wk thru xmas or no $$."

Brandon didn't respond, focusing instead on an incoming text from Josh. "The club tonight late – guy u got to meet. what u need = connections. capisce?"

"[Martini Glass]," Brandon replied. They agreed to meet at midnight.

After a round of handshakes and a scout's honor selfie, Brandon and Luis entered the decommissioned church. It was a Puritan's dream—unadorned wooden pews with hymnal racks and white walls interrupted by arched clear glass windows. The smell of pine-scented wax wafted up from the wide-plank floor. Two rows of bare-bulb chandeliers ran in parallel down the middle aisle. Where a crucifix might have once been nailed to the far wall, tall multicolored stained-glass windows hung decorated with wholesome scenes from Pilgrim America—the landing of the *Mayflower*, a sun-splashed, all-hands barn-raising, a bountiful Thanksgiving feast complete with smiling natives bearing gifts of maize and fish.

Brandon hadn't been inside a church for more than six years. Sheila would've hated this one. No stage lights or fog machines. With Luis shooting from the choir loft, he walked toward the altar, bouncing his hand against the pews and recalling when his head barely peaked over the seat backs. The faithful used to stretch their hands toward the aisle just to touch the square shoulders of his JCPenney navy blazer. He climbed three steps to study the trio of New England idylls. "Spayed and neutered, like I like it." He sat at a baby grand to the left of a naked altar and accompanied himself in the beginning of "Alice's Restaurant," segueing to the first stanza of "What a Friend We Have in Jesus."

As soon as he stopped, lazy claps echoed off the vaulted ceiling. Alda stood behind the back row. "Don't let them catch you sanctifying in here, or they'll have to call in a strict Unitarian to exorcise all the holy ghosts. Considered an invasive species."

"You'd like Black Sabbath better?" Brandon slammed a pair of two-fisted dissonant chords and jumped from the keyboard. Rays of sunlight streaked his face as he walked down the center aisle, imitating a solemn priest swinging incense and blessing the congregation. When he reached Alda, he gave her a playful shoulder shove. "They can't catch me anyhow."

"Where's your sidekick?" she asked.

Brandon pointed straight up. Luis waved from the railing. "What's with the spandex? I was expecting one of those pleated plaid skirts."

She glanced down at her outfit, black leggings and a light gray Arc'teryx fleece. "Today's my day off. Besides, I'm no Catholic."

"I wasn't trying to find out if you were Catholic. I'm just saying, most girls might've made more of an effort before meeting up with you know who."

She shifted her weight to one hip and rolled her eyes. "Sorry, your highness. I left my quivering lips at home."

"Where's your pal, K-pop? Bet she'd have been all decked out."

"*Hilarious.* That's *so* funny and totally not racist. Her name is Charlotte, Charlotte Ahn, and she's at an ice hockey tournament in New Hampshire. She's so over you already."

"They got cheerleaders for that?"

"Seriously? Listen, Turnip Truck, she plays on a travel team."

"Dude, she's like ninety-five pounds."

Alda's eyelids fluttered with impatience. "Everybody knows Koreans can't get into Harvard with perfect SATs and a violin case anymore. It's like 'been there, done that' to the power of a thousand. Char says it's not so bad, but I totally know she hates it."

Brandon had stopped listening, looking past Alda toward the chapel's front doors. "Where's the surprise?"

"You're not gonna find it in any church."

"I already know what it is. Glee club's gonna flash-mob me with a medley from that shit album the network made me record."

"I always liked 'Slow Motion Squeeze,'" she said. '*Taking my time. Ready for the replay—*'"

Luis, who had come down from the loft, echoed "*Ready for the replay*" in a pitchy falsetto.

"Stop it, please. Jesus, that crap sucked so bad. I'm serious, Backrow. I don't do patience."

"It'll be worth it. I promise."

Brandon craned his neck to inspect matching rows of glossy wood beams holding up the roof. "Everything here's a little too perfect, like a set of brand-new fake teeth." He smiled wide to shine two strands of impeccable implanted ivory. "How about a little plaque, some grunge around the edges?"

"My dorm hasn't been renovated for years."

Luis put a fist over his mouth to smother laughter. "Shari would have a coronary. A security camera clip of you sneaking into a prep school girls dorm looping over and over again on *Entertainment Tonight*. Very Jerry, though. You have to admit."

Once outside, Alda grabbed Brandon's forearm. "Maybe you want to hear some of my ideas first, about the movie?" He stared at her hand without responding. She popped open her grip and stepped back. "I sort of prepared some stuff, you know, in case." She pointed to a pair of freshly painted green benches in front of the chapel. "It's a good spot, isn't it?" A low wall of pruned bushes speckled with bright red dots of autumn fruit provided the backdrop, and an array of fallen leaves decorated the foreground. "Lighting's good too, right?" She swung an open hand toward Luis.

"What's Daddy gonna say about all this exposure?" Brandon asked.

"An IMDb entry totally jumps right off the page of a Brown application. Douglas will so learn to love it."

"Shoot first and ask questions later," Luis said.

Brandon twirled an upright finger in the air and sat down on one of the benches. "Now you're finally starting to understand." Alda joined him and waited for Luis's cue.

"It's a truth *almost* universally acknowledged that *The Catcher in the Rye* is really a war novel, a response to the psychic trauma Salinger experienced in World War II. He carried his typewriter across battlefields, putting words into Holden's mouth and exposing him to horrific sights, like pimple-faced kids getting blown to chunks and stacks of death camp corpses, images no teenager should ever see." She tilted her head back as if to contain welled tears. "But what if it's more than survivor's guilt or shell shock that made Salinger check into a psych ward at the end of the war?" She stared beyond the camera as if the answer might be found in the long meadow stretching from the chapel to the athletics complex.

Brandon leaned forward, locking fingers between his thighs. "What's survivor's guilt got to do with *The Catcher in the Rye*?

"You don't mean the obvious stuff?"
"Try me."
"Seriously?"
"Cut." Brandon bounced to his feet. "Explain it to her, Lu."

Brandon lit a cigarette and took a step back toward the chapel to check his phone. During sessions with his rehab therapist, he had come to understand how the Oklahoma City bombing had been the big bang that gave shape to his universe and how his own survivor's guilt had linked him to Holden Caulfield.

At first, young Brandon heard only a choir of cocksure holy rollers singing praise for the Lord's special plan, admonishing him to fulfill his heaven-sent role. He embraced the perfect harmony of their blessings. The hymn was so loud, so constant that his callow, untrained ears could perceive nothing else. By April 19, 2000, however, his hearing had sharpened. He began to detect discordant notes sounding in a darker key.

At nine years old, he and his mother returned home for the somber dedication of the Oklahoma City National Memorial. Sheila had wanted her son to perform but couldn't get him on the program. Rows of empty chairs, one for each person who had died, consecrated a fresh-cut lawn. Nineteen smaller seats symbolized each child lost. Brandon would have made twenty. Only a few of the parents greeted him. He kept his head down, avoiding eye contact even when they tried to shake his hand or hug him. Sheila scolded Brandon for not looking at people when they spoke to him. One mother nearly squeezed the breath out of his chest.

Sheila had scripted the response her son would parrot to the media, a verse from the Book of Matthew about children being the greatest in the kingdom of heaven. While he was quoting scripture to a local TV reporter and assuring her that the children were with Jesus, a man pushed his way through the crowd and began yelling at Sheila, who stood off camera. "You think God had a different plan for my little girl?" He had a picture of his daughter pinned to his lapel. It was surrounded by pink lace. He ripped the photo from his suitcoat and pressed it hard against Sheila's face. "Do you?" he shouted. Event security hooked his arms and dragged the sobbing man away.

A year later, Sheila had managed to get an invitation to witness Timothy McVeigh's lethal injection at the federal penitentiary in Terre Haute, Indiana on June 11, 2001. Brandon stayed in the warden's office playing a Nintendo Game Boy until it was over. A picture of the warden shaking hands with the president was surrounded by wall-mounted fish, their mouths open as if gasping for air. Following the execution, Sheila, her arms wrapped around her son, spoke with a pool reporter, praising the cleansing power of "sacred retribution" and reminding the world of Brandon's special mission to spread the good news. He thought of the small empty chairs and the pink lace little girl. His mother's steadfast assurances clashed with the piercing echo of that distraught father's wails.

Exactly three months later, while traveling the mega-church circuit, Brandon sat on a king-size bed at a Topeka La Quinta Inn, eating an A&W burger and fries and watching the news. It was September 12, 2001. Sheila was in the shower; otherwise, she would have turned it off—a story about the Children's Discovery Center, the day care at Five World Trade Center. The teachers had saved all of their kids that day. Not one was lost. He had nightmares for weeks, dreams of Jesus playing with him and his dead friends at the water table or the book nook. He always spotted the bomb in the classroom before it went off, a papier-mâché longhorn steer skull, an alarm clock sprouting wires between the horns. He screamed "get out," but his friends kept laughing while Jesus knee-slapped a raucous tambourine. After the blast, he stood in the rubble, alone with the Lord. "Why weren't you here?" Jesus asked him.

The seeds of doubt about divine intervention being the guiding force in his life had taken root. What began as a niggling sense of injustice grew in tandem with his burgeoning fame, his success not evidence of an invisible hand but of the unfairness of chance. He later wondered if that same kind of doubt made it too hard for his father to live with Sheila's self-centered self-righteousness.

Brandon had never told anyone about the childhood nightmares until he went to rehab. He confessed to his therapist he'd been afraid to share them with his mother. "She'd just blame Satan and get more grubby hands laid on my head." The therapist had helped him to see that the roots of his drug abuse had anchored themselves in the post-traumatic stress that he, much like his father, had suffered since the bombing. His condition, she had said, tied him in a knot of conflicting symptoms—denial and duty, self-sabotage and ambition, insecurity and arrogance. She explained that he had been grappling with the dilemma of wanting to be praised and forgiven, judged and condemned at the same time. His mother's drive for him to achieve superstardom had only intensified the internal battle of his polarized emotions.

After reading *Catcher*, he told the therapist that he no longer felt like the sole survivor. There was a bond. He felt understood. He sent a copy to his father with a note about how it had helped him, more than anything else had, but in the few times a year they had spoken or texted, Chuck never mentioned it. Brandon could never bring himself to ask if his father had read it.

Luis sat next to Alda on the bench while Brandon stood behind them scrolling through text messages and social media posts. "Brando likes where this is going, but you got to play along. Of course, he knows Holden and Salinger share a guilty conscience. Teenage Panzer fodder got wasted daily while good old Sergeant Salinger of the counterintelligence corps lived safe and sound, doing shots of schnapps with Papa Hemingway. In *Catcher*, the pure, perfect, innocent little brother, Allie, dies, and Holden, the perverted, delinquent older brother, lives."

"And the self-flagellation," Alda said.

"That too. Holden wants to be punished for living so he taunts his roomie into tagging him in the choppers, and then does the same thing with that greasy elevator pimp, Maurice, at the no-tell hotel." Luis picked up a fallen winged seed from a maple tree, held it high above his head, and let it twirl to the ground. "You see what he's doing?"

"Yeah, I do, I do, but not totally, I guess."

"Here's another SAT word: exposition. Brando's playing stupid so you'll explain all that background shit for the audience. When it works, you don't even realize it's happening. Got you to explain Hinkley and Chapman in the first minute you two met."

"*He* was doing *that?*"

"*Ye-ah*," Brandon said, glaring at Alda for emphasis before submerging back into the depths of his phone.

Luis lowered his voice. "Don't be fooled by the boyband stare and the backlot GED." He held out his hand for a fist bump followed by silent, slow-motion fireworks fingers.

Brandon returned to the bench to reshoot the exchange. Alda traced the Salinger-Caulfield guilt parallels, and after Luis shot B-roll reactions, she launched into her unique analysis. She speculated that Salinger had been molested as a child, an experience that had shattered his innocence, even before the war, warped his sex life, and echoed through Holden's troubled adolescence.

Brandon felt his cheeks flush. He cleared his throat and snapped his head to crack his neck as if to reboot. His voice, soft and slow at first, grew steadily in pace and volume. "That would explain . . . Jesus, Salinger too . . . I mean it's not only what happened with that fondling perv, Antolini, on the couch. Holden tells us it happened to him like twenty times since he was a kid. The last line in that chapter is about how he couldn't stand it. He even wonders if Jane Gallagher's stepfather was a molester. Why else would he be so fixated?"

"Exactly," Alda said. "It can't be a coincidence. Not just what Holden says, but what Salinger himself does with those young girls. It's a vicious cycle of abuse. Between the two of them, there's way too much smoke. When you play that part, you got to carry all of Salinger's squalid baggage through every scene."

Brandon let his head drop as if in silent prayer and swiped a stiff horizontal hand to end filming.

"What did you think?" she asked.

He palmed his knees to press himself up and turned away to light a cigarette. "Sure as hell didn't expect that. Sort of prepared, huh? You canned that lecture hall routine from your mom."

She raised a foot to the bench to retie a neon pink sneaker. Even with her head down, he could see the blush on her cheeks. "Some of it, sure, but not all of it, not everything. I mean, I knew you were coming, so obviously, I—"

"You might be onto something, it not being all about the war. Nothing can scar you like childhood."

He got a text from Josh. "don't bring anybody tonite"
"???"

"My friend hates crowd. Shy type."

Luis asked them to wait while he shot more B-roll. Between wide shots of the campus and different angles of his subjects, he said Alda's analysis was trying too hard to be clever. "That the shit-show in the Belgian forest and seeing the concentration camp definitely left him *requetejodido*. Totally fucked up. Don't you think that's more than enough?" He wound his finger counterclockwise. "J.D. just wanted to turn back time to some kind of pre-war Eden. Driving around with those high school kids in Vermont in the Fifties, going to their basketball games and the soda fountains, that's comic strip world, Archie and Jughead malt shop crap. If Salinger had been in *Total Recall* or *Men in Black*, he would've one hundred percent volunteered to have his war memories erased."

Brandon checked his phone and texted "NOOOO" to a second plea from Shari to do a remake of Disney's *Herbie the Love Bug* in a Toyota Prius. He elbowed Alda. "What happened to the surprise? You got the glee club hiding in the dining hall?

"The library," she said.

"I'm not here to check out books. Let's see the dorm, then we scoot."

"But what if the surprise is in the rare book room? Say a first edition of a certain novel maybe, triple mint."

"Picture on the back?" Brandon asked.

"Scary Jerry himself."

"That could be good, Brando," Luis said. "Display case?"

"Of course. The room's a fishbowl, usually locked, but the book's set up so you can see it through a glass wall."

Brandon searched the ground and cracked a hickory nut with his heel. "*Catcher* two times untouchable, or so they think."

8

A call to campus security was all they needed to bypass the reluctant young woman working at the circulation desk, an exchange student from Pakistan unfamiliar with and unimpressed by Brandon's fame. In less than five minutes, Rudy Dunbar swaggered into the lobby, a mishmash of keys fanned out in his fist like a martial arts weapon. Brandon caught him near the door. He whispered that they wanted a shot of Alda holding the first edition *Catcher* because it was her mom's favorite book, a perfect addition to the anniversary montage. He said he didn't want to tell the truth or reveal that they were related.

Rudy hiked up his belt. "I got this." He explained to the desk clerk that Brandon was acting under his direct supervision. There would be no log of the visit. He would write a special security report.

The young woman tapped a binder. "It says here you'll need archivist gloves if you're going to touch any of those books." She rummaged through a stack of drawers, eventually pulling out a fistful of white cotton fingers pointing in every direction.

Brandon held up his arms, twisting his fitted hands back and forth, switching from surrendering cat burglar to pre-op surgeon. "We look like the four lamest mimes at a community college improv class." He pretended to be trapped inside a box.

Alda took dramatic aim with a long rifle and fired. The mock recoil thrust her arms upward. Brandon pressed hands to his chest and stared in horror at blood-soaked palms as he fell to the ground. "I was shattering the case for you to escape, drama queen."

Rudy shuffled through keys at the entrance to the Westmoreland Family Rare Book Room. After a few failed frantic efforts, he invited them in with an apologetic grin. A rectangle of glass display cases lining the perimeter held first editions of *The Adventures of Huckleberry Finn*, *The Red Badge of Courage*, *On the Road*, and *The Grapes of Wrath*, among others.

"Heard of a couple of these, even read half of the Steinbeck," Brandon said. "About Okies, like me and Woody G., heading west."

Luis hovered over a copy of *Portnoy's Complaint*, pointing his lens at the cover.

"What the hell is *Portnoy's Complaint*?" Brandon asked.

Luis started to laugh and lowered the camera. "Sorry, Brando. I can't help myself. Neither could Alex. It's about this." He shook a half-closed hand in front of his crotch as if he were about to roll dice. "Portnoy was this teenaged, massively obsessed midget-beater." Luis couldn't stop laughing. "There's a movie, but it's total crap. Left out all the fun."

Rudy joined in with high-pitched giggles. "A regular meat-grinder, eh? Jerkin' the old gherkin?"

Tears pooled in Luis's eyes. "Brando, maybe you can do the remake, the critics would love it, 'strokes of genius,' they'd say." He could barely catch his breath.

"Enough already." Alda put hands on hips. "The little boys' locker room is on the other side of campus."

Luis and Rudy both apologized as they struggled to regain their composure. "I zoomed in for a reason. Portnoy and Holden and Salinger. Like Alda said, *Catcher* is this war novel pretending to be about teenagers, right? And waspy Holden is really a secret Jew, dressed up like a gentile. He's a Portnoy in disguise. And there's more. Crazy connections. Salinger had a ball that never dropped and so did Portnoy. *Two* half-sacks? Bro, that *cannot* be random. Somehow Roth, the author, must have known. Plus, Portnoy and Salinger both lost their shit over *shiksas*."

"Like Hitler," Alda said. "The one testicle thing."

Brandon asked Luis to repeat his explanation. He took time to describe in more detail the character traits Holden Caulfield, Alex Portnoy, and J.D. Salinger had in common. Brandon, leaning back against the door, listened with eyes closed. "Ok, I got it. Let's shoot." He positioned himself next to the display and delivered a flawless summary of Luis's analysis. "Cut. Now where's the hot tamale?"

Alda led them to the far side of the long, narrow room. With a soft spotlight overhead, a first edition of *Catcher in the Rye*, wrapped in a pristine dust jacket, sat alone in its own case made of thicker glass. To the right of the book, a color copy of the jacket lay flat, the blood-red horse, twice impaled by the carousel pole, its body beginning to shrivel, Manhattan retreating deep into the background. To the left, a copy of the title page with a faint pencil autograph.

"You didn't say it was signed." Brandon spread his fingers wide on either side of the case. Luis made a semicircle around him. "Look at Salinger. Those ears, they're so round, so hard-rimmed. They look like, I don't know, like handcuffs."

Alda tapped the top of the case. "And those dark black-hole eyes. They suck in everything and spill it out through his fingertips."

Rudy held up a small silver key. "Ready?"

Brandon lifted his hands from the glass and shot his palms forward as if casting a spell to unseal an ancient tomb. "Open sesame." After Rudy had lifted the lid, Brandon cradled the book with two hands, removing it like a preemie nurse lifting a newborn from an incubator, or an archaeologist extracting a desiccated infant mummy from a tiny crypt. "Rudster, would you mind stepping out for a minute? Luis here is going to need more space to frame the right shot with me and cuz."

"No problemo. I'll guard the entrance."

Brandon waited until Rudy had shut the door. "You two stand in front of me so he can't see."

Alda glanced back at Rudy. "You're not gonna steal it?"

"I'm no thief, just a vandal." He pulled out a half-pencil he'd swiped from the circulation desk and began flipping through pages.

"Brando, what are you doing?"

"Her mom would know. I think they call it literary criticism. Here, here's the spot. Handsy pansy Antolini, trying to feel up Holden when he's asleep." In all-caps block letters, Brandon wrote "FUCK YOU" in the margin. "How do you like that, jerk-off?"

"You're gonna get me expelled."

"It *is* really funny, if you think about it," Luis said. "And it's only pencil."

"Shit, if I autographed it, that would only add another ten grand to the price tag. I'd be doing them a favor. Now, let's get to work." Brandon held the book above his left shoulder, tapping the cover for emphasis. "This is exactly what I'm going to do for Holden. They had this book in an all-glass prison, solitary confinement, like Magneto." He waved a hand around the room and then stepped aside to allow Luis to get a tight shot of the empty display case. Once the camera returned to his face, Brandon continued, "I'm about to set the ultimate mutant loose. I just freed *Catcher*, and next up I'm gonna free Holden." He stayed mannequin still until Luis gave a thumbs-up.

Brandon said good-bye, again, to Rudy and excused himself to go to the restroom. He settled into the middle stall. Its beige metal walls had splotches of paint a few shades too light to match the factory color. They were irregular blobs, like splashes on a Holstein or a Pinto. As he grimaced and shifted, Brandon began talking to himself, a habit of distraction since childhood. Though alone, he still kept his voice low. "Janitor must have painted over graffiti he couldn't scrub out. Usual horndog crap." He let out a laugh that bounced off the walls.

An abandoned red rubber band the size of a bracelet rested at the border of an adjacent stall. He called out "hello" twice to make sure he was still alone and picked it up, twisting it in his fingers before slipping it over his bicep. The light tension across his skin gave a hint of the old rush. He couldn't possibly count how many toilets around the world he'd shot up in—from a spotless lobby loo at The Savoy to a rancid porta-potty at Burning Man.

He was convinced that Holden, who had already been drinking too much, would've become hooked if he hadn't gotten help. The hard stuff would have become irresistible. Brandon knew what that undertow felt like. He once described *Catcher* to his therapist as a series of one-on-one interventions. "No one in the entire novel ever asks Holden Caulfield for his advice," he'd said. "The advice runs in only one direction." That was another reason he had felt such an immediate and intense connection.

Brandon took a deep breath and yanked on the rubber band, breaking it, the ends snapping back against his fingers. The brief but intense pain came as a relief, like a broken curse. He dropped the band in the water and put his head in his hands, thinking about how, to get Holden right, he would have to let the demons back in, relive the pain and the powerlessness, allow himself to be tempted by a siren song of relapse luring him to the edge of a cliff where he would have to remain, teetering helplessly above the void. He understood, for the first time, that sharing an authentic Holden with the world would require a measure of self-sacrifice that could jeopardize much more than his future earnings.

9

Brandon met them outside the library. Alda was sitting on the lip of a concrete planter while Luis demonstrated camera functions. Vanishing sunlight, wedged between buildings, painted a strip of light at their feet. Gusty winds had swirled fallen leaves into a tight pile near a catch basin. Two boys in matching reflective yellow vests zipped past on racing bikes as if they were in a time trial. Alda led her guests to a dumpster behind a tall picket fence, ordering them to stay put while she scouted ahead to make sure her hall was clear of Instagram snipers.

After a brisk, surreptitious tour of the perfectly unrenovated dorm, Alda invited them to dinner. She rattled off a list of Darlingbrooke favorites—coal-fired gourmet pizzas, a farm-to-table tasting menu, Asian fusion with a same-day sushi guarantee. "Lots of second homes up here," she said.

When she got to a hole-in-the-wall in a downriver town that smoked its own meat and had homemade fruit pies with lard crusts, Brandon cut her off. "That'll do. I could use a little self-medication."

"They won't keep their distance like getaway New Yorkers too cool to approach."

"I came prepared."

Alda rode in the front passenger seat while Brandon hunched in the back, adjusting a jet-black, shoulder-length wig, a faded Sooners baseball cap, and a pair of bulky drugstore glasses. They drove through downtown Darlingbrooke, passing beneath a series of banners announcing Octoberfest attractions—a chili cook-off, a Halloween costume parade, and an ugly pumpkin contest. A lone minuteman on bended knee, holding a rifle, guarded the town square's bandstand. Antiques stores and coffee shops with names like Patina Cantina and Parade Grounds lined Main Street sidewalks.

"That used to be a really old general store." Alda pointed to a stand-alone two-story that had been converted into a cryotherapy spa on the ground floor and a college counseling center on top. "Even had real hitching posts. It's where I go for SAT prep. My tutor, he's the absolute best. He went to medical school, but now he's a freelance coder. Char swears he's got a side hustle with the NSA."

"Concierge services," Luis said. "Funny how the free market makes so few people freer."

Brandon threw himself against the backseat. "Here we go."

"Brando, that's exactly why I got no love for your BFF. Caulfield says he hates everybody in his lily-white, private school, Upper East Side world, but truth is, that kid loves it." Luis stopped the car across from a clapboard Congregationalist church. Its walls, illuminated by a ring of spotlights, glowed pure ivory as if they had just been painted. "That roommate, the one who says Holden and his swanky leather suitcases are 'bourgeois,' nailed it. You ever notice how Holden claims to worry so much about the cost of taxis but never dares to slum it with the unwashed masses in the electric sewer until the very end, when he'd have to use Phoebe's Christmas money? And what about when he lost the fencing team's swords? Why the hell did he have to keep getting up to look at a subway map? The dude *grew up* in the city. By the time I was twelve, I knew four different ways from the Heights to *mi abuelita* in Coney Island." Luis looked over his shoulder at Brandon. "Even you learned how to get around. Twenty years later, I guarantee Senior Vice President Holden V. Caulfield would be propping up his shoe-shiny wingtips in a corner corporate office, banging his outer borough secretary, and complaining about those uppity negro caddies who talk too much whenever you're trying to read a green."

"That's not right, Lu. He's no racist."

"He's not? Really? What about Ernie, the so-called 'big fat colored guy' who played the piano and had his own club? All Holden could see was how old Ernie put on airs while he entertained a packed house snow white as that church over there. Have you *ever* spent a minute thinking about what Ernie—probably had grandparents born slaves—had to go through to get his own club back in those days?"

"No, but—"

"Exactly. Neither did Captain Country Club. Ernie could've been the kid from *Invisible Man*, got lectured in his school chapel and expelled too, like Holden, except for bullshit reasons that weren't his fault. Ran away to New York. Jerry probably ripped it off like copycat Elvis. The best Holden could do was call Ernie a 'terrific snob.'"

"Holden might not be a progressive," Alda said. "But *Catcher's* no social commentary."

"You sound like his friend Josh."

"Holden's a kid, like me, and massively flawed, like all of us. He's nobody's hero. Heroic is the last thing anybody should call him." She paused to speed-type on her phone and flashed the screen toward Luis, its display glowing with a Wikipedia entry. "*Catcher* came out a year before *Invisible Man*, so, yeah. Hold the salt."

Brandon smacked the headrest. "Exactly. He's just an equal-opportunity critic with a color-blind bullshit detector."

Luis shifted into gear. "Hating everybody is a cop-out excuse, Brando. Maybe if Salinger had more than one good ball, he would have been stronger, written something more honest about the war, about what it did to people, what it did to him." Luis twirled a finger next to his temple. "Stop hiding behind ivy-covered walls and complaining you're allergic to weeds. *Coño,* do I really need to see you kicking an empty toothpaste box down the hall with your sheep-lined slipper? Tell us what you *saw* in battle, what you *did*." Luis banged the heel of his hand against the steering wheel. "Don't give me candy-ass frustrations as code for the horrors of combat. Show me fresh blood soaked through the pages of a Dear John letter."

Brandon clamped a hand on Alda's shoulder. "Didn't expect to spend the day with Groucho Marxist, did you? That's what Josh calls him. Hey, what's that?" He pointed to the marquee of the town's one-screen theater. It advertised a special, weeklong run of *Knife in the Water.*

Luis and Alda exchanged looks as if bargaining over who would answer. "Roman Polanski," Luis said.

Alda pinched her forearm as if measuring its thickness. "Yeah, before he developed a taste for undercooked meat."

"What the hell's wrong with you?" Brandon asked.

"Figured I'd lighten the mood."

"*Hilarious.*" Brandon imitated the elongated way Alda had pronounced the same word back on campus. "Enough talk." He took out his phone and pumped Garth Brooks through the SUV's speakers. "Us Okies got to stick together."

"Ralph Ellison was born in Oklahoma too," Luis said.

"Who's that?"

"Nobody."

They descended a winding river road lined with abandoned factories, their crumbling brick sides whispering faded advertisements for ladies' shoes and gentlemen's hats. After crossing railroad tracks and entering the Town of Rilex, they passed a VFW hall, St. Bridget's Catholic Church, its parochial school shuttered, a Dollar General, a check-cashing storefront, an out-of-business pet shop, and a medical supply company promising full Medicare coverage for all scooters.

"Even the name of this town is dreary," Luis said. "Like some gray, flaky construction material that causes cancer."

"These fine folks march to the multiplex for every one of your block-busters," Alda said. She tapped the dashboard. "Probably paid for this sweet ride."

Brandon stuck his head into the front. "And your last spree at Bergdorf's."

They parked in front of a restaurant sitting on the high bank of the river. The familiar design gave away its prior incarnation—a dethroned Dairy Queen. The sign-tower out front read "Meats 'N Eats." Alda said that the letter "M" had been burned out for so long that the locals called it "Eats and Eats." "We call it E² at DH."

Brandon's phone chirped a reminder tone. He grabbed it from the center tray. "Shit, it's Rosh Hashanah. Totally forgot."

"Not gonna find a synagogue around here, Brando."

"Don't be an idiot, Lu. Every year I call Shari and sing her a song. She loves it. Wrote it myself." Brandon sang it for them and made them practice. With his agent on speaker, they caroled:

We wish you a Shari Mishkin.

We wish you a Shari Mishkin.

We wish you a Shari Mishkin.

And a Happy Jew Year!

"Sha-na-na *tovah*, SM. Shofar show good, right?"

"A real *shonda* of rhymes, Brandon. Wouldn't be the holidays without it. I got a few minutes before dinner. Listen to me. FEMA wants you to do a PSA. I know how you feel about the disaster stuff, but—"

"No way. If I turned down all those telethons . . . I was a poster child long enough."

"Who's the girl? Sounds statutory."

"Luis's cousin."

"Where the hell are you?"

"Location scout."

"Take me off speaker. Damn it, you wanted a meeting with the lawyers. I got you one. Cost us another ten grand to hear what I already told you. It's a no-go. Total career killer. Jesus Christ, you're lightning in a bottle of Dom, and you want to throw all that juice away searching for Bigfoot? When you come out of the woods, empty-handed, head-to-toe in rashes and ticks, you're gonna be hearing goddamned crickets ringing in your ears *for-ever*, from here to the 405. Nobody waits for the prodigal son anymore. You understand? They'll just right-swipe to the next golden calf."

"Save it for Passover, Shari. I know what I'm doing."

"Come to my office next week. Let's really do something. Your vision, definitely, one hundred percent, but projects we can actually accomplish."

Brandon trailed them into the restaurant. He yanked on the bill of his grungy baseball cap and, even if with the thick, smudgy glasses, kept his head down.

Alda pointed to a menu board hanging behind the cash register. "You order at the counter, and they bring it out. No vegetarian options. Lots of animals harmed in the process."

After filling their own drinks and getting a greasy laminated number card slotted into a metal stand, they picked a corner booth near the front of the restaurant. Split red vinyl covering exposed yellowing foam cushion, like someone had hacked the benches with a machete.

Two little boys in knee-length Patriots jerseys stood on their seats, pointing toy laser pistols at random diners. "Hey, Miss UFO. Here's my IOU," said a gap-toothed crewcut as he pretended to zap a mother wiggling chubby infant legs into a high chair.

Alda nudged Brandon. "Isn't that one of yours?"

He braced his elbows on the table and pressed his forehead against the heels of his hands. "*Martian Rangers.*"

"You and that actress, Brando, that was for real?" Luis asked.

"No way. Chum for the barracudas. She's with Shari. Not a big fan of the...," he glanced at Alda, "I didn't really have a shot."

Alda tore paper towels from a roll on the table and handed them out. "You got a title? For the documentary."

Brandon slipped a cigarette in his mouth. "Not yet."

"No smoking in here, mister," a server said. "Got an ash can out front."

Brandon waved the cigarette in the air. "Not lighting up."

"Gotcha. Adult pacifier." The young woman slid a round plastic tray under her arm. "You and me both. Did the same thing until the patch kicked in. Need any refills?"

Luis held up a red hard plastic tumbler with a textured surface and sat up to read her name tag. "Thanks, Luanne. Root beer." She had burnt orange hair, like a Crayola color, wire crimped around each ear, and a tattoo of a curvy, Medusa-haired sorceress on a bony arm.

"Something with 'catcher' or 'catch' in it," Brandon said, "like that DiCaprio flick *Catch Me If You Can*."

Luanne put her hand on Brandon's shoulder. "That's a good one. Seen it on Redbox last month. You know that man was real, the one who did all those phony check schemes."

"How long you been clean?" Brandon drew back his sleeve in anticipation of her response.

"Nine months. You?"

"Two years."

"Tell me it gets easier."

"Sugarcoating's what got us into the shit, right? Different day, same temptation. You never really leave the desert."

She sighed and shifted her weight against the serving tray. "You're not from around here?"

"No, ma'am." He hunched over his cup. His Oklahoma inflections were on full display. "Long-hauler. Load of produce way out from Yuma. This here is Alberto. Unloads them avocado crates quicker than Speedy Gonzalez."

She thrust her chin toward Alda. "What you doing with these two, sweetie?"

"My daddy owns the trucking company." Alda mimicked Brandon's accent. "I go to boarding school over at DH. He has his boys take me out for dinner whenever after they make a delivery up here. They always bring me a big box from Momma, you know, care package from home and all."

Luanne, apparently satisfied with the answer, scooped up the other two glasses. "Be right back."

"Who's the drama queen, now?"

"You started it."

"Seriously, Brando? Speedy Gonzalez, the undocumented produce packer. That's really nice. Real Cesar Chavez of you."

"I never said you were illegal."

"You've spent too much time in Hollywood. All you know is typecasting."

"Yeah, you're right. Why do you think I'm trying so hard to break the mold?"

While devouring meaty slabs of slathered ribs, they discussed their favorite parts of *Catcher*. Luis broke down the chapter when Holden first checks into the grungy room at the Edmont Hotel—the most cinematically significant scene in his opinion. He described Holden's peeping-tom observations of an aging closeted transvestite and a salacious couple spitting an unknown liquid at each other as a kinky voyeurism reminiscent of Hitchcock and anticipating the work of Spanish filmmaker Pedro Almodóvar. "Dude even put an early Hitchcock in the book, *39 Steps*, the one Phoebe knows by heart."

Alda wondered if Holden's admiration for the two nuns at the luncheonette foreshadowed Salinger's subsequent embrace of a "cloistered, ascetic existence." She proposed fast cutting, back and forth from the breakfast scene in Grand Central to Holden in the mental institution. Two nurses, two nuns.

Luis seconded her proposal, reminding them it could start even earlier because Holden had asked Ackley, the pimply kid from his Pencey dorm, about joining a monastery. "You really think Holden even cared about the actual good his donation to those two nuns might do? The poor folks in real need? Not a chance. That ten bucks was the most self-centered gift ever. He wanted to connect to their lifestyle, not their charity."

Brandon reserved judgment on their directorial suggestions, choosing instead to revisit Salinger-Holden parallels. "J.D. must have known he'd end up committed like Caulfield. He had a choice to make. Build his own nuthouse or be shipped off to an institution. So, he decides to design a padded cell in the New Hampshire woods, ended up being his own warden."

Luis tossed a stripped bone into a galvanized metal bucket. "For a man obsessed with eastern philosophy, he's like its worst disciple ever. He hated letting go of anything. If Salinger could've bought back the publishing rights and all the copies, I swear to God he would've." Luis held up his hands, palms out, thumbs perpendicular, like he was framing a shot. "One bio I read says he even used to drink his own urine. *Por dios,* Jerry couldn't stand the thought of letting his own piss go. Freud would've had a field day with that kind of retention."

Alda covered her mouth as if she were about to gag and cleared her throat. "What about *If You Want to Know the Truth?*" she asked, changing the subject back to the question of the documentary's title.

"Sounds too much like a news show," Brandon said. "Wait a minute. I got it. That's it." Brandon grabbed Alda's head like it was a basketball and planted a kiss on her forehead. He checked the diners for reactions and lowered his voice as he shrunk back into the booth. "You ready for this? No, you're impossibly not ready. *You Can't Catch Me.* It's perfect. Better than perfect. It's unstoppable. It's inertia."

"Not bad, Brando," Luis said, "but the trust is still gonna take you to court, soon as *Variety* gets a whiff."

Luanne returned with another round of refills. Brandon touched the serpent-haired tattoo to keep her at the table. "You think that courts treat celebrities same as everybody else?"

"'Course not," she said. "I did a week in County for mouthing off to a cop who tried to slide his hand up my shirt. That O.J. Simpson slashed two people to death, got a victory party for it. Now, you take some Holly-wood hunk, like that Liam Hemsworth, he would have to shoot a cop in the middle of New York City, broad daylight and videotaped to boot."

"Or what about that Brandon Newman?" Alda asked.

"Sure enough. Him too, even after all the drugs."

Brandon slapped Luis's thigh under the table as if to confirm her assessment. Luanne scooped up the bone bucket and slung an array of wet wipes on the table as she left. Luis ripped open a packet to scrub his fingertips. "Yeah, I see what you mean, Brando, but you do know the Juice's been locked up in Vegas for like seven years now? Still holds a couple of track records at my alma mater. And even *he* got caught. You really think you're faster?"

10

After the last pie crumbs had been forked, they dropped Alda back at school and returned to New York. Brandon changed into a vintage bowling shirt, black with white front panels, and a black leather jacket with a studded collar. He took a taxi to Handel, traveling alone as instructed. Without explanation, Josh had further instructed that it was "important" for him to text upon arrival and wait outside the alley entrance. Brandon lit a cigarette and propped himself against the side of a Chinese take-out shop the size of a telephone booth with a retro neon "chop suey" sign. The pavement, cracked with spider veins and patched with squares of blacktop, glistened from a midnight shower. The cool air condensed his smoke. Deeper down the alley, lit by light leaking through angled blinds, a raggedy dumpster diver performed a series of foraging handstands. Josh emerged from the unmarked door, dressed in coal black jeans with twin ladders of vertical gashes and a white CBGB t-shirt.

"What's with all mystery, Hitch . . . *cock?*"

Josh wrapped an arm around Brandon's waist, pulling him close as they walked. His lips nearly kissed Brandon's ear. "I closed the backroom early just for you, buddy. Private session. Who I'm introducing, you don't go in like it's nothing, 'cause it's not. And no matter what, this didn't even ever happen. You got me?" He reached inside Brandon's jacket pocket and pulled out his phone.

"What the hell?"

"No phones allowed."

"Since when?"

"Since Sallie."

"Sallie who? It's some chick?"

"Sallie's no skirt. *Sal-va-tore* is doing me," Josh tapped his own chest, "a personal favor by meeting you."

Brandon's eyes grew wide, his jaw unhinged. "Are you shitting me?" He shoved Josh against the wall. "A button man?"

75

Brandon had binge-watched *The Sopranos* in his trailer during breaks from shooting season three of *Mock Trial Club*. He'd always wanted to star in a mob movie, but the casting directors politely and uniformly informed his agent that he didn't have the right look. "You know what that means, Brando," Shari had said. "Mayo and marinara don't mix."

"I'm not saying he's anything, Brando. That's thing one. You heard nothing from me, nothing. He's got businesses in Brooklyn, Queens, knows everybody. *Everybody*. But you don't ask him any personal questions, like what he does for a living, where he lives, his family. *Niente*." Josh swiped a finger across his lips. "You need a permit? He gets it. You need a vacant warehouse? He finds it. You need help on the docks in Bayonne? Troubles on the job site? He waves his hand like Christ Almighty and stills the waters. You need money, and that I don't recommend, but he's got that too. Please, you should see this guy at the Indian casinos up in Connecticut. They treat him like he's the Duke of Urbino."

"Why haven't you ever—"

"Because I never had permission before. His is not a name you drop casually at the bar. Are you mental?" Josh grabbed Brandon's head with two hands to shake it. "Loose lips one day, concrete piggies *mañana*."

"He's like a boss?"

"You see that, exactly what curiosity did to the cat. Nine lives didn't help that nosy pussy for shit. Sallie's connected everywhere. They call him the human Amazon. Nobody says no, and nobody asks why. And none of that hot shit celebrity swagger either. You go in humble. You let *him* ask the questions. He likes to get to know who he's doing business with. He's not what you're expecting."

Just inside the door, they were met by a tall, twitchy beanpole, early twenties, New York Giants away jersey, shaved head, silver chain hanging from beltloop to back pocket. He swept Brandon with a metal detector. Josh surrendered Brandon's phone. The Beanpole jerked his head toward the far corner of the empty room where a man sat alone at a four-top, reading. The overhead lights beamed like it was closing time. A muffled mix of house music and an occasional shout bled through the wall from the public side of the club.

"Brandon, let me introduce a good friend of mine, Sallie Choo Choo." The man put down a copy of *The Catcher in the Rye* but remained seated at the table. As they shook hands, Brandon's eyes bounced between Sallie and the book. Josh must have given it to him. The open paperback, spine up, rested on the table like a gymnast stuck in the splits.

Sallie wore a perfectly pressed white button-down shirt with a pink Vineyard Vines whale logo, khaki pants, no creases, and mossy brown penny loafers. Well-defined crow's feet marked him as mid-fifties, but he kept his back straight, his shoulders square, his face clean-shaven, as if he'd been in the military. He had thick black hair cut short and wore round wire-rimmed glasses. "Look at this kid, staring at me. Not exactly what you suppose, am I right?" Despite his clean-cut appearance, Sallie's accent was pure street-corner. Brandon blinked and shrugged but stayed silent, heeding Josh's commands, even though he was bursting to ask about Sammy the Bull, Donnie Brasco, Henry Hill, and the entire Gotti clan. "Alley cat got your tongue? Let me guess. Joshua warned you not to run your mouth?"

"Something like that."

"Pfft." Sallie waved an impatient hand. "This jittery *goombah* loves the theatrics. Permission to speak granted. At ease, Brandon. Mind if I call you that?"

"Not a problem, um, ah—"

"Call me Sallie, or Choo Choo, whichever you prefer."

"You like the railroads, I take it?"

"Yeah, most people assume that at first, to tell you the truth. When I was a kid, the springtime, I had the hay fever so bad, sneezed my way to the nurse's office more than a couple times."

Brandon gripped the back of a chair with two hands. "Good-looking outfit by the way. Josh told me we were going midnight yachting, so—"

"I asked for that one, didn't I?" Sallie tapped the pink whale on his chest. His broad smile revealed a set of caps that outshone Brandon's. "You're right, JF, this kid's a regular Pistol Pete, a real *Pagliaccio*."

Brandon looked to Josh for an explanation.

"He means a comedian."

Brandon waited until all eyes were on him. He cocked his head. "What do you mean, like I'm a clown to you?" He was mimicking a whiny Joe Pesci from *Goodfellas*. "I'm here to amuse you?"

Josh shrugged his shoulders, palms up. "You walked right into that one, Sal."

"Settle down, Abbott and Costello. Grab a chair why don't you."

"Mind if I smoke?"

Sallie tapped the side of his nose. "You'll have the train running all night. This joint reeks bad enough already." He tilted his head toward a shoulder and bounced two fingers at Brandon. "You don't know *Pagliacci*, I take it?"

Brandon's eyes rolled up as if searching for an answer. "Was he one of the guys killed off in the first season of *The Sopranos?*

"Not an opera fan. Got it. That Leoncavallo rips me up every time, swear to God." He made the sign of the cross. "It was all that Tonio's fault, fucking stool pigeon." He scooped a handful of air for Brandon to lean closer. "We come from a freaking *via appia* of clever *paisans*—Rossini, Da Vinci, Marconi, plus Julius Caesar and all those other Roman bastards. The Heebs, they got nothing on us."

"Good thing Josh didn't tell me I was coming to night school or I might've cut class."

Sallie, smiling, rested his forearms on the table and sat up taller. "You were expecting, I suppose, some Sergio Tacchini tracksuit-wearing *gavone* with a checkered napkin stuffed inside his shirt and a fat face buried in a platter of macaroni and gravy. Am I right?"

"All I know is from the movies, so—"

"Joshua, you got any tea?"

Brandon checked over his shoulder. "Tea? Seriously? This has to be a setup. Where's the camera?"

"Not a chance, Brando," Josh said.

"I can't take the caffeine this late. See if you got the chamomile." As Josh headed for the kitchen, Sallie summoned him back to the table and asked for a slice of lemon and a drop of honey. "Where were we? Disabusing prejudices, I think. I love that word 'disabusing.' It sounds like you're tossing some *jadrool* a beating, but it means the complete opposite. My lawyer is always using it in the courtroom." Brandon glanced at his watch. "You putting me on the clock now? You know I don't exactly bill by the hour." Brandon twitched his head in denial and slipped his hands under the table. "Just like me, impatient. Good. Let's get down to business. Speaking of business, I was a semester short of graduating." Sallie held up a hand like he was about to take an oath. "Serious as a heart attack. Management degree. They gave me a football scholarship to Iowa State. Fastest white kid on the squad, a cornerback. All those years running numbers must've been." He winked. "None of the cops from my neighborhood ever laid a finger on me. There I was cooling my heels in my mother's cellar before they ever busted down the policy bank's front door." He clicked his tongue and sighed. "Tore up my knee senior year."

"Iowa. That must've have been like moving to Mars."

"Can you imagine going from the New Utrecht in Bensonhurst, I'm talking guindaloon freaking central high, to Field of Dreams U? Great people, the best, lousy food. Everything tasted like Wonder Bread and corn." Sallie's face twisted like he'd eaten a sour grape. "It's like feeding a Chinaman a grilled cheese sandwich. You know, the lactose intolerance? They don't have the genetics." He snapped his fingers. "Vincent." The Beanpole hopped from a barstool to provide an airplane-size packet of cashews. "I caught the hypoglycemia last year." He looked at his copy of *Catcher*. "I cut my share of classes too," he tapped its spine, "but I've always been a reader. My Uncle Nunzio, typical Jesuit, was always pushing paper on me. Loved the Westerns, all the classics, *The Virginian, True Grit*. Frontier justice. My old man was mostly at Fort Dix back in the day."

"He was in the army? So was my dad."

Sallie stood up and patted Brandon's shoulder as he walked behind him. "Not that part of Fort Dix. The FCI part, federal correctional institution. Now your friend over here is just like my uncle, giving me reading assignments like he's handing out penance."

Josh had returned with a cup of tea, a glass of single malt for Brandon, and a Sierra Mist. "Except Sallie actually cracks them open."

Brandon took a sip of scotch. "I don't really have time to read about surviving the next asteroid strike."

"This is where you're wrong, Brandon." Sallie sat down and took a tentative sip of tea. "That's exactly how Joshua and I met. Can you imagine that? Of all things, I'm at an outdoors convention at the Javits Center, standing next to a booth on tilapia pond gardening. Circle of life they call it. We strike up a conversation, come to find out our grandmothers lived two towns apart in Sicily."

"You're a prepper?"

Josh stopped mid-sip. "Even Holden wanted to run for the hills and chop wood."

"I got news for you, Mr. Brandon Newman. The ugliest pile of bull elephant shit you've ever seen is most certainly gonna hit the ceiling fan. Could be any day. Take your pick—CME, EMP, nukes, gamma-ray burst, mutant Chinese virus, North Korean mustard gas, or a comet shot out of the blue. It's coming, definitely. Who's gonna be ready?" Sallie pointed two thumbs at his chest. "Guys like me, that's who. I got this place upstate, Ulster County. You'll come see it." He turned to Josh. "You'll bring him. It's inside this huge cave. Never find it in a million years." He swept a slow crossing-guard hand in front of Brandon's face. "Built under budget and ahead of schedule. You can suppose I've got a couple, three friends in construction."

Josh scooted closer to Sallie and held out his hands, fingers spread like he was about to perform a magic trick. "You should see the storage units and the flooring. Concrete's all M70-rated. Industrial-grade steel doors. He's got the best lock guy money can buy. And supplies like you wouldn't believe. I don't even know where he puts it anymore. Freaking Quartermaster General's like some bum with a shopping cart compared to Choo Choo. It's coming out of his ass."

Sallie, beaming like an angel, put a hand on Josh's forearm. "Kindness of strangers. He's telling the truth though. Propane tanks, solar panels, hazmat gear, night vision, generators, pallets of food, building supplies, and whatever else I might need to defend what's mine." Sallie wagged a stiff finger at Brandon. "Don't get any ideas. The self-defense toys are all legit, a thousand percent, every single piece, all the paperwork to back it up. I got this Spanish kid, ex-Green Beret, comes out once a month for training sessions. Close combat, small arms, forest edibles, fire-making, first aid. Only time I ever missed was when that cocksucker state court judge had me on the ankle bracelet for ninety days. Beat the case but caught a hell of a rash." He stuck out his leg to show Brandon the faint ring scar above his foot. "Me and my friends, nobody's getting over on us. Warlords in waiting Ramirez calls us. You want a revelation? I'll give you one right here." He pounded a rigid pointer into the table. "What's Wall Street gonna do for you when the lights go out?"

"Nothing," Josh said. "Please, this guy's gonna be a regular Mad Max." He eyed Sallie up and down. "Better dressed though."

"The preppy prepper don," Brandon said.

The room froze when he let it slip. He searched Vincent and Josh for a lifeline, but their fugitive eyes had already abandoned him. "Sallie, that's my bad, I'm sorry, I mean, I didn't mean anything by—"

Sallie had put down his tea and sat back in the chair. "We'd only have a problem, Mr. Newman, *if* what you said was true, and *if* you was a walking walkie-talkie for the rat-infested feebs. Now, that's not the case, is it?" He watched Josh as if Brandon's answer would also determine his friend's fate.

"No, definitely not. One hundred percent."

"Good. Glad we cleared that up. When the end times come, if you're smart, you'll stick with Joshua. We got a network." Sallie flipped the book over and turned to a page near the beginning. "Before we go nailing down the brass tacks, I got a couple, two questions about this Holden of yours." Sallie shook the bag of cashews. "He's at the cuckoo zoo, right?"

"Some sort of psychiatric facility."

"Correct. But why tell us that smack on page fucking one? I mean, why not tell the whole story, and then, boom, we find out at the end he went the mattresses?" Sallie made a clicking noise and pretended to fire twin finger pistols at Vincent, who was nursing a drink at the bar.

"Sal, you're killing us with that *Godfather* shit already. Don't you know any better? We don't beat a dead horse." Vincent swung a stiff axe hand. "We just chop off its fucking head and put it to bed."

"*Madon*, you see why I love this kid? He's got a pair on him." Sallie held out his hands like he was cradling a watermelon. "What's the shit that Wolverine's made of?

"Adamantium," Josh said.

"Exactly. So, what about it, Brandon? Why give away the suspense?"

"That's a pretty good question, honestly. Maybe Salinger wanted us to know Holden was broken from the beginning so we can understand what led him to the breaking point. You know Salinger checked himself into a psych ward at the end of the war. Definitely a connection."

"It's less about surprise," Josh said, "and more about what Holden went through, more of how he ended up losing his marbles."

Sallie took off his readers and poured the last few nuts into his mouth. "Still, if I was you, not that I'm any expert on the subject, I'd leave that fact out until the very end. Then it's sort of like a fresh slap right in the face." He punched an open palm for emphasis. "Like when we come to find out that Bruce Willis was a ghost the whole time in that movie with the kid who could see the dead people. Or, you know what? I'm gonna tell you one better. Don't even mention it, the funny farm business. It's not even necessary to tell you the truth."

Josh stared at Brandon, eyes wide with warning. "I'll think about it, Sallie. For sure, I will. In fact, mind if I take my phone back to write some notes?"

"Sorry, kid. If a tree falls in this forest, ain't nobody gonna know it hit the ground." Sallie brushed the pages of *Catcher* with his thumb, front to back, like he was shuffling cards. "Moving on to new business, from what I can see, you mostly need locations—cheap hotel, couple of clubs, a luncheonette, we got lots of those. That's all easy street. Josh says you got the prep school covered. And the outside stuff, the park, street scenes, that's on you. I could shut down a block in Mill Basin or Middle Village, no problem, but in Midtown, even I got my limitations."

"We'll shoot the exteriors at daybreak," Brandon said. "Use a skeleton crew, make it seem like an amateur student shoot."

Sallie rested clasped hands on the paperback. "The old-time taxi cabs, on the other hand, that's a piece of cake. As you might guess, I got a few fingers in a couple of livery operations. And as far as the skating rink goes, they got one in Prospect Park. I can get you in there off hours. My cousin's got the concession. I figure you do the wide shots at Rockefeller and the close-ups for Brooklyn."

Brandon squinted and scratched the side of his head. "This can't be your first movie." Josh gathered the empties and headed for the kitchen.

"Tell you the truth, Brandon, it really is. Between what I do and a movie producer, I don't think we're altogether that much different. It's like I see everything rolled out on a carpet runner, right in front of me, all at once. You got to have, what would you call it, Vincent?"

"Vision, Sal."

"Bingo. And while we're on the subject of the park, Brooklyn Zoo is a piece of shit, but they got the sea lions, so you should probably take a look. Place is always empty, which is a plus. What Brooklyn has got over on Manhattan, I don't mind telling you, is the carousel. Makes that knock-off in Central Park look like a supermarket birthday cake decoration. And I'll tell you another thing that's gonna make your head spin. You know who runs that one in the city? Humpty-Dump Donald Trump. Honest to God." Sallie put a fist to his mouth to smother laughter. "I'm still splitting sides every time I think of that beat artist from Queens trying to con his way into the White House. This clown prince runs a sure-thing casino into the ground, but he's supposed to run a country." Sallie huffed and rolled his eyes. "The stories some of my friends could tell. Don't get me wrong, most of them would love to see Donnie Boy win. Fox in the henhouse time, if you know what I mean."

"Fox News, you mean," Brandon said.

"Vincent, what did I tell you? I told you. We got a live one here. He's a regular Buddy Hackett." Sallie put a finger in the middle of the table as if indicating a location on a map. "Matter of fact, my pops used to run out to Buddy's place in Fort Lee back in the old days. I'm talking way back. Used to belong to Albert Anastasia." Brandon didn't understand the reference, a fact apparently made obvious by his expression. "He was a very important man, powerful, respected, got too close a shave one day in a barber chair at the Park Sheraton Hotel, back in '57." Sallie crossed himself and bowed his head for a few seconds of silent prayer. "Getting back to the nitty-gritty, my wife's cousin has got the maintenance contract for the Brooklyn carousel. You ever seen it?"

"Never."

Sallie kissed his fingertips like a French chef. "Old-world craftsmanship. The carving on those wooden horses. It's like they're flying in the air." He stretched out a hand toward the rafters. "The lights and that old-time organ, whirling around. Never be another one like it."

"I'll have to check it out."

"We'll set something up for you, definitely. And what about the train station? Have you scratched your noggin about that one yet?"

"Actually, I think New Haven might be easier."

"Great minds. Exactly what I been thinking. And you'll use my friend for the commissary, of course."

"I'm sure that'll be fine."

"What about the natural history museum?"

"I was planning a voice-over as we watch Holden walking across Central Park to the museum. Maybe use a drone for some overhead shots. We want it to feel low budget, operating outside the system, renegade-like."

"I get it, Brandon, outlaw-style." His eyes darted as if being watched. "Not to be outdone, however, I happen to think going inside is pretty important. This kid, Holden, he doesn't want to grow up. That's really the whole ball of wax right there. You follow me? We got to *see* that." Sallie bounced a hand on the table as he spoke. "He wants to stay a little kid permanently. End of story. Flunking out of all those schools so he never graduates, playing with his kid sister all the time, and how nothing changes with them Indians behind the plexiglass. He's trying to give Father Time the slip."

Josh returned with more scotch and tea. "But, Sal, the kid's always lying about his age with all those older women he's trying to make time with."

"He pretends to be older, Joshua, because he's got the overheated hormonals, but he doesn't really *want* to be older. When he had the chance, a fucking sure thing, with that whore in the hotel room, what happened? I'll tell you exactly what. *Stugotz* is what happened. All he could do was *blabahdee, blabahdee* and no action, zilch." Sallie held up curved fingers to make a zero. "He's exactly that kind of basket case."

Brandon's gaze drifted above Sallie's head to a photograph hanging behind him, a barbershop quartet, young mustachioed men dressed in old-time Victorian swimsuits, horizontal stripes, like convicts, and short straw hats. They posed, arm in arm, on the beach at Coney Island, the two at the ends curling muscles like sideshow strong men.

"You with me, kid? I'm boring you now?"

Brandon shook his head. "No, not at all. Sorry. It's just those men, in that picture." Sallie turned to look. "They must've been like my age. Now they've been six feet under for years, decades probably."

Sallie faced front and sipped more tea. "Fuck 'em. Like I was saying, this Holden, he's a grade-A pussyfooter if you stop to think about it. I guarantee you he'd be watching a top-notch skin flick and complaining the whole time about the lousy artwork hanging over the headboard. Or, even better, listen to this one." Sallie reached across the table to slap a hand on top of Brandon's, as if to fix his attention. "I'd lay any odds you want he'd be watching alone and never even unzip, spend the whole time crying about some droopy-faced pooch tattooed on the shoulder blade of some chick getting rear-ended."

Vincent's cheeks burst with laughter. "You got it, Sal, a special delivery from the pipefitters union." He thrust his bicep against a cupped hand before rubbing away tears.

Josh applauded with slow claps. "You two, you're like modern-day Petrarcas with that love poetry of yours."

Sallie tossed his head back and snapped it forward to lock eyes with Brandon. "What this boy really wants is *to be* that little sister of his, or even that dead brother, a kid forever. He hates the Hollywood brother because that one double-crossed them by turning into an adult. And when the sister asks him to name one thing he'd like to do with his life, he starts bawling like a baby and says he wants to be some kind of full-time lifeguard." Sallie slammed stiff fingers on the table like he was playing a final pair of piano chords. "That's all bullshit. This fruit loop doesn't want to be some catcher in the rye. He wants to run off to Never-never Land with that *mezzo-finook* Peter Pan." Sallie pushed himself back against his chair. "It's your movie, of course. I wouldn't presuppose, but I can get you in there, the museum, off hours. Cleaning crew. You get me?"

"I do, seriously." Brandon ran a hand through his hair and exhaled deeply. "Christ, Josh wasn't kidding. Who knew I was going for a master class at the Actor's Studio? But you got some solid ideas, Choo Choo, for real." Brandon finished his second drink and lowered his voice. "Now, how exactly would I pay you for all this . . . assistance?"

"No points on the backend, that's for sure." Sallie held up his hands as if to surrender. "You found me out, okay? I'm guilty." He trembled in mock fear. "Never thought you'd hear me say that one, eh, Vin? I did a little j-edgaring before the powwow. That Wikipedia, they even got an article on me. A few very unfair characterizations, but they had all my college statistics one hundred percent correct—tackles, interceptions, everything. No offense, Brandon, but I'll need payment upfront. You got to be careful with the period films, so they say."

"I meant more like, you know, method of payment."

Sallie flicked his wrist like he was shooing a mosquito. "We're transitioning away from cash fast as we can. We got high hopes for the Bitcoin. Got some Ukrainian kids out in Little Neck working on it. My lawyer set up some LLCs with a holding company in Bermuda. I'm your consultant—business opportunities, dispute resolution, real estate. We even got a website. Naturally, I'm a silent partner. Check or wire transfer. All signed, sealed, and delivered. Whichever you prefer."

"So, if you don't mind me asking, why bother with…?" Brandon angled his head toward Vincent.

Sallie raised an eyebrow. "We got a few what they call 'legacy businesses' that partner with the laundromats and the car washes." His lips split into a reptilian grin. "Cleanliness is next to godliness." There was an impish twinkle in his eye. "And of course, now and again, some of my more eager beavers have got a couple of ultra-orthodox methods of getting to 'yes.'"

"Got it."

"But it's all in a transitional phase. That's the main point. The old-timers, they're like the dinosaurs, extinct or dying out in some rotten cell in Allenwood or Lewisburg." He picked up *Catcher* and waved it in the air. "It was a book that did us in, hit us smack between the eyes like that asteroid in the Gulf of Mexico. Fuck that fucking self-hating guinea bastard Mario Puzo. That book of his was the beginning of the end for this life." Sallie tossed *Catcher* to the table and folded his arms. "You think it's any coincidence they passed that RICO racketeering law in 1970, exactly one year after *The Godfather* comes out? Puzo laid it all out for them, gave them a fucking blueprint." Sallie pretended to unroll drawings on the table. "Brother Mario was really the first rat. And then that John Gotti and his renegade coup, thinking he was a movie star, put the last nail in our coffin. Make yourself into a joke, learning how to live the street life from the pictures instead of from your elders, and you stick out like a sore thumb." He held up a thumb like he was about to push in a tack. "And then you go one better and you jab that infected finger right in the government's eye." He mimed repeated thumb stabs for emphasis. "All of the sudden, with the RICO Act, you walk down the street, couple three blocks, with the wrong guy, they got you on the videotape, bam, you're in the jackpot, an 'ongoing criminal enterprise.'" He made air quotes. "That law's like fucking flypaper. You follow me? Or would you rather me say '*capisce*' and pinch your cheeks like a good little altar boy?" He slurped more tea. "All that *cosa nostra* crap is yesterday's news. The books, the movies, they ruined everything."

He pushed away from the table, chair legs squeaking across the floor, and stood up. "A few of us realized that what we needed, as they used to say in management class, was a paradigm shift. Matter of fact, my daughter is always telling me I'm what those talking heads on the Discovery Channel call a 'transitional fossil.'" He leaned forward, flat palms on the table, watching Brandon. "You understand what I'm trying to say to you?"

"I heard of dropping dimes on somebody, Choo Choo, but never a *pair of dimes.*"

Sallie nodded with pressed lips. "When you're right, you're right, Joshua. This kid's a regular Norm Crosby. 'Pair of dimes.'"

Brandon laughed even though he had no idea what was funny. "So, what exactly would be the next step?"

"Other than maybe at the bat cave, you won't ever see me again. You'll deal directly with my head of operations, Rosalie. But you'll know I'm the engineer cranking away the gears. She's got an office in Long Island City, best spot, near the water. Our building, naturally. Joshua will make the arrangements. She can draw up the contract, take care of everything."

"I'll probably let my agent handle it, if that's okay."

Sallie rolled his lips inside his mouth and made them pop. "This agent of yours, let me take a wild guess. He's a Jew?"

"*She* is."

Sallie palmed his face and sighed. "They don't make your capable Semites, like Lansky or Siegel, anymore. They've all gone soft." He dropped his hand to lock eyes. "Don't tell that agent word one about me. Rosalie and the LLCs, that's something else. But not me. Understand? Under no circumstances."

"Of course, but she's like family. You wouldn't—"

Sallie held up a finger as if to scold. "She's not like *my* family. Soon as Special Agent Elliot Ness puts his paws on the thermostat, I guarantee it's Let's Make a Deal time. We speaking the same language here?"

Brandon knew better than to raise any further suspicions about his own bona fides. "I understand."

"Good. Now I'm gonna tell you three things about dealing with Rosalie. Number one: She's my daughter. Number two: She hates being called 'Rosalie'; call her 'Rose.' Rose Eddington. I swear she married that deadbeat just to get his baking powder last name. Thank God he's not in the picture anymore."

Vincent hopped off the barstool and pretended to swing a baseball bat. "No disrespect, Sal, but I had a bad feeling about that kid from day fucking one. Never looked me in the eye. Always wore that fucking backwards-ass *moulie* hat. Made my whole year to say *sayonara* to that piece of shit Jell-O mold." He crackled his knuckles.

Brandon's eyes zigzagged from Sallie to Vincent.

Sallie's body shook with laughter. He waved his forearm like the pope giving blessings from a motorcade. "This kid, he's seen way too many movies."

Vincent returned to his perch. "Been in too many, you mean."

"My ex-son-in-law, *ex*, Bradley, was a sculptor. Ran off to live in a mud hut with some swami in India. I warned Rosalie, 'You marry a boy from one of them artsy-fartsy northeast colleges, they're like dust in the wind.'"

"What's number three?"

"Number three: She busts more balls than a Turkish prison guard with a Louisville slugger."

"I'll make sure to wear a cup."

Sallie pinched Brandon's cheek. "Good boy." He picked up *Catcher* and flipped to a dog-eared page near the back. "Before you go, only other thing that bothered me." He sat down to read a few lines. "Again, I'm not trying to tell you how to do what they might call your artistic nuts and bolts, but I can't understand this ending here. It's not clicking." Sallie scratched an ear. "Tell me how come the story didn't end right when the kid was watching his sister on the merry-go-round. That's the spot. That's when it all dawns on him like a ton of bricks."

"How do you mean?"

"'How do I mean?' How I mean is until then he's still fliting around in fairy tale land. Remember that stuffed shirt prick friend of his from the bar who was banging the Chinese girl? He asks your hero not once but twice he asks when is Holden gonna grow up. At the carousel, he really sees it, knows he can't ever be a kid again. You understand? He finally gets it through his thick skull. It's like watching her through prison bars." Sallie held splayed fingers in front of his face to demonstrate. "Some shit can't ever be undone, like time. Me and my friends might know a thing or two about that. There's your money shot, if you understand what I'm talking about. The kid tries to sound happy, but that's a con artist hustle. Don't forget this sad sack warned you from square one that he was what?"

"The biggest liar you ever saw," Brandon said.

"Correct." Sallie tapped the back of his wrist and pretended to listen for ticking. "Reliable as a Rolex off a Times Square Nigerian. So, what's he really doing? He's practically bawling that's what. And that music. The music playing on the ride—did you notice?—ain't exactly 'Happy Days Are Here Again.' It's 'Smoke Gets in Your Eyes.' My old man

used to whistle that tune whenever he was around. Sounded like a
bird dipped its beak in crack. That song, let me tell you something,
it ain't no rainbow ending if you know what it's about. Deep down
he knows the truth, finally. That carousel just keeps turning in one
direction, like a clock. The rest of it, afterwards, it's like," Sallie slid
a thumb back and forth over his fingertips as if conjuring an answer,
"it's like a big stupid red bow. You give a kid a pony for her birthday
she doesn't need some goddamned bow on top of its head. It's the
pony for Christ's sake."

Josh was playing with a lighter, spinning it on the tabletop. "I practically said the same thing, Choo Choo. It's like smothering ketchup on
top of a perfectly grilled porterhouse."

Sallie spread his hands, palms up, to emphasis the point.

"But, Sallie, if I may, it's kind of important for us to remember that
Holden's sharing his story with us. He's letting us into his pain. Hearing
from him again at the end in the mental institution, that reinforces his
desire to connect, even after all his sadness and loneliness. Jesus, I sound
like Alda." Brandon slapped a hand on top of his head

"Who?"

"My cousin, her favorite book."

"As far as I'm concerned, Brandon, the pony would've been enough.
That author, he really left the kid in the park there if you ask me. Anyhow,
I'm sure you'll think about it and make the right decisions."

"I will. I promise."

"Good. Couple last things, housekeeping they call it. I almost forgot."
He rubbed his forehead. "You off the junk for good?"

Brandon held up the boy scout salute. "Two years clean."

"I managed to notice you're still sipping the sauce. That part of what
they call recovery nowadays? Joshua over here is a regular Osmond brother
with the Seven-Ups."

"I've got it under control, Sallie. It's kind of like the way they put a
little virus in a flu shot. I go to NA meetings all the time."

Sallie clamped a hand on Josh's forearm to give it a shake. "Not for
nothing, your friend here's vouching for you."

Brandon knew from the movies what that meant. Josh would have to
pay for his sins if he ever double-crossed the mob. Brandon stood and
extended a hand. "You've got nothing to worry about."

Sallie smiled and gave a firm shake. "I knew I could trust you. You've
got one of those big, honest mugs, like all them freckle-faced cornpones
down there in Iowa."

Just inside the door leading to the alley, Sallie explained how they would stagger departures. Vincent first, followed by Sallie five minutes later, followed by Josh and Brandon ten minutes after that. "It's what the feds call being 'surveillance conscious,'" he said. Brandon thought it wasn't that different from the way he often had to slip out of restaurants, nightclubs, and charity events. Decoys, misdirection, and backdoors.

After Sallie and Vincent had left, Josh asked Brandon to take an oath of *omertà* to never reveal anything about Sallie. When Brandon started laughing, Josh kicked over a barstool. "This is no joke, Brandon." He rarely called Brandon by his full first name. "This is not some Studio City soundstage, and those two did not just go back to their trailers. Never mind what Sallie said about times changing. Out here, people can still disappear." Brandon, sobered by Josh's earnest reproach, held up a hand and swore to keep quiet. The concession wasn't enough. Josh insisted on a blood oath "to make it official." Without a stash of holy cards at Handel, he had to improvise, dripping droplets from Brandon's finger onto the face of a queen of hearts—the best stand-in for the Virgin Mary they could find—and then burning the card in a bowl that had been emptied of mixed nuts. Apparently satisfied with the makeshift ritual, Josh took Brandon outside to wait for his ride.

"Does Sallie know which team you play for?" Brandon asked.

Josh led him toward the curb, away from a crowd of rowdy patrons waiting behind the velvet rope. "Not much slips past that old alley cat. One day, he came into the club, told me he was flipping through cable when *Brokeback Mountain* popped up. He scratched a finger in the air for me to come closer, so he could whisper. 'Don't you think they should've called it *Bareback Mountain*?' Sallie started shaking with the giggles. I said, 'I wouldn't know, Sal. Haven't seen it.' Which was a lie. He stopped laughing and stared me straight in the eye. 'Really?' he asked. He stayed mute for what felt like a full minute. Then he patted me on the shoulder and said, 'Wouldn't have mattered if you did. Don't ask, don't tell. Am I right? Good rules for this life.'"

"If I was twenty years older, JF, I swear to God I'd give my left nut to play a guy like Sallie. I could live with one in the chamber, like single-shot Salinger, for a chance to do that."

On the ride home, Brandon caught up with social media and text messages. Other than a late-night Mishkin barrage about an appearance on a celebrity home improvement show and a stint as a guest judge on *American Idol*, he had only received two new texts since Josh had taken his phone, one from Alda and another, two minutes earlier, from her mother.

"Sounds like you've had a big day, Mr. Newman. I think it rather important that we meet. I'd prefer not to involve your lawyer, but that's easy enough if necessary. I have office hours on Monday from 10-12. 1150 Amsterdam Avenue. Meet me at 11. Call when you're downstairs. Maeve Kelley-Blackburn."

"gonna get call/text from mom. [sorry face] said a little too much-swore you were perfect gent! chaperone whole time. just being momma [teddy bear] dad doesn't know. turn on the charm [heart, flowers, violin] call to war game."

11

"Come in, Mr. Newman."

Brandon entered the professor's office wearing a white Joe Cool hoodie with Snoopy in blackout shades and a red turtleneck. A pair of wrap-around Ray-Bans with copper-tinted lenses sat on the bill of a Yankees cap. The sky blue JanSport backpack draped over one shoulder completed the collegiate disguise.

"The latest in fan-proof apparel, I presume? A little too Big Ten, if you ask me." She wagged a reproaching finger. "Not nearly enough *weltschmerz* for these parts." A blank look must have betrayed his confusion. "Never mind, what's the ballast?" She reached over her shoulder to tap her back.

"Couple of scripts. Rejects."

The office was cramped, windowless, messy—a cluttered desk, a wooden bookcase, nicked and scuffed, its shelves stuffed with door-stop books and its top covered with a teetering tower of journals. A creased anti-apartheid "Divest Now" placard and a framed poster from Springsteen's Tunnel of Love Express, April 1, 1988, Nassau Coliseum, hung side by side. Professor Kelley-Blackburn had faded freckles on her cheeks and forehead and small pouches under her pale green eyes. She wore faded blue skinny jeans and a black wool sweater with a loose turtleneck collar. Her shoulder-length auburn hair was soaking wet, and she smelled like the antibacterial soap dispensed in locker room showers.

"Back from a workout, Professor?"

She touched the top of her head. "Call me Maeve. It's Irish. A quick dip between meetings. My hair must be an absolute mess. I didn't have time to blow dry. Do you mind the music?" Her docked iPhone played a choral piece. She lowered the volume and sat down to sip a large iced coffee through an extra-long green straw. "It's Gregorian chant. Lately I've been completely obsessed with the Benedictines."

Brandon stared at a worn, spindle-backed chair serving as a makeshift shelf for a thick manuscript titled "Finding Meaning Where It Isn't: A Probabilistic, Quantum-Mechanical Approach to Neo-Structuralism."

"Sit down, please." She cleared the seat and explained that through a combination of Douglas's indiscreet pillow talk and Alda's eagerness to impress, she had learned about Brandon's project, its legal challenges, and the "potentially worrisome" friendship with her daughter.

A 5x7 of Alda on bended knee, clutching a soccer ball, sat on the desktop, angled toward a similarly framed photograph of a lean, blond, freckle-faced boy holding a lacrosse stick in the middle of a turf field. "Alda has a brother?"

Maeve picked up the frame. "Didn't mention him? I'm not surprised. He's three years older, a first year, plays for the Air Force Academy. Alda's still furious."

"Why?"

"Because she idolizes him, a proclivity of hers we'll no doubt discuss further, and she's afraid he'll end up shot down over Syria or Afghanistan. Chase wants to be a pilot and an astronaut."

"Take it from me; it's a lot safer to play one on TV."

"Alda hasn't spoken to her brother since he left for Colorado Springs. And now you come along to fill the void. That girl simply abhors a vacuum."

"I never had a kid sister, only an idiot older brother, walk-in chiropractor king of Tulsa. Cheats at golf every Wednesday and drinks like a channel cat. Only time he ever calls is to see if I'll do commercials." A puff of air burst through Brandon's lips. "I'd rather pitch Scientology."

Maeve put down her coffee and turned off the music. "You can't be surprised that I've summoned you here. Only the most shameless of stage mothers would be thrilled by the notion of a heartthrob playing footsie with her underaged, star-struck daughter." She had hands on knees, her chin dipped, her piercing eyes fixed. "Do I need to get a restraining order, Mr. Newman? Because you know I can get one quick and on the cheap."

"Call me Brandon." He tapped two fingers against his chest. "I'm no J.D. Salinger, not a snowball's chance in hell." He stood and stepped behind the chair, bracing his hands on its back. "I'm all about Holden. Period." Brandon swiped at the air with a knife-hand before resting it over his heart. "I would *never* do what Salinger did."

Maeve sucked up the last drops of coffee. "Why not? You snap your fingers for front-row seats and presidential suites." She scooted to the edge of her chair and snapped her fingers twice. "What's more alluring than forbidden fruit to the young man who can have everything?"

"Sorry to disabuse your prejudices, Maeve, but after what I've been through, you really think I need more tabloid covers? Or even worse, a nice, long staycation at the nearest state pen? You've got nothing to worry about. Besides, I've got a strict celebrities-only policy. A lot safer for guys like me." He patted his stomach and pulled his phone out of the hoodie. A text from Alda. "Excuse me. It's my agent. Contracts she needs me to sign or something." He sat down to read the text. Maeve put on glasses and opened an e-mail window on her desktop.

`"going OK?"`

`"Waving shotgun on porch [winking face] keep the faith I got this"`

Maeve turned away from her computer screen. "You'll forgive me, Brandon, if I remain skeptical. You've made some awful choices in the not-so-distant past, showed a completely reckless lack of control." She rested her hand on the desk telephone. "Why shouldn't I end all this with one ring to Douglas, or perhaps a whistle blown in the direction of Salinger's trust?"

Brandon smirked and held up crimped fingers. "Momma Bear's got some sharp claws." He mimed a bow draw and let one fly. "I've been clean two years. Arrow straight. Went to a meeting yesterday. Bunch of recovering actors. You know what they call twenty-four hours under the spotlight in prison? Torture. Probably do that shit in Gitmo. If you saw us, sitting there, you'd think we're doing a table read for some lousy Lifetime series." He pretended to hold a script. "But it's the most real thing we do. You don't have to worry about me falling off any wagons. Us Sooners are practically born with Conestoga reins in our hands. Plus, nobody dances the twelve-step better than I do." He tapped his feet to simulate a kick ball change.

Maeve seemed unfazed by his attempted humor. She stared at him over the tops of her readers. "What if you're merely trading one vice for another? Perhaps your current obsession with this particular book is a distress call from your superego."

He didn't understand what she meant, but he knew he still had to convince her that Alda would be safe. In pregame texts, she had warned him that Maeve could make Saint Thomas look like an easy mark. Brandon picked up a nearby stack of student essays and flipped through them, each one streaked with red ink. "What a surprise? No easy As." He flung the papers to the floor. "Yeah, I know, all of us actors have these giant egos. I get it. You want proof? I'll give it to you. I've really got no time for this." He shot up and pressed his back against the door, one hand clamped on the doorknob. "It's because nobody could lock a dressing room faster than I could. Okay?" He glared at her, unblinking. "I knew plenty of kids who weren't so quick." He looked away, wincing from the memory of narrow backstage escapes. "Alda—*you*, I suppose—might be right about what happened to little Jerry Salinger. Actually made me feel bad for the guy. But I swear I didn't turn out like him . . . stuck in some fucked-up fetish feedback loop. I might have ninety-nine problems, but *that*, I guarantee you, ain't one of them."

Maeve rested her chin on bridged fingers bowing under the weight, pausing a few seconds before speaking as if to acknowledge the gravity of his revelation. "I appreciate your candor, Mr. Newman, Brandon." She looked up at a Darlingbrooke Hall wall calendar turned to October. A brick-red covered bridge stretched over a narrow, rushing river dotted with gray granite boulders and lined with bushy maples in full color. "So, it's more than just survivor's guilt you share with our woebegone friend."

Brandon sat with hands clasped loosely in his lap. "I'll stay away from Alda if that's what you really want, but she's perfect for the documentary. She knows that book better than my momma knows scripture. You should see what we've shot so far." He slid to the edge of his seat. "You understand why having a bright-eyed teenage girl is perfect to take on a lech like Salinger." Brandon pretended to throw jabs. "Karma's a bitch, right? You've read—"

"All of it, of course, minus whatever the trust keeps hidden in its precious time-release capsule." She removed the lid from her iced coffee to crunch on the last cubes and put the empty cup in a recycling bin beneath her desk. "I have to confess I'd always hoped that whenever Salinger arrived at the pearly gates, he'd be met by a scowling little girl, some rosy-cheeked cherub clutching the golden keys instead of a doddering old Saint Peter." Maeve opened a desk drawer and took out a tin of Altoids. They each took two. She hesitated before closing and pulled out a butterfly paperclip. "When Alda was little, she used to call these 'angel backs.' See, the twin tops look like wings." She held it up to point them out and made it dance before his face. "A sly angel with braided pigtails consigning J.D. to the flaming lake." She inhaled deeply. "I'd pay a premium to see that." She tapped the paperclip against Alda's frame. "You must know by now what I think. What that man could have accomplished if he'd put as much effort into his writing as he did into luring young women to that spooky boondocks lair. Imagine a female author living like some self-indulgent siren, crashing little boys against the rocks. You think she'd be as worshipped?" Maeve twisted the paperclip into a gnarled snake as she spoke.

Brandon slapped his thigh and pointed at Maeve. "You have got to be one of my talking heads."

"Flattery, Mr. Newman?" She deposited the contorted metal in the trash. "I'd happily agree to sit for a Salinger documentary *if* you promise to leave poor Holden alone."

Brandon's eyes popped. "Why would I do that? He's the whole point. Sorry, just a sec, my agent's rattling my change again."

```
"Shotgun down yet?"
"phase II. abt to take me [movie camera] school."
"[trophy] [heart eyes]"
```

"I'm really sorry about that. Shari is so pissed. I told her I absolutely refuse to be on any more Comic-Con panels. It's all robot alien salutes and ET yakety-yak. I D-N-D'ed her." He zipped the phone inside his backpack. Alda had warned him that Maeve would probably want to give her opinion about his project and that hearing her out was the best way to avoid any problems with Douglas. "Go ahead, Maeve, I think you were about to stomp on my dream."

She stood up and rested a hip on the edge of her desk. "In my opinion, for artistic and not legal reasons, you should allow *The Catcher in the Rye* to remain in its original form, a novel." She moved next to her packed shelves and pulled out a copy of *Catcher*. "You can't be surprised to hear that from someone like me." The paperback's pages were frayed like a worn-out toothbrush. She shuffled them between her fingers, just like Sallie Choo Choo. "I know you think Salinger and his trust are keeping Holden Caulfield locked up, but aren't you simply trying to become his latest jailor?"

Brandon sat back, scanning the room as if searching for a cue card. "You lost me there, Teach. All I been trying to do is bust him out. I'm not the one who won't share."

Maeve reached into her purse and pulled out a makeup compact. She kept it unopened in a closed fist. "Holden, up to this point, has never had a face. Neither has Phoebe. The characters, the settings, the sounds—they pop into existence, uniquely, in the mind of each reader. The possibilities aren't infinite, of course, but they are legion. There is an unparalleled richness in that—the chance for intimate, singular engagement. Once you film, the variety of perspectives collapses into one vision, yours." She opened the case and turned the mirror toward

Brandon. "Holden Caulfield becomes fixed, locked in." She snapped the case shut and pointed to the bulky manuscript she had moved to allow him to sit. "It's like quantum mechanics. A movie freezes him in you and your interpretation. Your film becomes reductive, eliminating the inimitable alchemy that occurs each time a reader turns the page. Tell me: Is one solid state truly freedom for a character as meaty and meaningful as Holden Caulfield?"

Brandon took off his ballcap, brushed a hand through his hair, and replaced it, backwards. "No offense, Maeve, but that sounds like a bunch of ivory tower mumbo jumbo. I'm not changing any part of his story. That's the whole point. If I make the movie, millions of people who don't know about him, who wouldn't ever, will get to meet him. If somebody wants to pick up the book afterwards and imagine the boy two inches taller or with a deeper voice, be my guest. You can't begin to think about what he looks like if you never even heard of him." Brandon pulled a copy of *Great Expectations* from her shelves and shook it next to his face like a fire-and-brimstone preacher wielding the Bible. "Seriously, are you planning on investing in a bookstore or a publishing house anytime soon?"

She shrugged. "At least you didn't grab *Fahrenheit 451*. That would have been some classic Tinseltown schlock." She tossed *Catcher* to the desk. "To borrow a metaphor from your preferred medium, let's cut to the chase." She sat in her chair with one leg folded under her body. "It's not merely a question of literary virtue. As I believe Douglas explained, you will be sued into bankruptcy if you produce a faithful version. If his firm says there's no way around it, believe me you don't need a second opinion."

"Opinions aren't facts, Maeve. I'm not giving up."

She smiled and sat back, her arms folded. "I do happen to have an alternative for you. I've been thinking about it ever since I heard you wanted to turn the novel into a movie. Why not, instead, make something that's edgy, current, original, and frankly, much more commercially viable? A contemporary story *about Catcher* that becomes transformative, which, I understand, is legally significant in the copyright realm. They'd probably still take you to court, kick and scream, but ultimately they couldn't stop you."

He looked at his watch. "The elevator doors just closed, Maeve. You're on the clock."

She stood to make her pitch. "Imagine a movie about the three assassins inspired by *Catcher*, three interwoven storylines where you play all three roles, Chapman, Hinckley, and that man who killed the young sitcom actress. What was his name?"

"Bardo. Robert John Bardo." Brandon had almost raised his hand before answering.

"Was that really his name? Jesus, you can't make this stuff up. You know what 'bardo' means, don't you?" Brandon remained silent. "The bardo is a Buddhist purgatory, an impermanent state of existence between death and rebirth. Hell of a last name for a murderer. You tell their three stories all tied together by *Catcher*, have them reciting parts of it aloud to themselves, like Vedas, cutting back and forth, one starting a sentence, another finishing, each one taking the same incantatory meanings as their obsessions grow and they pursue their targets. And then," she grabbed a pencil and skipped it in the air like an orchestra conductor, "the classroom. The last thread should be a small graduate seminar engaged in a close reading of the novel." She sat down and held *Catcher* with two hands on her lap, the cover facing Brandon. He'd never noticed the streetlamp that looked as if it had skewered the carousel horse's hind leg. "The professor and the students would share insights on the assassins' favorite passages, showing the audience where the madmen occasionally get it right but mostly get it wrong."

Brandon tuned out the rest of her proposal as he stared at the cover. The horse seemed like it was falling. Had it been shot by the arrow tattooed on its front leg? Mr. Antolini tells Holden that he is "riding" to a downfall. Brandon saw himself gripping the wooden horse's mane as they plummeted together into the abyss. Even the background sketch of the cover's New York City skyline foreshadowed a great collapse—two tall twin towers appear to soar above the pencil-sketched skyline decades before the World Trade Center came tumbling down. His mind flashed with photographs of the people jumping out of windows, falling to their deaths, like the boy who died wearing Holden's sweater.

"What do you think?" she asked.

Brandon felt he had shown more than enough patience. "Why does everybody want to change my movie?" He pointed to Alda's photo. "She would never agree with this. Why should I make a movie *about Catcher* before I make the original? I don't want to play a deranged assassin, let alone three. Your script would turn Holden into an extra." His backpack rattled. "Sorry. Shari's got an emergency number when she has to reach me."

"done deal?"

"got spiel on why TCITR won't work. [Circle with a slash] [worried face] the classic IS LIFE."

"[crying eyes out]"

97

"Sorry, Maeve. I've got this phone call later with a studio exec. He wants me to play Hawkman. Hollywood is really scraping the bottom of the superhero barrel these days. No way I'm running around in another pair of tights *and* a pair of stupid feathery wings."

She pulled another butterfly clip from her drawer and flew it above her head. "You know what happens when you soar too close to the sun?" She plunged the clip into her lap.

Brandon knew what she meant—a terrific fall—but deflected with a joke. "Sunburn?"

Maeve frowned and wrapped a hand around her jaw. "Maybe Douglas *was* right about you."

"About what?"

"Underestimating risks. It's a pretty long way down from such lofty heights."

"They don't call it a leap of faith for nothing."

12

Brandon met Shari on a Friday afternoon in mid-October at the midtown heliport to fly to the Hamptons for a product launch, a new cologne called "Grecian Fire." Brandon was in the last year of his contract with a multinational cosmetics firm. Once they were strapped in, he fingered the fabric of Shari's burgundy pantsuit. "The latest from the Hillary Clinton collection?"

She tugged on the lapel of her gray knee-length sweater vest. "Vintage Bea Arthur."

He flipped palms to show his confusion.

"The tall one from *Golden Girls*. Died about five years ago."

"That's one way to get out of appearances."

"You got to love the tag line, Brando. 'For passion that burns all night.'"

"I'd rather be getting a tooth pulled. Shit smells like ginger beer and burnt leaves."

"I asked the pilot to take us over Green-Wood Cemetery in Brooklyn. Something I want to show you."

The helicopter followed the East River toward the Manhattan Bridge and veered left, heading up Flatbush Avenue. The sun, already low in the western sky, washed rows of apartment buildings in smoky amber. Brandon asked the pilot to fly them over Prospect Park. When they passed above the great arch at Grand Army Plaza, the park's main entrance, the pilot, who had obviously done his share of skyline tours, rattled off trivia: 526 acres, designed by the same architects who created Central Park, opened in 1867.

Brandon pressed his hand against a window. "Is that the zoo?" He searched for the sea lion exhibit.

Shari pressed against him to get a better look. "Yep, went there as a kid. My *bubbe* lived in Inwood, used to take me. They had this scrawny-looking polar bear, Snowball. Its mangy coat looked like three-day-old street snow, clumps of sooty gray. Sad sack kept pacing in circles. She always bought me Italian ices, cherry flavored. Afterwards I'd stick my bright red tongue out and howl at the baboons, trying to get their attention."

"Where's the carousel?" Brandon asked.

The pilot pointed out an unremarkable, hexagonal brick building south of the zoo. "You can't see much of anything from up here. Built in 1912, fifty-three hand-carved wooden horses, a giraffe, a lion, and a deer. She really whirls." He twirled his finger upward.

"Is this more goddamned location scouting? That's exactly why I want to show you the cemetery. Something so much better for you. It can't miss. Something you can do *today*. You'll die for it."

"That why we're headstone shopping?"

"Fat chance, funny boy. Look, there it is."

"Green-Wood Cemetery was founded in 1838," the pilot said. "Four hundred seventy-eight acres, designated a National Historic Landmark by the Department of the Interior in 2006. Boss Tweed, Horace Greeley, and Leonard Bernstein are among its more famous permanent residents."

"You know who else is buried in there, Brando? The guy who's gonna win you an Academy Award, that's who."

"It ain't Salinger."

"Nope, it's Giuseppe Gallo."

"Some dead opera singer? You know I won't sing in movies anymore."

"Not it, my little okie artichokie. It's Joey Gallo, also known as 'Crazy Joe Gallo,' notorious Brooklyn gangster."

"Never heard of him. They wouldn't cast me anyway."

"That's the point. Now *you're* the boss, bankrolling your own projects. This is the one to do. It's a grand slam, straight out of the park."

"What's his story?"

"1972. Legendary mob hit. Whacked having dinner at Umberto's Clam House in Little Italy. He and his brothers were running around like madmen in Carroll Gardens back in the Sixties. Over there." She pointed to the northwest. "Protection rackets, bookmaking, you name it. You've seen that famous picture of Albert Anastasia, the mob boss shot dead in a barber chair?"

"Of course." Brandon hadn't, but he recalled Sallie's recent description.

"Guess who did that piece of work. Crazy Joey, that's who."

"You might be interested to know," the pilot said, "that Mr. Anastasia is also one of Green-Wood's perpetual tenants."

Shari tapped the pilot on the shoulder. "What do you say you keep your eyes to the skies, Lindbergh? We're discussing business here." She sat back to resume the pitch. "This Gallo kid was a diagnosed schizophrenic, but he was also a certified genius, like some kind of rain man. He went to prison and started reading all these existentialist French philosophers— Sartre, Camus, and a bunch of other frogs." She slapped Brandon's arm. "I'm not kidding. He even gave philosophy lessons to some of the inmates. Painted watercolors and learned contract bridge too, became a world-class player."

"Sammy the Bull liked to play chess when he was locked up," Brandon said. He imagined Crazy Joe and Sheila painting landscapes together in a cellblock.

"On top of being this jailhouse intellectual, Gallo saved a correctional officer during a prison riot. The guy testified for him at his parole hearing, and Joey gets sprung. Back on the streets, he becomes the darling of the New York social scene, palling around with celebrities, best friends with Jerry Orbach."

"Who's that?"

"Who's that? Jesus, I'm getting too old for this. Orbach, Broadway legend, Tony winner. He was that Joe Friday detective from *Law & Order*."

"The one who looked like an undertaker?"

"Exactly. Gallo lived too fast and made too many enemies with elephant memories. Died in a hailstorm of bullets right before the tiramisu. Forty-three years old. Born and died on the same day, April 7. It's one hell of an arc. Balls-out mobster becomes this bookworm in the joint but can't escape his past. That's your movie. Can you believe it?"

"You know what? I think I can. These wise-guy types are full of surprises."

"What do you say?"

"Got a script?"

"I got a guy. He knows Pileggi from *Goodfellas*. You can't get any better. He wrote a shitload of other mob books. He's long in the tooth, but they say he's still banging away. We can get him help if he wants. He's interested, definitely they tell me. With his name and this *punim*," she pinched Brandon's cheek, "we can't lose."

The helicopter flew low along Long Beach, its beige sands and snack shacks deserted until spring. "Get me the script, but it's still gotta toast back of the stove."

"What is it gonna take to change your mind?"

Brandon knocked a fist against his own head. "It's gonna take Dr. Frankenstein with a circular saw."

A Black Lincoln waited in Southampton for the short trip to the beach-front estate that had been rented for the cologne kickoff. They walked along a gleaming white marble path lined with burning Olympic torches and a dozen young models dressed like vestal virgins, laurel wreaths in their braided hair, greeting guests with smiling "*kalisperas.*"

Shari elbowed her client. "Some Saudi prince uses this place for three weeks in the summer, otherwise it sits vacant the whole year." The massive three-story structure looked like a mirrored ice cube. The last rays of sunlight warmed its west side, making it glow like a fading ember. The house was surrounded by grass cut golf-green short and accented by shrubs pruned in precise geometric shapes—pyramids, globes, and cones. Two enormous gleaming sculptures framed the main entrance—price-less red balloon dogs by Jeffrey Koons, according to Shari. "House was designed by Philip Johnson, piece of shit architect he was. Big Hitler lover in the Thirties, adored that anti-Semite priest, Father Coughlin. Bastard said he was sorry decades later, built a synagogue in Port Chester, as if that makes up for it. I'd have no problem casting a few jagged stones through his precious glass houses. How'd you like that kind of *Kristallnacht*, Phillie boy?"

Brandon braced a hand on her shoulder. "That's good enough for me. Let's split."

"Forget it, Brando, contract says we got to." They were directed to the back of the house near the pool. She dragged him straight to an audi-ence with the majority shareholders from Singapore. While they posed, arm in arm, for an inordinate number of group pictures, muscular male models in short togas poured drinks from faux amphorae carried on broad shoulders while furry-legged Pans, playing pipes and lyres, skipped and twirled among tall-hat aluminum patio heaters.

Brandon, his arm sore from almost being shaken off, excused himself by pretending to need a drink. "We done, Shari?"

"Not yet. The step-and-repeat is over there." She pointed to a vinyl wall stretched along a short side of the rectangular pool and emblazoned from top to bottom with images of the Grecian Fire logo. A pack of photog-raphers wrestled for position as they snapped pictures of a man Brandon later learned was the top-rated polo player in Argentina. "You're up next."

Brandon fluffed his hair and approached the melee with a professional sashay. He spit his gum into a clump of blue hydrangeas and checked his face in a magnifying mirror held by a young woman stationed at the edge of the wall. She had a last-minute makeup kit hanging around her neck. He waved off any touch-up. "To the firing squad," he said, stepping into the camera sights. Accompanied by a chorus of rapid clicks, he smiled, pointed, joked, posed, and sprayed a few puffs of cologne from a bottle handed to him by a stoic Nordic Aphrodite. At the end of the wall, Brandon coughed as if he'd been holding his breath too long and searched for Shari in the crowd. As he reached inside his suitcoat for a cigarette, a meaty hand clamped down on his shoulder.

"Brandofsky." The husky male voice belonged to a pudgy Broadway producer who'd been pestering Shari for weeks, trying to get Brandon to star in a musical version of *1984*. He took Brandon by the hand and pulled him into an empty cabana facing the ocean. "You can't avoid Big Brother forever. He's everywhere." The producer spilled half of a cosmopolitan on himself as he laughed. "We've got the absolute A-plus list: George Wolfe, Susan Stroman, and, shhh, listen to this." He stood within millimeters of Brandon's face. His breath stunk of cigars and liquor. "Sondheim," he whispered. "I'm not even supposed to mention it yet. His people tell me he's definitely in. You can't miss the last rodeo." The man stepped back and raised his voice. "I had lunch with Donna last week, you know, Bernadette's sister, said you'd be absolutely perfect, the best. Couldn't stop talking about you. Mr. Smith, Winston Smith, goes to Broadway. Heard you want to get away from that cookie-cutter crap they serve out west. Why not make it a clean break? Cold turkey. Legitimate theater's the ticket. How about it, Curly McLain? What do you say? Show me a little sweet charity." He mock-punched Brandon's bicep.

"I think it's way too dated. That's what I've been hearing." Brandon fled toward a buffet table near the beach, but the persistent producer heeled in close pursuit.

"Dated? No way, Count von Brandenburg. Now's the time, it's like a fine Bordeaux. They buried real news in Cronkite's casket. Today it's all propaganda. That's just the way it is. Network stooges need content so bad they gobble up whatever the party feeds them. What'll it take? You want me to beg? I'll beg. I'm begging you." He seized Brandon's hands.

Brandon shook free of his grip. "Sorry. I don't have time now. My pipeline's too clogged." He spotted Shari standing alone near the beach, phone pressed to her ear, waving a skewered prawn. "I gotta go." He spun around after a few steps. "I'll think about it. I will. Shari'll call you." Brandon quickstepped to his agent. "Let's get out of here."

Shari mouthed "my mother" as she finished the call. "Ma, I told you they'll replace it if you want. No cost. It's covered. I'll send them tomorrow." She slipped the phone into her purse. "Bought her a massage chair, top-of-the-line recliner. Ma sets it on 'high' and peed herself." Shari made the headless prawn quiver. "The vibrations. Golden years all right but nobody tells you that means piss everywhere."

"What's *1984*, the book, actually about?" Brandon asked.

"It's about this dictator state, government controls everything—news, history, even your thoughts. Clocks strike thirteen and two plus two equals five. And you don't question it. You don't *want* to question it."

"Perfect place for Holden," Brandon said. Shari let her head go limp against her shoulder and pretended to yank a rope above her head. "Hilarious, Shar. All you've been wanting to do this whole time is off that poor kid." Brandon faced the gentle evening surf. Enough sunlight lingered to create silhouettes of anchored sailboats bobbing in the sound. "Let's take a walk before we go."

"All I'm saying, Brand, is why waste prime time chasing windmills? The trust is going to snatch your wallet and make you and me look like a couple of laughingstocks."

"I've been rethinking my strategy. I want to get sued, the sooner the better."

"You got a screw loose up there?" Shari woodpeckered a finger against Brandon's temple. "You heard Blackburn. A judge would freeze everything on day one."

"But how can you stop the movie before you've even seen what it is, before it's even finished?"

"Brando, if you tell the world you're gonna torch my house, a judge doesn't have to sit around until you pour the gasoline and strike a match. He can curtain the show, act one, scene one."

"But what if I tell them it's a fresh look? You remember what Doug said about how I could make fun of *Catcher*, or do an X-rated version. Hold on." Brandon texted Maeve. "What was that transformation thing again?" They stepped onto the sand to avoid a pair of joggers. "What if we tell them we're doing something different, a total remix?"

"I'm nobody's IP lawyer, Brand, but I think that depends on how different."

Brandon's phone buzzed. "Transformative use. If you change a work of art enough in making your own comment on it, you may not be violating the copyright."

"Let's say I tell them I'm making a mash-up, my own interpretation. What if it's like this artsy reboot, completely transformative?"

"But you've been like Johnny One Note with this thing all along, telling the world you want to shoot *Catcher* like a Muslim reciting the Koran, word for sacred word."

"So, what if I'm a goddamned temperamental artist? People don't ever get to change their minds about anything?" He let his posture slacken and eyes droop. He cocked his head, lids shut, frowning, as if summoning a distinct voice from an internal repertory troupe. "My momma done learned me back yonder that that there cousin Saul of yours did one doozy of a U-turn along the dusty dirt road to Damascus."

"Oh, really."

"Damn straight, he did. Praise the Lord." Brandon bowed his head and held a testifying hand to the sky, striking a familiar pose from his youth. As soon as he looked up, the homespun evangelical had slid back down inside, rejoining the company in residence. "And like some other Hebrew know-it-all once told me, 'don't snub free pub.' Let them sue me, long as we win. Think of the hype: headlines, paparazzi, talking heads, social media. All we got to do is to convince a judge to let us stay in production."

"Now you're really getting up a little too early for my night school law degree."

"Get Doug on the phone."

She called the firm. "They say Doug's in Sag Harbor. Can it wait until Monday?"

"That's perfect. Tell them we'll be at his house in thirty minutes."

Brandon texted Alda. "You in Sag Harbor?"

"How'd you know?"

"On my way to surprise daddy-o. [fingers over lips] More war gaming. Play it cool. Tell Momma [bear]."

He texted Maeve. "Coming to Sag to ambush Doug. Legal powwow. A's gonna warn you."

13

Floodlights triggered by motion detectors illuminated the Blackburn second home, a stout two-story with cedar shake siding and white trim. Inside the spray of light, a quartet of forest green Adirondack chairs surrounded a stone firepit off the back deck. As the car turned into the circular drive, the headlamps flashed across a net hung between tall pines. Brandon had just finished a frantic text exchange with Luis. "They don't seem like the volleyball type."

"Come off it, kid," Shari said. "That's badminton. Probably got their sticky wickets set up around back."

Brandon imagined playing badminton with Alda on a hot summer day. It would be a close, lively match—long rallies, lucky breaks, snarky banter, do-overs following spirited rule disputes. But it wouldn't end well. She'd scold him when he smashed a shuttlecock into her chest. "What are we even playing for, then?" he'd say. "You want me to let you win?" Her cheeks would be pink from heat and anger. She'd claim it wasn't about winning and that he didn't understand her at all. Then she'd demand that he bring her some fresh-squeezed lemonade from the kitchen. Brandon would end the scene with a bitter Salinger-esque observation about the frustratingly unsolvable mystery of women.

Douglas Blackburn opened the front door and popped out on the porch before they had a chance to knock. "Hi, Doug. You remember Shari. Sorry about the pop-in. We were just down the block. Didn't have time to grab a bottle. You can charge me time and a half."

"Apologies for the sneak attack," Shari said. "On *Shabbos* no less. He's kidding about that last thing."

Douglas wore weathered brown loafers without socks and a gray NYAC sweatshirt. He offered them bowls of his "famous" campfire chili. Brandon said they'd already eaten. Douglas led his guests through a living room with a glossy black Steinway grand piano, a brick fireplace painted white, standing-room-only built-in bookshelves on both sides, and an oil painting of the Blackburn family hanging over the mantel, Douglas and Chase in matching navy blazers, Maeve and Alda in white cotton summer dresses. She must have been about six, front teeth missing. Douglas stopped at the butler's pantry to take drink orders. Shari examined a bottle of Hendrick's gin. "This seems like a pretty good spot for a martini." Brandon opted for Johnnie Walker Blue Label, neat.

"The way you're dressed, Brandon," Douglas said, "I'd have pegged you for a martini man. Shaken, not stirred, if you get my drift."

"Newman, Brandon Newman," Shari said in a garbled British accent that sounded like a mix of Mel Brooks and Mel Gibson.

"That's a slipper I've got plenty of time to grow into, Doug."

Drinks in hand, they proceeded to a den off the kitchen. Maeve and Alda were wrapped in matching tartan plaid blankets, ensconced in a pair of sandy-colored couches, overstuffed like billowing clouds. They were watching *Napoleon Dynamite* on a massive flat-screen. "My Alda is quite a fan of yours. She's seen all of your films."

"Pleasure to meet you, Alda." She stood up, and they shared an arm's-length handshake. Alda wore a baggy gray sweatshirt with the outline of an island that looked like an upside-down pork chop and a pair of cotton candy pink pajama bottoms with "DH" on one thigh. Brandon shot his chin at the screen. "Nobody understands poor Napoleon. His friend Pedro is the best. He kills me. Which one is your favorite? Of my movies, I mean."

"They're all so good. I really like that one about the bullied immigrant kid who becomes a chess champion, *Czech Mate*, but if I had to pick, it would definitely be *Secret Skater.*" Alda turned to her father. "Brandon, Mr. Newman, played this teenaged skateboard champion who doubled as an undercover CIA hacker. What was the tagline again?"

Shari lowered her voice. "Skateboard by day, keyboard by night."

Brandon stepped toward Maeve's couch to shake hands. "Nice to meet you, Mrs. Blackburn."

"Maeve Kelley-Blackburn, but you may call me Maeve." She remained seated and apologized for not having put out any food. She offered to whip up a tray of cheese, crackers, and fruit for the unexpected guests.

So far so good. They had all played it cool. Douglas typed on his phone, oblivious to the improvisation being performed in his honor. Brandon held up his drink. "Thanks, Maeve. We're all set." He apologized for interrupting their evening, explaining that he had some new thoughts on an urgent legal issue.

Maeve re-wrapped herself to tighten the blanket. "Please, Douglas rarely gets to use his home office. Trust me. He's thrilled."

The study had a nautical theme, framed antique sea charts and sconces with caged lights. A model clipper ship and a miniature lighthouse sat on the floor-to-ceiling shelves lining the wall behind a two-ton antique wooden desk. Opposite the desk hung a painting of a giant ocean wave topped with white sea foam that looked as if it were made up of a million bony witch fingers. A pair of French doors led to the back deck. Douglas stared into the darkness, tapping on the glass. He said they would soon be pulling the sailboat for winter storage. He rested a hand on a spotting scope atop a tripod and described the daytime view of the bay as "absolutely spectacular."

Brandon stood next to a short, stubby paddle hanging near the doorjamb. "What kind of boat is this one for, Doug?"

"Not for the water, that one. It's a pledge paddle, the old Tri-Kap days, my fraternity."

"What were you, like, the chief ass-whooper and towel-snapper?"

"Not quite. Purely decorative. Our hazing was more psychological than corporal."

"No goat *shtupping*?" Shari asked.

Douglas looked like he'd swallowed a fly. "Um, no, the worst we did was blindfold pledges and make them squeeze overripe bananas floating in library toilet bowls. Strictly puerile pranks."

Brandon imagined Josh, tears streaming down his face, roaring at the thought of Holden pledging a fraternity. "I got another Oscar winner for you," Josh would say. He'd propose a slasher parody—Holden, lowest pin in the pledge class, putting on his people-shooting hat after a brutal hell week and mowing down the entire frat house, except for the diabolical rush chairman, who'd be forced at gunpoint to do a perfect half gainer off the frat house roof. Douglas would probably give the green light for that one. Brandon finished his drink in one gulp. "Mind if I swap this out for some sparkling water?" It was a ruse to meet with Maeve. He had just texted her. He excused himself and returned to the den.

Maeve had discarded her blanket and was sitting up, waiting. Brandon cranked his arm in a tight circle and headed for the kitchen. Alda stood up to join them, but he twitched his head and pushed a palm down to exclude her.

They stood at a vast island topped with white marble streaked with twisting strands of gray. She handed him a bottle from a refrigerated beverage drawer and put his empty glass in the clean-up sink. He asked if anybody knew about her pitch, the three assassins and the college class. She assured him no one knew. "Good. I thought all this time it was about being a fugitive, staying one step ahead of the trust, but listening to you, I started seeing a better way." He explained how he intended to abandon a faithful *Catcher* and present her pitch to Doug as his own latest inspiration. "You got to promise you're not gonna say I stole your idea."

She gave a quick, constricted nod. "I understand. The answer is no. No problem, that is. I would never have done anything with it."

"You're cool with opening night tickets?"

She extended her hand to shake on it. "What should I say to Alda?"

"Tell her the truth. That I wanted to run my new version by you, how to sell it to Doug."

"She'll be jealous."

"Good. By the way, you have got to write the treatment." He bolted from the kitchen before she could respond.

When Brandon returned to the office, Douglas and Shari stood shoulder-to-shoulder facing a framed document, swirls and loops of faded calligraphy with a faint red seal at the bottom. Douglas's glasses had been raised to his forehead. "Brandon, come take a look at this. I think you'll find it fascinating."

Brandon joined them, imagining exactly what Holden would say about it being "fascinating" in that surly, exasperated whine he'd been secretly working to perfect.

"I'd wager you've probably never seen one of these," Douglas said. "It's a royal land grant. Old George gave my family a large tract outside of Princeton. We had it for nearly two hundred years until one of my excessively benevolent greats left it to the college. Rumor has it he was unusually fond of the provost." Douglas clucked his tongue. "Athletics practice fields now. Not even a placard." He gestured toward two guest chairs upholstered in anchors and sextants. "Shall we get down to business?" He dialed a number on his landline. "I want Wong on with us."

"Sorry to ruin your Saturday, Ernie boy."

"Not a problem, Brandon. It's only me and Xbox tonight."

He explained his new concept, just as Maeve has described it, parallel story lines featuring the three assassins inspired by *Catcher*. Wong's keystrokes clacked through the speaker. "I know it's not poking fun, but it's totally different. You think they'll still sue me?" Brandon expected Douglas's answer would be "yes." He was counting on it.

"Your proposal does give us something interesting to work with, a lot actually, but I've got to be honest. Those corporate trustees are the worst overprotective Jewish mothers you can imagine." He looked at Shari. "No offense."

"Are you kidding, Doug? My mother sent me to college with a portable fire escape ladder, and I lived on the first floor of a concrete building."

Douglas predicted that as soon as the trust learned of the film, it would waste no time in launching a furious legal offensive, particularly in light of their prior cease-and-desist demand. The trustees would likely view any film based on *Catcher* as the beginning of a descent down a slippery slope resulting in "a material degradation of the copyright." The trust lawyers would send a second, more indignant cease-and-desist letter with a very short deadline. Once the date passed, they would file a complaint seeking a permanent injunction along with a request for a temporary restraining order and a motion for a preliminary injunction. "The TRO freezes you immediately until we have a preliminary hearing, and if we lose that, you're frozen solid until the case is finally decided. Then it could be months, or years, until it's finally over."

Shari took a pad of yellow Post-its from the desk and put them on an end table to use as a coaster. "Sounds like a headache and a half. So many other projects you could do. That thing we discussed in the whirly-bird." Shari turned to Douglas as if to translate. "I get calls from Netflix and Amazon every day, pleading to hand this kid not just a fat check but a morbidly obese check for new projects. I'm talking Orson at RKO kind of sweetheart deals."

"What about transformative use, Doug?" Brandon asked. "Doesn't that make it a slam dunk?"

Douglas let his jaw drop. "Have you been cheating on me? I thought we were going steady." He winked at Shari.

"I LegalZoomed it. This movie isn't *Catcher*. It's about psychotic stalkers who think they've finally found their first true friend. How can the trust convince a judge it's even close to the same? What about my freedom of expression?"

"It would depend on how truly distinct your interpretation is, how much you really create something that transforms the original artistic work." Douglas plucked a golf ball, St. Andrews logo, from a full glass jar on his desk and reclined to cross his legs. He rolled the ball in his fingers as he spoke. "I know their counsel all too well, and I have to confess I'm not too sanguine. Pack of feral hounds they are, and their mission is to fight tooth and nail. They won't even negotiate. They'll argue you're co-opting the unique essence of Salinger's creation until they're blue in the face. Even if it's a losing battle, the CPLT will go down swinging, and its attorneys, I assure you, will happily bill thousands of hours in what promises to be a very drawn-out process."

"But couldn't you stop the freeze at least while I'm working? Until it's done?"

Wong cleared his throat. "Excuse me, Doug. We would have the prior restraint analogy."

"What's that?" Brandon asked.

"Go ahead, Ernest."

"The First Amendment case law on publishing and defamation would be favorable to us. The Supreme Court has repeatedly held that it disfavors a prior restraint on the release of a book or newspaper article when someone claims potential defamation. An injunction that stifles a story before publication too severely impinges upon the core First Amendment rights of freedom of the press and of speech. Only in the very clearest of cases, where, for example, national security might be irreparably compromised by publication, will the courts issue a preemptive order preventing publication."

"That's what I want. Support the Bill of Rights, go see my movie."

"Hold the publicity campaign," Douglas said. "We could buttress the First Amendment position with a justiciability argument, given the lack of ripeness in the absence of a finished product, but this isn't a breaking news story with political implications. A court sitting in equity would, at the end of the day, very likely prevent you from distributing any film until it has had an adequate opportunity to review the final cut, receive briefs and hear arguments from both sides, and rule on the ultimate question of copyright infringement. And of course, there's always the possibility of a lengthy appellate process even if you were to win round one."

Shari put down her martini and placed a hand on Brandon's knee. "And if you lose, all that time and money," she flushed air through his lips like a worn-out stock horse, "straight down the crapper."

Brandon snatched a gold-plated letter opener from the desk and thrust it to within a millimeter of the back of her hand. "That's how they took out Luca Brasi, remember?" He dropped the dull blade in her lap. "Doug's just got to get me a window. By then, we'll have all the momentum we need. The trust will be waving a white hankie way before the judge even has to make a decision. Look what happened with that tightrope walker, Petit. Port Authority didn't even prosecute him for trespassing, gave him a lifetime pass to the observation deck instead."

"Ernest and I would obviously need to vet the script to give you a more particularized assessment of your chances to finish the film and actually distribute it."

"I don't have it yet. Just a treatment."

"Well, that's the first order of business then, but if it's what you've proposed, we've got at least a fighting chance. Ernest, do you concur?"

"I do, Doug, provided, of course, the film is not a thinly veiled effort to retell the original story or simply an attempt to put Salinger's original characters in new settings."

"Precisely."

Brandon texted Alda. "about to come out take me to the boat before I go"

"[checkmark]"

When the three men returned to the den, Maeve and Alda were still watching *Napoleon Dynamite*. Uncle Rico was videotaping himself throwing a football. Brandon planed his face and half-closed his eyes, aping the sleepy body language of the title character. "I hate Uncle Rico and his stupid schemes. I'd like to throw that football into his stupid face. Idiot!"

"Bravo," Maeve said. "Spot on."

"My mom used to peddle Amway, so, it's like, bringing back all those fond memories."

"That actor, Jon Heder, was an Eagle Scout, like Chase and me."

They all stared at Douglas.

"Like fun he was." Alda traded a wink for a smirk with her mother.

"No, I'm serious. I read it a couple of months ago in *Eagles' Call.* He was even a scoutmaster. Gosh!"

Alda covered her face with two hands. "Oh my God, Dad. So embarrassing. Mr. Newman, I'm so sorry you had to see that."

"It wasn't too bad, Doug, but I wouldn't garage-sale the briefcase or the collar stays quite yet."

"I thought maybe I could show Mr. Newman the Catalina before he goes."

Maeve took Brandon's empty water bottle. "Honey, it's getting late; it's too dark."

"We've got dock lights, Mom. I really think he might like to see it." She turned to Douglas. "Mr. Newman did an amazing movie about a boy who sailed solo around the world. He falls in love with a deaf-mute Polynesian girl on a remote island in the Pacific. *Two if by Sea.*" Brandon agreed to take a quick look. Shari accepted Maeve's offer to prepare a mesquite turkey and avocado wrap for the trip back to Manhattan.

Beyond a storage shed, a long walkway—weathered wooden planks framed by telephone-pole pilings with mounted guidelights—led to a thirty-five-foot sailboat moored in a patch of moonlight splashed across the water. They sat near the stern on opposing vinyl-covered benches. The tranquil bay offered little more than a faint wobble.

"You know Salinger swiped that line," she said.

"Like fun he did."

"Totes. My grandmother completely adores *The Philadelphia Story.* We watch it whenever we're in Narragansett. I practically memorized the dialogue by the time I was ten. Came out years before *Catcher.* Connecticut socialite, Tracy Samantha Lord, played by a young Katherine Hepburn, mocks her boyfriend with the exact same line. No doubt Jerome ripped it off. He did love movies after all. Of course, probably sounds a little different when Sunny the prostitute says it."

Brandon had picked up a loose rope and was looping it around his forearm. "Sounds transformative to me. I met Traci Lords once at a wrap party in Malibu. Totally cool person. She's one O.G. survivor. We swapped stories about our screwed-up childhoods. She won. Old J.D. would have totally loved her, worked underaged in a bunch of pornos." He tossed the coiled rope to the deck. "You know what? She'd be perfect as that older woman Holden meets on the train, when he's escaping from Pencey." He pulled out his phone to save the idea: `"Traci Lords = Mrs. Morrow."`

"Hold on, Skipper. Mom told me you're taking a whole new tack."

Brandon moved closer, leaning back against the transom. "Can you keep a secret?"

"Haven't I already proven that?"

"But this one is way bigger."

"Try me."

"I lied to your parents."

"What lie?" She folded her legs up onto the cushion, kneeling in expectation.

He lit a cigarette. The wind streamed smoke off the stern. A squadron of low-flying gulls strafed the boat with piercing shrieks. "I told them I had this flash of inspiration, about the three assassins obsessed with *Catcher,* a fresh look at why the same old novel held a grip on their insane membranes."

"I know. Mom told me. It's good."

He took a noisy drag. "I'm still making *Catcher* exactly as is."

"Wait, that's the lie?" She thrust a hand against his shoulder. "Oh my God, I love it, but how?"

He stood to face the bay. "I'm gonna give them one script and shoot another."

"But they're gonna find out eventually, and way before it's released. Then some nice judge might be so entertained by your little caper that he offers you a free cot and a charming roommate in a cozy little windowless studio upriver."

Brandon waved to the shape of a fishing boat outlined by dots of light as it cruised past. "I hardly ever get to wave like a regular person." He flicked his cigarette to the water and sat down. "This buys me time. I would never get away with shooting undercover, hit and run. Let's say I get halfway done, and it leaks. They sue, right? Get the prints. I'm done for, according to pops. But if they *think* it's gonna be different. If a judge tells them to wait until I'm finished, I *get* to finish. The ball's rolling so fast by then—"

"But you could still have a leak. Then what?" She stomped a foot twice on the deck. "Bilge pump's not gonna work."

"I thought about that. I'll shoot a couple assassin scenes early to throw everybody off. Plus, the lawyers aren't gonna be on the set, which will be closed. We'll get NDAs all around. I'll only give out pages on a need-to-know basis, lots of changes. We'll shoot totally out of order, churn the crew with freelancers. I can do some of the outdoor scenes in Chicago or Toronto if I have to. It's mostly me anyhow. Nobody will ever put it together, not while it's happening. Not even Shari at first."

"This is so epic, but why tell *me?*"

"Because, number one, you're a part of this, and number two, I need a spy in the camp, keeping tabs on Daddy, plus, number three, you can be my double-secret *consigliere*, like Little Steven in *The Sopranos*."

"And what are you gonna do when the judge wants to see the final cut?"

"See that, Backrow. You can't even really ask that question until there *is* a final cut. That's more than enough progress for now. What is it they used to say at Facebook back in the day? 'Move fast and break things.' Inertia worked out pretty good for them."

"Don't forget, Mr. Newton, that movement is only half of inertia. Paralysis is the other. The bigger they are, the harder it is to make them fall."

"Newman, not Newton," he said.

"Slip of the tongue. Sorry. What about your documentary?"

"What about it?"

"The trust lawyers, soon as they sue, are right off the bat gonna ask a judge to make you turn over any and all related documents, including but not limited to film, stills, videos, screen tests, storyboards, call sheets, treatments, scripts, *et cetera*. That's what Douglas would want. It's a problem."

"Why would the judge give it to them if I tell them I'm doing something different?"

"Because they're not going to *believe* you. They'll argue that you still want to make the original *Catcher*, and that you are simply trying to disguise the movie enough to slip it past the court. They'll say whatever you already have in the can proves your true intent."

He sat with elbows on his knees, head in his hands, as all the incriminating scenes crashed together—the petulant gym phone call with Shari, the dirt bike dialogue in the Pines, the road trip monologues, the Darling-brooke Hall library. And there was more. Luis had shot a few late-night smartphone takes of Brandon on the way home from clubs and parties. He had insisted on trying to re-create *Catcher* taxi scenes with actual cab drivers. He'd feed them a few lines, but it never worked. Once, a Guatemalan woman became so distracted when she recognized Brandon in the rearview mirror while crossing Gansevoort Street that she had to slam on the brakes to avoid hitting a young woman already hobbling on crutches. On another predawn ride, an exceedingly polite Sikh man thought Brandon had asked about the "fucks" in Central Park and said they would have to go way uptown to find any. The documentary was more than a smoking gun; it was a bazooka. His head popped up as if resurfacing. "What if I trash it, all of it? The only thing I want to give them is the treatment, if I have to, not even a script. That's why I gotta get sued as soon as possible, so we can be the ones who freeze out the trust."

Alda stood to lean against the boat's wheel. She bowed her head and pressed an index finger against her lips. "So, what I'm understanding you to say is that because you want to do a distinct and modern interpretation on the impact of *Catcher,* the documentary has become wholly irrelevant to this entirely new artistic endeavor. Am I hearing you correctly, Mr. Newman?"

This time, Brandon was the one who couldn't follow her lead. "I don't think so."

"Hold on a minute. I think I am, actually." She took two steps to port and spun around. "Because if you were to say, hypothetically speaking, that you intended to destroy potentially relevant evidence to prevent its discovery by future opponents in foreseeable litigation, you would, in concept at least, be flirting with a theoretical claim of spoliation, obstruction of justice, even a conceivable criminal charge. Now, Mr. Newman, that's not what you're suggesting is it?" She yanked a small flashlight from a cradle mount at the helm and flashed it in his face.

Although he reflexively shielded his eyes, he had managed to see the light. He felt like he was back on the set of *Mock Trial Club.* "Of course not. I'm all about getting back to the drawing board, square one. Blank slate."

She held the flashlight right below her chin and pointed it to the sky. "Right. So, it's purely a creative decision, correct?" She put him back in the spotlight to cue a response.

"Of course, that's all I ever had in mind. I'm constantly changing my mind, throwing out bad ideas all the time."

She clicked off the beam. "That's exactly what I thought. So, if you were called to testify at a preliminary hearing about the documentary . . ."

Brandon sat up, his head slightly lowered and turned toward an imaginary judge, as if he were on the witness stand. "I realized, Your Honor, that I needed to take a totally radical approach, something that doesn't re-create *The Catcher in the Rye* but creatively interprets its impacts and effects on these three deranged individuals." He pretended to take a slow sip of water, slurping near the end. "When I got this exciting new concept, I realized immediately that the raw material I'd shot before would have to be scrapped. Happens all the time in this business. You can't imagine how many projects get shit-canned, my apologies, Your Honor, dumped, even with two outs in the bottom of the ninth inning."

"That makes so much sense, Mr. Newman. In fact, your decision to discard the documentary is further proof of your commitment to a bold, new direction, correct?

"Absolutely."

"No further questions."

He stood up, braced his hands against the side of the helm, and whispered, "I'm still gonna keep a copy squirreled away for once the trust gives up."

Alda stepped toward the dock, resting a foot on the gunwale. She shook her head and pounded a flat palm against its side. "Damn this swimmer's ear. Too many laps at the club this morning. Couldn't hear a thing you said. In fact, we've been talking about sailboats the whole time, best as I can recall."

14

They took an Uber to Prospect Park on an early Sunday morning in late October, using Luis's account, as usual, to hide Brandon's identity. He wore an Oklahoma City Thunder ski cap, a four-day goatee, and dark shades for urban camouflage. During the trip to Brooklyn, they discussed how best to provoke a lawsuit. The night before, over a new Chinese app with disappearing messages, Alda, still playing the cautious counselor, had proposed a straightforward press release announcing the new project. Brandon dismissed it as having no "viral potential." Luis, an eager recruit to the *Catcher* conspiracy, suggested an ambiguous teaser posted on YouTube for two days then taken down, something "more *Blair Witch*" that would blend a scene from the novel with interspersed micro-clips of news stories about the Reagan and Lennon shootings. Both agreed no one would recall the murder of sitcom actress Rebecca Schaeffer, or her stalker, Bardo. "It could dissolve into a wide shot of you, from behind, putting on that red hunting hat, whistling down Fifth Avenue."

"Not iconic enough, Lu. It's all about the carousel. We start there, horseback POV, up and down, a happy little nursery rhyme playing, like "London Bridge," then we bounce back and forth to some breaking news coverage, the merry-go-round picking up speed the whole time. We cut to half my face. I'm smiling, watching the carousel." Brandon wound his finger in rapid, tight circles and slapped his own thigh. "The music changes suddenly to 'Smoke Gets in Your Eyes.' The carousel and the music slow down, almost to a stop. Final shots, close-ups, my fist crushing the red hat, then back to a little girl bobbing in super slo-mo, the music's low and distorted, then back to my hand, except now I'm gripping a pistol pointed to the ground, and then tight around an eye, a tear runs down my cheek—"

Luis grabbed his arm to interrupt. "Fade to white, your name in black, lower case, full-screen, circled by a bright gold ring with a zip sparkle effect, then we dissolve to the last frame, 'In the movie you thought you'd never see.'"

They exchanged a robust triple fist pound with a flared fingers finale. "I'll have Shari get that 'in a world' guy for the voiceover. 'Golden Ring Productions presents.'"

"That dude's probably been dead for years, Brando, but James Earl Jones is still kicking it." Luis surrendered his voice to the dark side. "Brandon, I am your father."

"Perfect," Brandon said. "This isn't gonna go viral; it's gonna go freaking Ebola."

———————————

As they walked past the Audubon Center on the eastern border of the park, Brandon tested the audio recorder hidden in his denim jacket. Taping someone like Rose was a big risk, but he couldn't resist. The dangerous gambit would energize his performance, and he didn't want to miss the chance to capture his first carousel scene. He knew he might never use the recording, but that was a decision for post-production. It was better to beg for forgiveness than to ask for permission.

Luis was to cellphone film surreptitiously, pretending to be a tourist. Brandon had kept his blood oath and lied about Sallie Choo Choo. He told Luis that Josh had hooked him up with Rose Eddington and that she had no business connections to her infamous father. That lie, however, only begat more deception. Josh couldn't learn of the unauthorized shoot, and that meant Luis needed a reason to keep quiet. Brandon blamed top secrecy on Josh's "paranoid" concern that one day some of Sallie Choo Choo's trusted associates might "deliver him an ever-so-polite thank-you message for all the unwanted publicity." When he gave the disingenuous explanation for sealing lips, Luis joked that keeping secrets had become Brandon's latest addiction.

As they neared the carousel, Luis split off at a fork in the footpath to outflank the circling cavalry and approach from the north. Brandon headed straight for the ticket window. A sign on the unattended booth stated the ride would be closed until nine thirty a.m. He peeked through the bars of a locked gate but saw no one. It was 9:05 a.m. He sat on a bench and texted Luis to check his position.

"10-4, all set. it's like identical to central pk"

Brandon had already reached the same conclusion about the lookalike rides but couldn't share the confusion caused by Sallie's Brooklyn boasts. "Josh swears it's faster. might not be getting in-standby"

Brandon circled the carousel to take a few photographs. The fencing between the brick walls would have to be removed to frame a decent shot of the horses. Even then, the heavy columns would be a problem. In contrast, the best set designer couldn't have laid out a better array of trees, vintage streetlamps, and park benches. From behind, a female voice said, "Sorry I'm late. Tested our competitor's new rideshare app. Won't make that mistake again." Rose Eddington—early thirties, dark brown hair pulled back tight in a clip—had dressed for a job interview. She wore a black knee-length skirt and matching jacket over a white, no-nonsense blouse. No makeup, no jewelry, no creases anywhere. She looked like Anna Kendrick in *Up in the Air* but older, a more prominent nose, bright green eyes. A black leather messenger bag hung over her shoulder. She thrust out a stiff arm. "The fall colors are amazing, aren't they? They just pop on a morning like this." She took a deep whiff with eyes closed. "I love the smell of wet leaves on the ground. Don't you?" Her accent sounded nothing like Sallie's. She sounded like Alda, but her speech was more clipped and lacked a teenager's sentence-ending uptones.

"A rose by any other name would smell better," he said.

She seemed oblivious to both his attempt at double entendre and his superstar status. "Give me a minute." She held up a finger while reading an incoming text. "Huge party at our catering hall in Cedarhurst, family friend." She sighed. "Ice sculptor slashed open his arm carving a swan." Rose speed-typed a reply, took a deep breath, and forced a smile. "Okay. A quick spin and then down to business."

"Looks like we picked a bad time to meet up." He pointed to the posted notice and texted a prearranged launch code to Luis.

"No, that's what we told them." She called out for someone named Neil. A white-haired man, stout and round like a Lego minifigure and dressed in dark blue pants, a light blue work shirt, and a cheap black windbreaker, appeared to open the gate.

"Remember me to that guy from Bath Avenue," he said.

"After you, Mr. Newman. Let's ride on one of the dragon chariots, shall we? Easier to talk."

"You didn't need to dress up for this. And call me 'Brandon.'"

"I run a business, Mr. Newman, Brandon, and you're a potential new client." She dipped her head as if to make a concession. "Plus, I'm on my way to my cousin's first communion."

Once seated, Rose signaled Neil, and the carousel began to turn. The short bench, meant for smaller passengers, pressed their thighs together. Her eyes brightened and a smile spread across her face when the music began. "'Sidewalks of New York.' Love it. So Gay Nineties."

He imagined her father holding sit-downs in the very same spot, the full-throated calliope keeping his conversations safe from the eavesdropping ears of the FBI. He raised his voice to speak over the music. "This sounds like one those tunes the nickelodeons used to play. They got about a dozen of them, antiques, in the basement of the Cowboy Hall of Fame, back in OKC. I was six, maybe seven, on this field trip once. When we saw the keyboard playing without a musician, I told this little girl next to me—she used to practically suck her thumb off at nap time—that the place was haunted, bunch of dead cowboys tomahawked by Cherokees. I guess she didn't see the tour guide crank her up. Started bawling her eyes out. Mrs. Crabtree made me copy down the golden rule like a thousand times until my arm turned into a Slinky." Brandon dangled a lifeless right arm to demonstrate.

Rose pointed to the support beams, covered in light bulbs, radiating out like wagon wheel spokes. "It's got over a thousand."

He cocked his head back to take in the dizzying display. "All of a sudden I've got this massive craving for a funnel cake. Used to go to the state fair every year, even before I started performing there." He licked his lips. "Hot ones right out of the fryer."

"Hoosier *zeppole*," she said. "Like the Feast of San Gennaro."

Brandon looked down and blinked to flush the afterglow from his vision. "Did he explain what we'll be needing?" He deemed himself clever for referring to her father with an undefined pronoun.

She grabbed his knee. His body stiffened. "This is my favorite part." She began to sing along. "'Trip the light fantastic on the sidewalks of New York.'" Rose was stone-cold tone deaf. "You mean Mr. Fiumara? Yes, of course, he explained your requirements." Brandon understood she meant to steer the conversation even further away from Sallie Choo Choo. "I think we can assist you with several locations, plus the taxis, but first we'll have to resolve a few threshold matters." Now she sounded like Douglas. He assumed she meant walling off any possible avenues to her father. A blur of Luis's gaudy, red-white-and-blue Statue of Liberty sweatshirt and bulging fanny pack whizzed past.

"You've read it?"

"No, I put one of my people on your project, wants to be a novelist." She patted her bag. "He worked up the proposal, even found an old steam train in Essex, Connecticut."

"You never read it?"

"Ages ago I skimmed some Cliffs Notes to get by in Intro to American Lit at Fordham. I was an economics major, but you know those Jesuits."

"You should really give it a chance." Luis now filmed from the other side of the ride. A few young children pressed their faces against the fence to watch the rhythmic, loping cavalcade of riderless horses. Brandon avoided eye contact with their parents.

"Seems like this whiny book for sexually repressed little boys, like the kind of nerdy kids who play Dungeons & Dragons on Friday nights. No offense, but I prefer nonfiction, action-adventure."

"Like what?"

"*Into Thin Air, Unbroken,* people being tested by the elements, surviving against the odds, adrenaline junkies. They're so inspiring. Last year, I started free climbing in the Catskills. What's my excuse, right?" She shrugged her shoulders. "Did you see *The Walk?* It's amazing. I caught it last week in 3D. That guy, Petit, he was all balls. He would've been a good part for you. Novels never get me off the couch. All they do is make me want to eat ice cream out of a carton in baggy sweatpants."

Brandon remained silent, his eyes fixed on the back of the lion, the bolts through its paws denying the once proud apex hunter even a momentary leap. The dizzying combination of rotation, recollection, and regret prompted a sudden urge to explain everything to Rose, what it meant to live with the burden of survival, the scars from a broken home, the chronic pain of child stardom, the rigid pigeonholes of Hollywood, the lifelong struggle with addiction. He wanted to defend *Catcher,* tell her how the book, a made-up story, had yanked him back from the ledge. As he was about to speak, the carousel's music changed. The lively song sounded familiar—a raucous, festive melody with emphatic drums and cymbal crashes on every beat. "This isn't from . . . *The Godfather?*"

She covered her eyes as if embarrassed. "It's the tarantella from Connie Corleone's wedding. Can you believe it? Neil's daughter, Lorraine, did her pictures here last year, reception across the street at the botanical gardens. She begged for months, had the whole bridal party hanging off horses. I had to ride the white one, over there. I felt like we were on an episode of *Jersey Shore.*"

Brandon didn't believe her. He knew Sallie Choo Choo's fondness for the shock of mob humor. That amateur producer's mischievous fingerprints were all over the winking musical selection, but he knew Rose would never admit her father had done it for his benefit. "So, you come here often, I take it?"

"Is that really your best pickup line, Mr. Newman?" She leaned away as if to size him up. "I have to admit I expected better from someone like you."

He huffed. "You want to know my one and only pickup line?"

"Try me."

"'Hi, I'm Brandon Newman.'" He stared into her eyes to let it sink in. "Our mutual acquaintance, Josh, calls it the 'skeleton key.' Works anywhere, anytime."

"Not here, I'm afraid."

"That's because I've got to *mean* it when I say it."

After the ride ended, Rose thanked Neil and asked about the health of his brother in Fort Lauderdale. A long line of parents, kids, dogs, and strollers waited by the entrance. Brandon and Rose moved to a nearby bench. Luis had positioned himself at the end of a picnic table, partially shielded behind a tree.

"Mr. Fiumara explained that you may be risking litigation with Mr. Salinger's trust by making your movie. Frankly, that's your problem, not ours, but we will obviously need certain assurances."

Brandon couldn't fault Josh's decision to opt for full disclosure when dealing with Sallie Choo Choo. "I'm not looking to cause you, or you know who, any headaches, if it's—"

"I'm not sure to whom you're referring, Mr. Newman, Brandon."

"You said 'we' before."

She flashed the patient grin of a kindergarten teacher. "The royal 'we,' Brandon, corporate speak. La Traviata Property Management LLP is the only party in interest here. I'm its general partner."

"So, what would *we* need, Rose?"

"A hold harmless agreement with a full indemnification provision, including the advance of any attendant attorney's fees and expenses. And, of course, a certificate of insurance from your production company before shooting could commence."

"That sounds standard enough." He had no idea if it was. It did sound a lot more by the book than he'd expected. Sallie hadn't lied about times changing. "*We're* gonna need an NDA," he said. "Closed sets and all."

She opened her bag and pulled out a three-ring binder. "Descriptions and photos of some of the locations you might be interested in."

Brandon paged through the offerings—high-ceiling pre-war apartments on Eastern Parkway, throwback lounges in Greenpoint and Astoria, dated hotel rooms in Brooklyn Heights, luncheonettes in Bensonhurst, and a Red Hook garage with three mint condition Checker taxis. His pocket vibrated. He assumed it was Luis giving him some direction to clean up the shot, but the text had come from Maeve.

"Almost finished. Used a great DIY site for indies. Have to thank u. I'll explain when we meet. Pick up at my office, Wednesday a.m."

"Not email?"

"Things to discuss, plus no metadata. Explain later."

"K"

Brandon made sure to keep his phone and recording device in different pockets. "My agent pitching some dating app commercial." He held up the binder. "This looks good. You got time to walk over to the zoo with me? Scout out the sea lions?"

She checked her phone. "We have to make it quick." She took back the binder to carry it in the bag.

On the way, they passed a group of shuffling middle-aged joggers, a rollerblader, and a yoga class cycling through warrior poses. Ultra-Orthodox Jews comprised most of the sparse zoo crowd—fathers in black suitcoats, white shirts with open collars, and fedoras, wigged mothers in long-sleeved blouses and ankle-length skirts pushing double strollers, and strings of children of descending stature trailing behind.

"Lubavitchers from Crown Heights," she said. "We know all the big *rebbes*. Lots of storefronts over there. They come here before heading off to Costco to bulk up." Despite what she'd said before, Brandon knew exactly who "we" was.

At the sea lion exhibit, a front row of Hasidic children chinning the rail cheered the animals whenever their muzzles broke the surface, louder if one thrust itself halfway out of the water. Brandon and Rose stood behind them. The first feeding wasn't until eleven a.m. One of the little girls, pale with twin blonde pigtails in a simple black dress—she could've passed for Amish in Pennsylvania—pulled at the loose shirttail of her disheveled older brother and said, "Their faces look like puppies. Why can't we get a puppy? I want a puppy."

He ignored her at first, kicking pebbles under the railing and into the water, but the little girl persisted. "Why can't we get a puppy?"

The boy stopped to respond, sounding like the impatient father he would one day be. "We're eight at home. Who has time? You have a fish. Be happy with that."

"But he hates me. Shmuley Goldfish never comes when I tap on the glass, only for food."

"Fish are for watching, like TV. They aren't for play."

"But I want him to play with me."

"So, when you're married, you'll ask your husband for a dog instead of a baby."

She shoved the boy into the side of their older sister, who blurted something in a foreign language. It sounded like words Shari used when she was pissed. Their father, alerted to the commotion, approached the boy. His round face grew red and tears pooled in his eyes. A few stern, unintelligible words and an aggressive finger shake were all it took. The boy's head sunk. Once the father had rejoined their mother, the boy mumbled, "You don't think I like dogs too?"

Brandon scooted closer to Rose. "If you knew Salinger, you'd know exactly what he would be thinking right now. He'd want me to follow that family home and then go out and buy the cutest puppy I could find, a golden retriever or an Alaskan husky. I'd wait—for days if I had to—for the little girl to be playing alone out on the front stoop. I'd watch her bouncing a rubber ball against the steps or skipping jump rope. I'd be bursting to surprise her with the new dog, but then, at the last minute, Jerry would stop typing. He wouldn't be able stand the thought of her father taking that pooch away and selling it back to some goddamned pet shop."

Brandon noticed a young orthodox couple, apparently newly married, no children in tow, rocking back and forth to get a better look at him. He asked Rose to take a quick walk through Barnyard World. The exhibit—a spartan display of common farm animals like cows, pigs, and chickens—had a makeshift, B-list quality, as if the promised shipment of exotic animals from Africa had never arrived. He explained his idea for a movie teaser and asked if the simple shoot could be done fast. "An easy one-off," she said. Neil would open up at daybreak on a weekday and have some Parks Department workers block off a few paths for an hour. As they walked past a straw-filled pen with two sleeping Canadian geese, she put her hand around his waist. "Don't turn around, but there's a guy who's been following us since the carousel." Brandon didn't have to look to know who it was. Luis had gotten too close to a subject who'd been schooled in the surveillance methods of law enforcement by no less than a mafia don.

"Probably paparazzi," he said. "Occupational hazard."

She grabbed Brandon by the hand and led him out of the imitation barn, back to the Sea Lion Court. "He looks like a Fed. They always pull their undercovers off the drug or gang squads to do their surveillance on people like us, think we won't notice if they're black or brown." She peered at the barndoor exit over Brandon's shoulder as she spoke.

"Anything I should worry about?"

"Not at all," she said, "but you might get a knock on the door in a few days. They'll throw a handful of 8x10s on your coffee table and start asking questions."

"Twenty-seven?" he asked.

"What? You're trying to guess my age now?"

"Never mind."

"They get you staring at those glossy prints and not thinking about what you should be saying."

"But I've got nothing to hide."

"Exactly. You don't."

"So, I tell them the truth then?"

"Of course. Same truth we've been talking about all morning, but I'll hold on to the binder, send it to you through Josh. No need to give them any more suspicions." Without warning, she seized him by the lapels and kissed him on the mouth. He froze in shock. Seconds passed before she pulled away. He worried she might have felt the recording device in his jacket.

"I don't understand. Why would you—"

"Because he's behind you pretending to FaceTime and because boyfriends are less interesting. These guys like to follow the money. Better to give them a little romance. Maybe it keeps them away. Besides, you've probably fake lip-locked like that about a trillion times."

The scripted kisses on set had never felt anything like hers. "What if you're wrong?" he asked.

"You mean paparazzi? Who doesn't like free publicity? Your image has gotten a little too squeaky clean lately. I only put a little smudge on it." She pretended to wipe lipstick from his mouth. "Everybody loves the bad boy." She straightened his hat and patted the fuzzy ball on top. He reached into his jacket for a cigarette, but she pressed his forearm to his chest to stop him. She seemed to survey his entire face, searching up and down, eyes squinting, as if she had missed something important. "I suppose if you're right about our Latin stalker over there"—Luis had moved into Brandon's peripheral field of vision, his arms extended as if to take a slow, sweeping panorama—"and you don't mind what comes out in the grocery store rags, maybe we could, you know . . ." She paused, apparently waiting for him to finish her sentence.

"I warned you about the skeleton key." He pulled out a cigarette pack despite an array of prominently displayed "No Smoking" signs. "Haven't found a lock yet that could resist."

"Not so fast, Mr. Newman. I got one bitch of a chastity belt."

"Oh yeah, what's it made of? Adamantium?"

"Funny. No, nothing like that, words is all. Stops 'em dead in their tracks, leaves 'em cold and shivering, every time."

"What is it?"

She stared at him just as he had when delivering his surefire one-liner at the carousel.

"Maybe you know my father, Sallie Choo Choo."

15

Luis spent the next week shuttling between the Central Park and Prospect Park carousels. Brandon insisted on redheaded little girls in braids, lots to choose from, shots from behind or side angles, no faces. Phoebe would be cast later. TV news reports from John Lennon's murder and Hinckley's near miss had already been culled and loaded for editing. Neil was ready to open the ride at six a.m. on any Tuesday, Wednesday if it rained. Shari had drafted an all-star team of Facebook and Instagram influencers to re-post the teaser once it went live on YouTube. Douglas predicted they would be served with a cease-and-desist demand within twenty-four hours of upload.

Brandon planned to issue a very short press release. No questions would be answered. The silence would both stimulate the media chatter and, according to his counsel, prevent the trust's lawyers from misconstruing any out-of-court remarks. Douglas repeatedly stressed that he needed the film treatment ASAP to prepare a response to the allegations of infringement in the CPLT's forthcoming court pleadings. Ernest followed up with apologetic reminders. Alda secretly reported that in contrast to his vague and hedged lawyer-speak, her father had let slip that a judge would "very likely" rule in their favor. Brandon promised Douglas a rewrite would be ready in a matter of days. He blamed the delay on a talented but unreliable ghostwriter. Maeve had postponed their meeting twice, saying she needed more time for finishing touches.

Of course, no photos of the zoo smooch ever showed up at checkout counters or strewn melodramatically across a coffee table. Brandon had been briefly tempted to leak Luis's front-page quality shot of the dramatic kiss, an electric image of young passion with a fat sea lion sunning itself in the background, but the timing wasn't right for that kind of publicity. It would have only served as a distraction from the teaser's imminent release.

Beyond keeping their first kiss out of the papers, he also had decided to keep their new romance a secret. Rose represented a significant deviation from his "celebrities only" rule, but he knew Sallie Choo Choo's daughter would be the last woman to gold dig or kiss and tell. They hadn't yet gone out in public, meeting three times so far—once at her apartment in Williamsburg for Indian takeout and twice at his loft for sushi and vegan dinners prepared by a part-time private chef. Rose's ex-husband had converted her into a strict pescatarian before he'd left. "Causes my mother fits at Sunday dinners." She consented to the discreet arrangement but assured him that Sallie wouldn't have a problem. "'Anybody but Bradley,' he always tells me. If that boy managed to waltz out of New York on two good legs in a pair of Birkenstocks, trust me, you've got nothing to worry about." Rose occasionally slipped into her father's rhythm and phrasing, displaying the same knack for colorful metaphor. Brandon kept the observation to himself, fearful she'd try to break the unconscious habit he had found so attractive. He explained that his motive for secrecy had more to do with staying on message than fear of her father's disapproval. All attention had to be focused on the media bomb he was about to drop.

Brandon had stopped recording her five minutes into the first date. By the end of the evening, he had revealed Luis's true purpose in tailing them. He promised not to use any of the video without getting her consent in advance. He left out the audio component, fearing that the notion he had wired up might scare her off, or worse. Rose confessed she'd never actually believed that Luis was a Fed. "I thought he was some gawky tourist. I needed to come up with a good reason to kiss you."

Brandon was careful not to pry about her family, or "the family." Rose seemed similarly reluctant to probe, perhaps the result of a tight-lipped upbringing, or because so much of his past had already been the subject of a slew of sensationalized slapdash documentaries on basic cable. At first, they talked superficially about celebrities, movies, the city's best ethnic food, and the exotic locations they'd visited. He showed her the small red scar on his big toe from the giant centipede bite he'd gotten while filming in Vanuatu. She described her two years with the Peace Corps in Belize where in one week she had both nearly died from a gut-wrenching bout of dengue fever and met her ex-husband.

By the second date, they tiptoed into deeper waters. Brandon volunteered anecdotes about the gimmicks his mother had picked up along every notch of the Bible Belt, from Springfield, Missouri to Lynchburg, Virginia: holy water solemnly collected from the pristine taps at Motel 6; Dead Sea mud reverently scooped straight from the banks of the Arkansas River; and pay-for-prayer websites with miraculously scripted testimonials.

"Some people," Rose said, "think that's the oldest racketeering there is."

She made few references to her father—no talk of their businesses, only his love of opera, which she didn't share, and his passion for doomsday prepping. She described the latter as ridiculous, "a daydream to fend off old age," but encouraged Sallie nonetheless, hoping his apocalypse watch might prompt an early retirement and speed up the corporate transition.

Brandon had always assumed there was no retirement from Sallie Choo Choo's line of work. The reflection sparked a scene-flash. Blue-and-white bodega coffee cups, one with tea, Brandon standing next to Sallie, overcast skies, squawking seagulls, cool mist on their cheeks, both men leaning over the bow railing on the upper deck of the Staten Island Ferry, the camera positioned behind them, all watched from above by the unblinking eyes of Lady Liberty but at a safe distance from the G-man's telephoto. "Kid, you leave this thing of ours in two ways, either face up on a lumpy Bureau of Prisons bunk in one of their all-inclusive gated communities or face down in the street with a pair of lead Ambien in your coconut." Brandon felt confident that Sallie had kept his daughter shielded from the darker aspects of the business, even as she became its manager, his legacy to her being a diversified and deep-cleaned portfolio of assets wrapped in a thick blanket of plausible deniability.

Between the second and third dates, Josh came over to watch Brandon's screener of *Star Wars: The Force Awakens*, a month before its release. "You know how much cheddar we could make selling tickets to your living room?"

"Not so fast, young Jedi. Mishkin says it's a straight-up rip-off of the original—female Luke Skywalker, bowling ball R2-D2 stuffed with a map instead of blueprints, and a killer star base instead of the Death Star. *So* creative. Nothing to do with box office or merchandising. Pure artistic integrity."

Josh had sprawled out on a plush home theater recliner. He tapped its control panel to dim the lights, sat up to pretzel his legs, put his hands, palms up, on knees, eyes closed, as if meditating. "Received you not the role you sought. Anger now you show."

"I didn't even try for it, ya string bean, pencil-necked muppet." Brandon cued the DVD player.

"Do or do not, young Brandon. There is no try."

Brandon plunked Josh with a throw pillow. "What do you say we do a shot every time Abrams recycles plot."

"Please. We'd be drunk as skunks by the end of Act One, but you know I'm still riding the straight edge. What about a round of 'Who's the Holden,' the stooge most likely to leave a sack of lightsabers in the cargo hold of the Millennium Falcon."

When the end credits began to roll, Josh wadded up his microwave popcorn bag and tossed it at Brandon, who lay half asleep on an Italian leather cinema couch, his hand dangling, a finger grazing the rim of his glass. "So, who was it, Brando?"

Brandon crooked an elbow to prop up his head. "I sure as hell know who Luis would say."

Josh counted down from three, and in unison they shouted, "Kylo Ren."

Brandon sat up and grabbed ice tongs from a bar cart to refill his drink. "But that's only the dark side of Holden. Sure, Ren's this frustrated Darth Vader wannabe, whines like an angsty teen, but there's none of Holden's sympathy, his search for honest, real connections."

Josh pressed a button that lowered the leg rest, raised the back, and lifted the seat to stand him up. "I'll tell you exactly who the Holden is. He's that die-hard O.G. *Star Wars* mega-fan, the geek who's been nerding out on the first trilogy since grade school, got a studio-quality storm-trooper outfit in his padlocked bedroom closet and recites full scenes from memory at conventions. You can hear that one, can't you, complaining? Veins popping about how Lucas and Disney gutted the franchise to make a buck. Please, our boy is a 'Han Shot First' true believer." Josh began to whistle "When You Wish Upon a Star."

Brandon held up his glass to toast the insight. He lit a cigarette and texted Rose. "want to see new star wars? got dvd"

"[yawn face] LMK when u get The Revenant"

The studio had said Brandon was too young for that part. He messaged Alda. "got new SW dvd. want to c it?"

"trying to netflix-and-chill me [winking face with tongue]"

"HILARIOUS nobody looks good in an orange jumper"

"how about blue coveralls? send to dh?"

"[Thumbs up]"

Brandon switched to cable and flipped as fast as he could past a block of news channels in their third day of round-the-clock coverage on the Paris terror attacks. He had tried to avoid hearing anything about the massacre, but the press had been badgering Shari for a statement. On her weekly radio show, Sheila had said the Bataclan audience members shot dead during the Eagles of Death Metal concert should have known better than to listen to "heathen hymns" like "Kiss the Devil," the song the band was playing when the massacre began. Brandon finally approved a short release Shari had drafted denouncing "his mother's callous and deplorable remarks" and reiterating his absolute lack of contact with her.

He settled on a *Food Network* rerun of *Young Celebrity Bake-off.* His overcooked peach blueberry cobbler had lost out to Emma Watson's spot-on treacle tart. "If Disney got their corporate hands on Caulfield, that focus-grouped doughboy wouldn't even smoke or drink. He'd feel aw-shucks sorry for his screw-ups, and right there in the front row at Phoebe's Christmas play, he'd vow to turn over a brand-new leaf." He stuck two fingers down his throat and pretended to gag. "It's a wonderful life, all right."

Josh picked up a daytime Emmy from a three-tiered display shelf stacked with People's Choice Awards. Brandon had won it for his role as Zak the Zookeeper in an animated special about endangered species. "You know nobody ever won a single acting or directing Oscar for any of the *Star Wars* movies. Not even nominated. Chick who played Rey was pretty good, though. Not my style, but not bad, right? Sort of familiar. Know what I mean?"

"Not really." Brandon had lied. He knew it from her first appearance on the screen. She looked like a younger, waspy version of Rose.

"Surprised to hear you say that, Brando. To me, she looks like the spitting image of Rosalie. You must've gotten a pretty good look at her by now."

Brandon kept his head down, swiping through Instagram. "I mean, yeah, at the carousel."

"Any place else?"

"You got something to say, Fiumara?"

Josh doubled over laughing. "I told you, Brando. This guy knows everything. He's got ears to the ground and dropping over eaves in every corner of Gotham City, coverage like freaking Wi-Fi hotspots. You seriously think he doesn't know you're dating his daughter? I'm a little offended, to be honest, I had to learn it from him."

"What happened to 'don't ask, don't tell'?"

"*Touché, mon frère.*" Josh zorroed the air. "You got nothing to worry about. Choo Choo's all aboard." He pretended to pull the string on a train's steam whistle. "Toot. Toot. Matter of fact, Sallie sends his regards. Says you and Rose take your time, keep it under wraps as long as you want. Our lips are sealed." Josh zipped fingertips across his mouth. "Sent me with something else too." He straightened his back and pretended to unroll a proclamation like a medieval town crier. "His excellency, the Duke of Urbino, graciously requests the glorious presence of Lord

Brandino at the *Grotta di Salvatore* on the twenty-fourth day of the twelfth month, anno domini 2015."

"The bat cave?"

"Correctamundo. You're gonna love it. Better than a reservation at Rao's. Feast of the Seven Fishes. Italian Christmas tradition, waiting up for the baby Jesus to drop. Choo Choo puts out a spread that would make Chef Boyardee jealous." Josh used both hands to pretend to stuff his mouth with food. "Seafood straight from the Fulton Fish Market, the freshest, brings in a cook from Palermo. Anchovies, sardines, *scungilli*, mussels, clams, *baccalá*, lobsters. My mouth's taking a piss just thinking about it."

"Does Rose know?"

"What? That *he* knows? She ought to. Nobody knows that shadow better than she does."

"We go as a couple?"

"No, she's up there all day with prep. He'll send a driver."

"It's a pretty secluded place, right?"

"Going to Sallie's is like wandering through the desert, not expected to see anything for miles." Josh used his hand as a sun visor and pretended to be lost. "All of a sudden, you turn a corner into this hidden valley, and boom, there it is, like finding that ancient city where they filmed *Indiana Jones and the Last Crusade.* Please, I still get turned around, and I been up there half a dozen times."

"Sounds like a good place to lose somebody, you know, permanently, like an unwanted boyfriend."

"Your throat getting itchy?" Josh rubbed his own neck. "Don't worry, Brando. This ain't the Corleone family, and you're nobody's Carlo. You got nothing to worry about."

"Tell him I wouldn't miss it."

At the start of their third date, Brandon told Rose about Josh's news and her father's invitation. She frowned and pretended to fire a shot into her temple. "I'm honestly surprised it took this long. I could never sneak around *anywhere*, with anybody, when I was back in school without getting an oral 302 the next morning along with my bowl of cornflakes." Brandon knew what an FBI 302 report was from a recent guest spot on *Quantico*. "On the plus side, Christmas Eve is the one holiday I can actually eat everything on the menu."

"You think it'll get out, about us?" he asked.

"'Good at gossip' is not exactly something my father's associates highlight on their resumés. They're all what he likes to call 'three-monkeys safe.'" She covered her ears, eyes, and mouth. "Even the preppers. Nobody would dare chirp a peep about you. They all know better."

After dinner, he gave her a tour of his walk-in closet. She said they could've ridden Segways. "Luis calls it my 'golf-in' closet." It looked like a factory outlet store—one wall stacked with shoe cubbies and a room-length rod hung opposite with a painter's sampler of blue jeans from periwinkle to midnight, all in various states of distress. "I get most of it for free. They send it, hoping I'll get snapped. The sponsors I have to tag on social media. More than I could ever wear."

"You give most of it away, I hope."

"My dogwalker is dating the Salvation Army driver."

Rose approached a life-size cutout of a smiling Brandon holding a surfboard and snatched the neon orange trapper hat he'd worn in the Pines from its flat head. She modeled it before a full-length mirror. "I didn't see any posts of you wearing this at Coachella."

"Have you read it yet?" Brandon had sent her an early hardcover edition of *Catcher* after their first date.

"I started." She replaced the hat on foamboard Brandon. "Why do we have to spend so much time in that awful prep school? It was a little cliché to tell you the truth. Every high school has got its jocks, tools, and nerds. That makes it like only a million other young adult books. Frankly, I don't see what's so special. Maybe you have to be a guy."

"But what about all the hypocrites? You must be Catholic."

"Everybody's always trying to find out if I'm a Catholic." She executed a perfect supermodel spin in a lab coat he'd worn on *Grey's Anatomy*.

He put on a Stetson from *Rodeo Camp* and pretended to ride a bull, one hand flailing in the air. "That Louis Shaney part's more than halfway through. If you did the whole Catholic school routine, you got to be able to relate. All those priests. Supposed to be protectors, not predators. If that's not the worst kind of phoniness, I don't know what is. That's exactly what Holden's getting at."

"But there must be something more important to talk about than his dork classmates."

"What about the death of his little brother, Allie?"

"Exactly. Why doesn't he talk more about that?"

Brandon took his cowboy hat off and held it over his chest. His voice drifted back to the dusty plains of Oklahoma. "What do you mean, little darlin'? He *never ever* stops talking about that."

After midnight, they lay side by side, staring at his bedroom ceiling. Brandon wore plaid boxers and a number 20 OU jersey, his father's favorite player, all-American running back Billy Sims. She wouldn't let him smoke, having inherited her father's sinuses. Chuck had given each of his boys an adult-size Sims jersey before he left for the Middle East. He promised they would grow into them. Sheila said the number 20 should always remind Brandon of God's special grace—that nineteen children had died on April 19, 1995, and that he would have made number twenty.

Brandon had stopped believing in her manipulative numerology years ago, but it always came to mind whenever he wore that shirt. He wondered if Rose had lost anyone in the 9/11 terrorist attack. He asked the standard opening question in the inevitable September 11th conversation, the exchange that arose, sooner or later, with anyone who had lived in New York City at the time. "Where were you when the first plane hit?"

She had been at school, Lourdes Academy, in Bay Ridge. She watched the North Tower fall from the park across the street. "Some girls lost their fathers, one lost both. My girlfriend threw up a bacon, egg, and cheese and a chocolate milk right in the middle of Shore Road." Rose described a "massive column of silent sooty smoke" drifting toward Brooklyn "like some Egyptian death plague from *The Ten Commandments*. The city smelled like burnt electrical wires. We even found some papers blown onto the soccer field. I picked up a scrap of resume, singed at the top, some guy who went to Penn, ROTC, loved sailing." He asked if she had known anyone who was killed. Her Uncle Joe from New Dorp, in Staten Island, her "real uncle" on her mother's side, had been a firefighter. "Uncle Joey died climbing stairs. I swear that church was like a river of tears when the priest called it a stairway to heaven."

The Newman boys had been deemed too young by their parents to attend the Oklahoma City funerals. Brandon remembered Chuck coming home, day after day, his tie getting looser and looser but his grip always vise-like around the neck of a bottle-shaped paper bag. Sheila kept an ironing board in the middle of the living room, pressing one of his father's two suits every night in front of the television. They had a terrible fight after the first day care memorial. Chuck screamed about how Sheila "had no idea what it was like to watch someone die." He broke down their bedroom door after she had locked herself inside. The brothers had hidden themselves under bunk bed covers.

Listening to Rose's 9/11 story, he recalled the contrast he'd drawn between the fate of his murdered playmates and the good fortune of the children who had all managed to escape the on-site nursery school before the Twin Towers fell. He fantasized about running inside to rescue those kids, showing utter disregard for his own safety. He could see himself in the next day's newspaper—a piggy-backing little girl, her round, chubby cheeks powdered white with blast dust, hugging his neck and two little boys in tattered clothes clutching his hands as they fled the flames and the debris, dodging body missiles raining down from the sky. He would go back in again and again until not one child was left behind. Later, he would refuse to accept any of the countless awards for bravery, barely even acknowledge the profusely grateful parents, his heroic status cemented forever in deeds and humility. Brandon turned toward Rose and propped up his head. "At least no children were killed. They all made it out."

She rolled up on her hip to meet him and massaged his shoulder. "You know there were little kids on those planes."

16

After another postponement, Maeve finally met him on a Monday afternoon at the Cask Room in the Collegiate Club on Fifty-Seventh Street. The Blackburn family, she said, had been charter members. She assured him no one would dare disturb the exclusive venue's "rarefied air" by acknowledging his presence. She had also hatched the perfect plan to neutralize the effect of any whispers that might echo in her husband's ears. After texting the proposed "stratagem" to Brandon, she asked Douglas to arrange the meeting. Her pretense was to coax the charismatic young movie star into serving as the celebrity emcee for an upcoming auction on behalf of a micro-finance organization for female entrepreneurs in developing countries.

She requested a corner table near the backgammon alcove. The intricately patterned dark wood paneling, the herringbone floors, the fading prints of Ivy League schools, the plush leather sofas, the short-jacketed, bow-tied waiters, the jumbo shrimp cocktails, and the steak tartare all seemed to have slipped through a time portal buried inside Salinger's novel. "I know it's a bother to dress up, but isn't this just the sort of place Holden's family would come to? I thought you should see it."

"No doubt," Brandon said. "And then he'd spend the entire time complaining about all of the terrific snobs in here saying everything is 'grand' or 'marvelous.'" They agreed that the club would never give him permission to film. Brandon also felt certain he'd be roughly escorted from the premises if management were to discover the tiny wireless microphone clipped to the underside of his Hermès tie. She ordered iceberg lettuce wedges with blue cheese, chopped tomatoes, and bacon. He picked the pasta of the day, linguini with porcini mushrooms and black truffles. "Seems like a swell place for an old fashioned," he said.

Maeve cupped a hand at one side of her mouth to form a sound shield. "They'd throw you out if you even tried to order a Tom Collins in this weather." She pulled a thin stack of stapled pages from her bag. "Sorry

I couldn't email it. These word processing programs apparently deposit a treasure trove of metadata in electronic copies, according to Douglas. No need for a trail of virtual crumbs leading back to your friendly ghost writer."

Brandon waved off the apology, still unclear about the incriminating nature of an email attachment. "Let's take her for a test drive."

He skimmed the first few pages. The treatment opened predictably with each assassin, alone, reading the same passage about Holden's people-shooting hat. Each man has a bedroom bulletin board covered with push-pinned pictures and cutout articles about Ronald Reagan, Jodi Foster, John Lennon, and the forgotten Rebecca Schaeffer. They clean their guns with "obsessive, ritualistic attention," pretend to be wounded in shoot-outs with the police, engage in "risky autoerotic behavior." They flashback to scenes of being bullied in grade school and suffering the adult frustrations of incompetent retail service and dismissive government bureaucrats. As time passes, they descend deeper into the novel, sounding more and more like Holden. Each shooter underlines and reads aloud Salinger's famous line about being able to call up a favorite author and have a conversation with him. The professor explains to her graduate class how Holden's desire for an immediate and intimate connection with a remote, idealized figure could be misunderstood as an "invitation to stalk, even an inalienable right to be heard."

"Well, there's a 'be careful what you wish for' lesson, Jerome," Brandon said. He continued reading. "Who's Bernhard Goetz?"

Maeve forked a full stab of lettuce into her mouth and spoke while chewing. "You can cut that part out if you like. You're too young, of course. It was the Eighties. Goetz was otherwise completely insignificant. Bit of a loner, an electrical engineer from Queens, he became known around the world as the 'subway vigilante.' Claimed four African-American kids had accosted him on the Number 2 train. He shot them all, two in the back. Made headlines for months." She put down her fork and wiped blue cheese from the corners of her mouth. "Goetz said it was self-defense, but he seemed to truly relish the chance to unload on all those young men." She pulled out a color printout headshot from her purse and surveyed the room. "The staff here has a conniption if they even see a cellphone."

Goetz looked like Edward Snowden, except older, his hairline in full retreat. "What's the connection?"

"After his 'payback is a bitch' moment, Goetz takes off down a subway tunnel, rents a car, and guess where he heads?"

"JFK."

"Vermont, where he said he buried the gun, and then to New Hampshire, where he eventually turned himself into the local police, nine days after the shooting, a shooting which took place *three days* before Christmas, December 22, 1984. Exact same time of year as *The Catcher in the Rye.* Can't you see our brilliant female professor positing a fascinating theory?" Maeve took a full gulp of sparkling water and spread out her hands as if to hold the attention of a crowd. "Goetz, frustrated, alone, the unavenged victim of a prior assault, rides the subway. Maybe he's read the novel a few times. Maybe he's thinking about the holiday season, tree trimming, that ending with Holden and Phoebe, or he's thinking about being a crusader, a savior, a catcher. A lifetime of simmering discontent, the accumulation of injustices both large and small, boils over in one volcanic eruption of violence. Where does he run?"

"Vermont, you said."

"Yes, but why? Where did John Wilkes Booth run? Due south, toward sympathy. What if Bernie Goetz did the same thing? Made a beeline to a certain reclusive writer's retreat in Cornish, New Hampshire, right on the border with Vermont?"

Brandon had been twirling the same clump of pasta while he sat captivated by Maeve's account. "He went to see Salinger?"

She ripped open an onion roll. "There's never been anything beyond my circumstantial speculation, but it's so tantalizing. So many parallels. The flight to sanctuary. The shared experiences. Goetz was half-Jewish, like Salinger, had troubles with women, and went to boarding school too, except in Switzerland. He was sent away when his father was accused of child molestation. Imagine the conversations those two would have had." Maeve gestured with a butter knife as she spoke. "There's Bernie, on the lam, expecting understanding, absolution, a shoulder to cry on, and Jerry, turning sheet white, overwhelmed by the unwelcomed and unexpected visit of another unbalanced Holdenite packing a worn-out paperback and a smoldering handgun." A waiter refilled her water glass. Brandon declined another old fashioned. She pushed her plate toward the middle of the table. "Maybe Salinger even convinced Goetz to bury the weapon and turn himself in. This story fits right into the 1980s timeframe of the movie. Lennon 1980. Reagan 1981. Goetz 1984. Schaeffer 1989. But perhaps it's too much, too far afield, that is. I'd understand of course."

Brandon placed his hands flat on the table, trying to look at her without blinking, hoping to appear genuine. "No, why not? I love it. I really do." Yet another thread did in fact seem a bit too much, but Brandon saw no reason to hurt her feelings. He had no intention of making her movie anyway, with or without the digression. "What did you want to thank me for?"

Maeve's face lit up as if she'd recalled a forgotten name. "This little homework assignment of yours has been a veritable wellspring. I came up with a dream of a theme for Alda's college application essay next year. She'll draw parallels between *Catcher* and the original *Curious George* story. You know, learning to love your cage, domestication and all. I hope you don't mind. I'm also writing a journal piece." Brandon shoveled in the last of his linguini as she spoke. "Comparing Kurt Vonnegut's *Slaughterhouse-Five*, Primo Levi's *If This is a Man*, and *The Catcher in the Rye*. I intend to contrast the clinical, decidedly unsentimental descriptions of the horrors of World War II in both Vonnegut and Levi with the suppressed rage of Salinger's war-torn alter ego. I hope to say something new about why readers fail to identify with Billy Pilgrim and Primo Levi in the same intimate, visceral way. It has to do with point-of-view, detached chronicler versus virtual reality gamer."

Brandon paid little attention to her academic gobbledygook as he finished his food and downed the last of his now-diluted bourbon. "Interesting. All square then. You're welcome." He flipped toward the end of the treatment, and after skimming a page, he began to read aloud. "'Deranged killers never have libraries. Their free hands can only ever manage to hold just one book.' That's good. The professor says that?"

"Right. Our three assassins are blindly obsessed with *Catcher*, but Holden, by contrast, is extremely well-read—Dinesen, Lardner, Hardy, Maugham, Fitzgerald, Shakespeare, and others. He has strong opinions about literature. Some critics may say that's merely Salinger's didacticism bleeding through, but a love of reading is true to Holden's sensitive, observant nature. The professor might contend that it even helped save him."

Brandon recalled Sallie Choo Choo's surprising love of reading, but his kills were different, strategic, not driven by deviant fixation, *una cosa di business,* as the Turk, Sollozzo, had explained to Michael Corleone. "Maybe Gideons International should be required to stick copies of *Huck Finn* or *The Grapes of Wrath* next to the good book in all those motel nightstands. Sort of like a trigger-lock." After more silent reading, he put his finger in the middle of a paragraph halfway down the second-to-last page. "You're shitting me? Schaeffer was expecting a script delivery, *The Godfather Part III,* when she answered the door and let Bardo in?"

"Absolutely. That's one hundred percent true. Such rich symbolism. Can you believe it? Here she is waiting for a career opportunity in a package of violence, a world where murder is represented by metaphor, a fish wrapped in newspaper or a brother's kiss on the mouth. Instead, she mistakenly welcomes in her own death when Bardo arrives with a copy of *Catcher* in his pocket and a .357 revolver."

Brandon sat back in his chair trying to process the unexpected intersections in his life. He felt like he was juggling torches—making *Catcher* into a movie, getting into bed with Sallie Choo Choo, and literally with his daughter. He saw himself back in the club with Sallie, strategizing—the secrecy, the intrigue, the schemes, the dangers. Producing *Catcher* would have to be a high-wire act across tenuous strands of legality, safety, and sanity. In that way, he would finally get to portray the aerialist Petit. When taking those last steps onto the skyscraper's roof at the end of the rope, he wouldn't disappear; he would transfigure. It was the necessarily narrow and harrowing path to liberation and fulfillment.

She asked a waiter to wrap up the rest of her salad. "You know, you share something quite unique with Billy Pilgrim, Vonnegut's protagonist in *Slaughterhouse-Five?*"

"Let me guess. He's from Oklahoma."

"Billy Pilgrim survived a major disaster, a passenger plane crash. Years before that, in the war, he was among a handful of survivors from the Dresden fire bombing, like Vonnegut was in real life. A prisoner of war at the time, he hid inside a meat locker. Now that's some stark irony, being saved from certain death inside a slaughterhouse."

"Yeah, not exactly what you'd expect. Kind of like when a country-fried terrorist uses a truckload of fertilizer to kill one hundred sixty-eight people. Can't exactly call that Miracle-Gro."

17

The carousel shoot was over in thirty minutes. With the news and park footage ready for editing, Luis only needed shots of Brandon near the ride, plus close-ups of the hat, the gun, and the tears. He had spent a full day rummaging through vintage clothing shops for wardrobe and an hour on Etsy for a red earflap hat. Brandon reused a prop revolver he'd kept from a guest spot on *CSI*. Rose brought a few of her younger cousins so the horses wouldn't be empty. Brandon's official website posted the teaser on YouTube on the Friday night before Thanksgiving.

Boosted by strategically selected social media amplifiers, the clip ricocheted around the globe at light speed. Within hours, outlets from *Buzzfeed* to *Al Jazeera* to the *Financial Times* reported that "Brandon Newman has broken the Internet." Downloads of "Smoke Gets in Your Eyes" spiked on iTunes. "Brando, my phone's not just on fire," Shari said. "It's the freaking China syndrome. I need asbestos gloves just to hold on to it." Brandon punched a clinched fist in the air. "Swear to God, Brand, the press are gyrating around like tops, hyped up like little kids who just ate the whole freaking candy store." She cleared her throat. "The *Megiddo* boys, on the other hand, are not so thrilled. We should've warned them. I told you that. They're pushing it to Memorial Day. I'm doing my best to spin this thing as pure *mazel*—any press for Brandon is box office for them—but they're not done ripping me new ones. I'm gonna be a freaking bag of doughnuts before this is over."

The press release, posted on Brandon's fan website at noon on Saturday, with Douglas's blessing, consisted of two sentences: "This film is my statement. There will be no further comment."

Shari called at 9:02 a.m. on Monday. A messenger had been waiting in the lobby of her building. The cease-and-desist demand resembled its predecessor, except the latest made ominous reference to "the swift and certain pursuit of all available remedies" and cited two unnamed sources from the entertainment community who were prepared "to testify that

Mr. Newman intends to make a film adaptation faithful in all material respects to *The Catcher in the Rye.*" The trust imposed a five p.m. same-day deadline for unconditional surrender. Brandon assumed the trust lawyers had scrounged up a couple of wannabe screenwriters who had sent unsolicited scripts in response to his original *Catcher* tweet. He even hoped the trustees might be bluffing, trying to fake him out the way Tom Cruise had posted a pair of know-nothing decoys in the back of the courtroom in *A Few Good Men.* Douglas warned Brandon to expect a banker's box of "love letters" by Wednesday.

The phonebook-thick stack of court pleadings arrived, as predicted, along with a copy of a signed TRO and a notation ordering the parties to appear for an initial hearing on the Monday after Thanksgiving. The matter had been assigned to the Honorable Idara Adebayo. In a conference call with Brandon and Shari, Douglas said they could have done much worse. She had been a judge for five years and before that, a legendary white-collar crime prosecutor in the Eastern District of New York, in Brooklyn. She'd won the DOJ's highest honor, the Attorney General's Award, for taking down a nest of sophisticated computer-hacking insider traders based in Massapequa, Long Island. "Idara is tough, likes to hand out maximum sentences. At the MCC, the inmates even nicknamed her 'the time machine.' On the plus side, she's a passionate lover of modern art, sits on the board of trustees at the Whitney Museum. Her son is a mixed media artist in Berlin. That's good for us in a case like this."

Shari had retained a security firm for the trip to the federal district court in downtown Manhattan. Brandon invited the bodyguards to help themselves to anything in the fridge. It was a sincere if hollow gesture. He had a typical millennial celebrity's Sub-Zero, half-empty shelves with a few bottles of Veuve Cliquot, door trays lined with Red Bull, a case of imported kombucha, and a Styrofoam take-out container with a half-eaten turkey leg and a slice of canned cranberries from the VIP tent at the Macy's Thanksgiving Day Parade. Before leaving the apartment, Brandon watched a local news report about his upcoming court appearance. The piece started with a clip of him at the parade, standing between swaying Keebler elves on top of a treehouse float while lip-syncing to a pre-recorded version of "Santa Claus is Comin' To Town." The story segued to a helicopter's overhead live shot showing spectators massing behind two parallel rows of police barricades that formed a narrow path to the courthouse entrance. After a quick preview of the hearing, the toupeed anchorman closed with a groaner about whether Brandon would be "naughty or nice."

A member of the protection detail handed him a clipboard with a liability waiver for his signature. "You sure you don't want to put on the Kevlar undershirt, Mr. Newman? Threat assessment says that book can make some folks go postal."

"I'm not expecting any special deliveries. I'll take my chances."

He insisted on a limousine so Luis could sit opposite to film and promised to pixelate the escorts. Brandon gave a rehearsed, passionate speech about artistic freedom and the importance for all "creative types" of his vindication of their rights in court. As the driver turned onto Canal Street, Brandon received a soon-to-vanish message from Alda. `"break a leg [red-cheeked face] check out my finsta. CPLT didn't sue michael scott! ROFL c u in court!"` Alda had one day left of Thanksgiving break before returning to DH. He opened her faux private Instagram feed, registered under the name @AlDuhNewz, and watched a clip from the American version of *The Office*, season four, episode eighteen, "Goodbye, Toby." The boss, played by Steve Carrell, explains to an ever-present but unseen documentarian that he intends to use birthday money sent four times a year by his forgetful grandmother to fund a farewell party for Toby from human resources, his sworn nemesis.

Holden would probably hate anyone from human resources. Brandon knew for certain that Salinger would. He cranked a finger at Luis. "Get this, sports fans. *The Office* ripped a scene right out of *Catcher*, when Holden explains how he had all that dough at Pencey. Exact same story. Senile granny and birthday money every couple of months. Maybe Doug should bring *that* up in court today."

Brandon would have to walk a long block to get to the courthouse. Pearl Street had been permanently closed to vehicular traffic, apparently a post-9/11 anti-terror measure. One of the bodyguards, a retired NYPD detective, had arranged for uniformed officers to meet them at the curb and reinforce the protective ring. Luis filmed Brandon leaving the limo but stayed inside. Back in Bushwick, Josh manned his post, screen-capturing live TV coverage from multiple channels for later promotional use.

As soon as Brandon stepped out, the familiar shutter clicks provided a background track to the clamoring reporters peppering him with questions. "Are you making *The Catcher in the Rye*?" "Who's going to play Phoebe?" "Will Spielberg direct?" "Have you spoken to Yoko Ono?" "What about Nancy Reagan, or Jodie Foster?"

Brandon waved with both hands and smiled in response to the shrieks of the crowd and the cries of "We love you!" "Marry Me" signs bobbed in the roiling sea of frenzied, mostly female fans. A few particularly enthusiastic admirers had hoisted giant foamboard cutouts of his head. He apologized to a cluster of "Newmaniacs" begging for autographs, explaining that "my lawyer told me I absolutely can't be late for this premiere." He was pleased with the size and spirit of the turnout, exactly the attention he'd hoped for. Two news helicopters whirred in circles above the scene. When his eyes returned to street level, they skipped over a rainbow of fangirl sweatshirts emblazoned with his face and locked on a pair of young white males who had managed to copy the teaser wardrobe, from the red hunting hat down to the two-tone saddle Oxfords. He made sure their hands clutched only the metal bars of the barricades. A reporter slipped through a narrow gap and thrust a microphone toward his face. "Did you know your mother would be here?"

His head swiveled back and forth like a startled owl. "Where?" The reporter jabbed the mic toward a revolving door entrance. He shrugged his shoulders and regained his composure. "You never know where Sheila's gonna pop up. She's like that *Where's Waldo*." He gave the camera a toothy grin, but he was seething. She wasn't there to show support. She had come to seize a golden opportunity to grandstand before a national audience. There were rumors on social media that she was planning a run for Congress. He instructed his handlers to move faster. As he neared the building, he spotted his mother in her signature white pantsuit and scarlet silk scarf, standing between a pair of similarly dressed women holding up large posters—one repeating the familiar refrain "Repent Now, John 3:16," the other reading "Godless Books Do Satan's Work. Two Dead, One Wounded. Who's Next?"

Sheila's face was stiff and bloated, like an angry pufferfish, so tight that cracking a full smile would have resulted in a trip to the emergency room. With a cameraman focused on her over-sculpted profile, she stretched her open arms over the metal barrier. "Brandon, he was a heathen, son, spawn of the antichrist. Remember what the Lord said, 'Get thee behind me, Satan.' It's time to come out of the desert." The shutter clicks multiplied exponentially. He kept his head down, refusing to make eye contact. He put his hand on a police officer's back and whispered a recommendation from Rose about obtaining swift courtroom access via the Marshals Service elevator.

Reporters clutching notepads packed the gallery. For once, he appreciated the relentless press, whose thundering herd mentality had left no seat open for his upstaging mother. Three sketch artists occupied the jury box, their chalks out, filling in backgrounds and zeroing in on Brandon's features. He sat at counsel table with Douglas and Ernest. Alda and

Charlotte perched behind them in the first row next to a paralegal rifling through color-coded tabs in a briefcase stuffed with documents. Shari took a spot in the back row to huddle with a reporter from *The Atlantic*, to whom, with Brandon's permission, she would speak off the record.

Two knocks on a door behind the bench brought the room to attention.

"Be seated, everyone. Haven't seen a full house like this since I got tickets to *Hamilton*." The audience erupted with ingratiating laughter. "I trust you all had a peaceful and fulfilling holiday."

"Good morning, Your Honor."

"Nice to see you again, Mr. Blackburn. Wasn't that a wonderful lunch the City Bar Association held last week for Judge Cahill?"

"Indeed, it was. Such a terrific turnout of former law clerks. We all thought he'd never take senior status."

"My colleagues and I finally convinced him to ride the circuit a little, snowbird in Miami, clean out some of that clogged-up drug docket." The judge next addressed the trust's counsel. "Good morning to you as well, Ms. Ricciardi. When you get back to the office, be sure to say hello to my old trial partner, Mr. Shapiro."

"I will, Your Honor. He's recently become the chairman of our executive committee."

"Can't be too good for his golf game."

"No, Judge. More than a few of us are hoping he'll drop a stroke or two before the next firm outing."

"All right, then. Let me state for the record what I've had the opportunity to review before today's hearing. I've seen the complaint filed by the Cornish Perpetual Literary Trust, the request for a TRO, which I granted last week, the motion for a preliminary injunction, which brings us here today, affidavits from the corporate trustees, and the memorandum of law in support. From Mr. Newman, I've read the memo in opposition and, of course, his affidavit." Douglas had drafted an initial version of the sworn statement, but Brandon, drawing on Alda's cautionary sailboat coaching session, insisted that it be more ambiguous, hoping to afford himself as much protection as possible against a subsequent claim of deceit or obstruction.

"Ms. Ricciardi, we are, as you are well aware, a passive judiciary, slow as a tortoise to stir, reluctant to get involved unless we absolutely must. My first question is this: Isn't your action premature, particularly in light of the fact that, number one, we have no artistic creation to examine, and number two, Mr. Newman's recently sworn denial of any intent to infringe? You have to admit the defendant's brief seems to have the better side of the law on that score."

"Your Honor, if there were no history here, I might share the Court's concern over jumping the gun. However, in the case at bar, Mr. Newman has made clear—through prior social media posts and to at least two witnesses from the entertainment community who are willing to testify—that he intends to produce a film fully consistent with the plot, language, and characters of *The Catcher in the Rye*. Of course, the plaintiff can prevail under a standard much lower than that of verbatim theft. We need show merely an infringement upon my client's property. The literary equivalent of trespass is all the law requires. Indeed, in the 1987 case of *Salinger v. Random House*, Mr. Salinger, then living, successfully stopped a would-be biographer from infringing on the intellectual property contained in his unpublished personal letters. He prevailed even though, as Judge Jon O. Newman, writing for the Second Circuit Court of Appeals, said—"

"No relation to you, is he, Mr. Newman?" Judge Adebayo asked.

Brandon stood up and buttoned his suitcoat. "No, Your Honor. None to Paul Newman either, though I may have suggested otherwise in a few auditions." The pews of reporters sounded like a sitcom laugh track.

"Very well. Counsel, you may proceed."

"Judge Newman, in considering the four-factor test for fair use, made clear that even the biographer's attempts at paraphrase still infringed upon the creative expression found in the unique combinations of otherwise ordinary words. Given the unparalleled artistry of Mr. Salinger, an author recognized as having a singular voice in American literature, Mr. Newman's general proffer of something, quote unquote, 'new and different' provides cold comfort. In truth, it is little more than *ipse dixit*."

"That's all well and good, but why not wait to see what he actually does? I know lots of films get made, edited, re-edited, and then never even released."

"Should the trustees let their guard down, Your Honor, contrary to the provisions of the trust, my clients may be susceptible to claims of estoppel, release, and/or waiver in future litigation. Given Mr. Newman's previously stated unequivocal intentions and our own investigation, we believe that an injunction is the only way to preserve the integrity of the trust's intellectual property. We are prepared to go forward with a hearing and identify our witnesses at the Court's earliest convenience."

Douglas rose and placed his glasses on the table. "Your Honor, if I may. We are not here today to dispute that Mr. Newman once expressed a desire to make Mr. Salinger's novel into a film. He's in very good company in that regard, as my always thorough adversary has noted in her papers. That's simply not, with all due respect, the matter before the Court. Indeed, we submit there is no justiciable case or controversy because, as Your Honor has rightly noted, there is no film. The screen remains *tabula rasa*. There is merely a concept that Mr. Newman has explained will be a substantive commentary on, and critique of, the novel and its unfortunately lethal ramifications. Moreover, the recently released movie teaser, which brought us all here today and is hyperlinked in the electronic version of our brief, certainly does not portend a faithful rendition. The transformative and critical creation to come is, we submit, fully entitled to the protections guaranteed to Mr. Newman under the fair use doctrine as interpreted in a mile-long line of Supreme Court decisions we've cited in our memorandum.

"What's more, if, under the justiciability doctrine, a ripe case or controversy is *sine qua non*, the price of admission, as it were, to this august public forum for dispute resolution, that requirement must be, *a fortiori*, indispensable where, as here, the inalienable rights of the First Amendment are at stake. What the plaintiff seeks, Your Honor, is nothing short of an unprecedented prior restraint on an unfinished, indeed nonexistent work of artistic expression. That makes the *Random House* decision wholly inapposite. There, the court had reviewable galley proofs of the proposed Salinger biography. That's a world of difference. The anticipatory equitable relief sought at this exceedingly early juncture, if granted, would not merely chill a host of writers, journalists, and artists from engaging in the vigorous cultural colloquy the Founders felt essential to a vibrant and healthy democracy; it would usher in the intellectual and aesthetic equivalent of a creative ice age."

"Thank you, Mr. Blackburn. I think we all know now why lawyers charge by the hour." A stand-up comic couldn't have hoped for a more responsive house. "You won't ever find too many fans of old Polonius down in the well of the Court."

"Your Honor, if I may respond, this action is not nearly so preliminary or theoretical as Mr. Blackburn suggests. We seek a much narrower ruling on very specific and unique facts. The artistic community will not find itself encased in the ice prison of counsel's rather vivid imagination. We understand as plaintiffs we bear the burden here and simply ask for the opportunity to receive limited expedited pre-hearing discovery, including Mr. Newman's deposition, to call our witnesses in open court, and to demonstrate that Mr. Newman's intent is to create something that, even if not a word-for-word version, will be a movie so imbued with the essential and proprietary aspects of Mr. Salinger's one-of-a-kind work that this Court can, even at this stage, order preliminary injunctive relief. We would then, of course, proceed to plenary pretrial discovery and be prepared to meet our ultimate burden at a full trial on the merits."

"What about that, Mr. Blackburn? A little limited discovery and a hearing with a short timeframe? What's the harm in that?"

Brandon waved his hand for Alda to lean forward. "A deposition? She can't let them do that. The documentary. And what about you?" He left the names of Maeve, Rose, and Sallie Choo Choo unsaid but not forgotten. "It would be a total nightmare."

"I wouldn't worry," Alda said. "The judge can't possibly let it get to that now, not with the denial in your affidavit. I think she's letting the other side have her say, a courtesy thing. You'll win the battle, but winning the war, that's something else. TBH, I hope you know what you're doing."

"I think I like you better when you're sitting in the back row."

"Your Honor, you won't be surprised to hear me say that my client, Mr. Newman, believes such a seemingly narrow ruling would nonetheless set a dangerous precedent. Not all artists, indeed precious few, enjoy similar resources. If this Court were to allow a copyright holder to bootstrap a few musings on social media into a court-ordered hearing and expensive and burdensome pre-hearing discovery, it would, forgive the extended analogy, blow a frigid gust over anyone hoping to reinvent, reinvigorate, or simply enter into a creative dialogue with the most influential and impactful literary works of our forbearers. What struggling, starving artist would take that risk? Would Andy Warhol have dared to paint his iconic 1962 pop art masterpiece *Campbell's Soup Cans*? I seriously doubt it. As an aside, the Campbell's Company loved the free publicity so much that instead of suing Mr. Warhol, they sent him cases of tomato soup with their compliments. Perhaps the trustees might take note of this enlightened response."

Ernest nudged Brandon and covered his mouth as he spoke. "Through our research, we discovered that the judge is on a planning committee at the Whitney Museum to mount a huge Warhol retrospective in 2018, including the soup cans. That will definitely catch her attention."

"My main point, Your Honor, is that allowing preliminary proceedings where, as here, there is not a final artistic work to evaluate would be a crippling and undue burden on free speech."

"I have to admit, Mr. Blackburn, I am a little concerned about your client's prior statements, and frankly, you don't give me much to go on in his affidavit. Pretty bare bones." She paged through papers on the bench. "Let's see here, 'will not be a word-for-word reproduction of the original work but a substantial reimagining of its message and the impact it has had on late twentieth-century American culture.' Can't you give us a little more than that?"

"Your Honor, the Court will understand that if we set out more detail of Mr. Newman's concept in publicly filed court papers, we lessen substantially the potential for the film's financial success. The fourth estate, apologies to those present, would have a field day with such description. Much of the box office draw will be in the film's mystery. If we lay the story out now for all to see, that allure will be gone forever. The financial impact would be, frankly, incalculable."

"I noticed in his affidavit that Mr. Newman acknowledges he has a so-called treatment prepared, correct?"

"Yes, Judge."

"Your Honor, if I may, this is another reason the trustees have legitimate and pressing concerns. We have offered to enter into a nondisclosure stipulation with Mr. Blackburn's firm so that we would be able review the treatment without any risk to the secrecy of Mr. Newman's ultimate production."

Douglas had wanted to file a copy of the treatment under seal to be seen only by the Court and trust counsel, but double-agent Alda reported overhearing her father tell Ernest that he believed they could probably win without it. Relying on his well-placed source, Brandon instructed Douglas to withhold the plot summary.

"What about that, Mr. Blackburn? Sounds reasonable."

"Your Honor, my position on that is of a piece with my prior argument. Copyright holders should not have the right to act as real-time censors, hanging over the head of a writer in the embryonic process of creation like a sharpened sword of Damocles. Rather, the presumption during the early stages of development, at a minimum, must be in favor of the artist. Should infringement occur in the finalized work, the offended party is not left without recourse. The cases holding that monetary damages and post-publication injunctions suffice as remedies for violations of the copyright laws are legion. We've included a string cite on that point from every circuit court in the country." Douglas stepped back toward the counsel table and Ernest slipped him a Post-it note. "That's found on page twenty-eight of our memorandum."

"I think I've heard enough argument from both sides, and I'm sure our friends from the papers have gotten more than enough for a column or two. I'd really rather not get into a ruling if I don't have to. Seems unnecessary at this time. My understanding is that before being released to the public, the Hollywood studios send out advance reviewer copies to all the major papers and critics. What if Mr. Blackburn would agree to send a copy to trust counsel at the same time? Wouldn't that afford the trustees ample opportunity to come back here, if needed, with a more concrete challenge?"

Douglas leaned over counsel table for a quick consult with his client. "Your Honor, Mr. Newman has advised me that he does not intend to send out any review copies to critics in advance. He believes it is crucial to the film's marketing strategy that it not be screened anywhere before release. No reviewers and no film festivals. I would note that this strategy, aside from its obvious commercial appeal, has the ancillary benefit of reducing substantially the risk that the film will be leaked or hacked or posted by a bootleg site on the dark web."

"Your Honor, this is simply one more reason the trustees remain legitimately concerned about what's transpiring, and frankly only further demonstrates the need for the preliminary relief we request."

"Let's take a brief recess, and I'll come back with my decision."

Upon her return, the judge denied the plaintiff's motion for a preliminary injunction but ordered Brandon's counsel to file a copy of the treatment, *ex parte,* and under seal with the Court by five p.m. Only Judge Adebayo would review it, and she would summon counsel for another conference within a week if she had concerns. She also otherwise stayed all proceedings in the matter "until such time as counsel for Mr. Newman reports to this Court and opposing counsel that the film has been finished. The Court expects that such notice will come no later than forty-five days before any public screenings."

Once the judge had left the courtroom, Brandon approached the bench and asked the courtroom deputy if his team might cut through the interior corridor to access the Marshals' elevator. He jabbed a thumb toward the throng of reporters leaning over the spectator rail and vying for his attention with whispered shouts. Douglas rushed to his client's side. "We'd love to get Mr. Newman out of here in one piece." She placed a call, and a court security officer emerged from the judge's entrance to escort them. Douglas announced to the press corps that there would be no further statement from his client.

Before leaving, Brandon spoke to Alda and Charlotte. "Thanks for the help."

"Looks like you dodged a bullet today," Alda said.

Brandon bobbed and weaved, finishing with an Ali shuffle. "Old J.D.'s probably in an underground spin cycle right about now."

"I don't think so. He's probably deep in meditation, trying to get reincarnated, coming back here as a . . ." Alda stopped and let her head drop.

"As a what?" he asked.

"As an obsessed fan," Charlotte said.

18

A week had passed since Brandon's court appearance and the submission of the movie treatment. With no new orders from Judge Adebayo, Douglas gave the green light to Brandon's second teaser, even while warning that its "highly incendiary concept would raise roof high more than a few hackles."

Most of the filming had to be done on December 8, the thirty-fifth anniversary of the murder that broke up The Beatles forever. Brandon dressed in a faded army jacket with a "Schmidt" name label, white-washed bell bottoms, and dark blue knit beanie with earflaps, braids, and poms. He wore an eight-day-old beard and a pair of rose-tinted "John Lennon" glasses he'd bought from an online retainer, an officially licensed version of the iconic pair with a laser-etched autograph. That Yoko Ono had been one true-blue capitalist. Salinger would have never authorized a line of Holden products: hunting hats, fur-lined gloves, sheep-lined slippers, hockey skates, figure skates, racing skates, premium luggage, cigarettes (Caulfields?), or baseball mitts with your favorite poem stamped inside on genuine cowhide.

Instead of accessorizing his outfit with the *CSI* prop gun, Brandon carried a loaded Ruger LC9s. The pistol wasn't part of his costume. It was for protection, not show. After his court appearance, the heightened sense of vulnerability he shared with fellow celebrities had mutated into the early stages of paranoia. Watching news reports about Bernie Goetz on YouTube had made him feel even more exposed. He also worried that his mother's publicity stunt—denouncing the book as satanic, a message she repeated on social media and on her weekly radio show—would get him killed. He feared a deranged disciple determined to punish him for his unrepentant disobedience just as much as a lonely lost boy in a ridiculous hat.

The possibility of arming himself had not been a new idea. For months, Josh had been nagging him to get a carry permit. "All the young guns are packing these days," he said. "It's like your black AMEX, membership in the Brat Pack. Plus, it might just save your ass." Until his recent encounter with Sheila, Brandon had always dismissed Josh's warnings as overblown. He'd dealt with a few minor-league stalkers, but none had posed a serious risk. One delusional groupie, a divorced mother of two from Toledo, had sent him an album of photoshopped honeymoon pictures. Brandon's face had replaced her ex-husband's in the infinity pool, on a Jet Ski, and beneath a beachside palapa. She showed up on location in St. Lucia, a copy of the album in hand, demanding to see "her husband," and was promptly arrested and deported. Another deranged fan, a mother from Little Rock who'd lost a teenaged son to suicide, baked breads and pastries with Brandon's likeness and sent them to Shari. A security consultant suggested they be sent for laboratory analysis. The black forest cake came back very positive for an elephant dose of Zoloft. The woman pled guilty to a misdemeanor and was ordered to refrain from further contact.

Brandon knew that publicly committing to a *Catcher* film meant superfan amateur hour was over. That book always brought out the heavy hitters. At his insistence, Shari begrudgingly located an expediter who specialized in obtaining concealed weapon permits for the rich and famous. Still, he would have to wait six to eight weeks. In the meantime, he borrowed the Ruger from Josh and kept the slim, compact, and unlicensed handgun snug in his waistband. On a recent overnight in the Pines, they had spent the morning dirt-biking and shattering long-neck empties for practice. The fear of a Caulfield zealot had motivated his preparation but didn't guarantee his performance. If he had to engage, he'd be acting without the safety net of a second take, no chance for a do-over if he hesitated or flubbed when the action went live.

Though he had no intention of flashing the firearm in the Lennon teaser, he believed that wearing it was critical, even for a movie he would never make. Its latent presence, its secret capacity for death, would connect him emotionally with the fractured psyche of the adoring assassin, the fan turned fanatic. The gun and the novel, the pen and the sword. He needed both, like the three men who went before him.

The day's first shoot featured Brandon roller-skating on a path bordering the east side of Central Park's Sheep Meadow, heading to Strawberry Fields, returning to the scene of the crime. A pawn shop guitar hung strapped over his back with a POW/MIA sticker and a psychedelic peace sign. He held a copy of Lennon's *Double Fantasy*, his arm straight at his side, fingertips crimped to cradle the album. Josh followed on roller blades, using a GoPro. Luis set up in the middle of the meadow to get the long take.

Shari had warned Brandon: "Better expect an AARP convention. Even I was once an angry teen with a pizza face and a tie-dye back in the Summer of Love." The commemorators, around a hundred, seemed even older than he had anticipated. Beer guts the size of pony kegs and widening center parts lined with parallel strips of wiry gray. Some day they would stop coming. Eventually, the park would need a plaque to tell visitors who John Lennon was. A few brave or clueless men, apparently untroubled by the chilly temperatures and the ravages of time, had appeared in John's iconic sleeveless "NEW YORK CITY" t-shirt. So did Josh, who could pull it off, except his variant read "NEW YORK FUCKING CITY." Most wore sensible sweatshirts with pictures of John and Yoko or The Beatles. They stood in a circle around the memorial's centerpiece mosaic, which had the word "IMAGINE" written in stone as both mantra and tribute.

The guitars, tambourines, and harmonicas grouped near the center and played a mournful jam session: "Come Together," "All You Need Is Love," "Strawberry Fields Forever." Brandon had tucked in the wheels of his retractable skates and wiggled into the heart of the musicians. He placed the album on the ground, face down, among a bed of scattered roses and votive candles. Luis had managed to position himself, crouched low, across from the performers. Brandon played along and sang quietly, making sure the camera angles were unobstructed. Josh skated around the edges of the scene, GoProing the crowd. The ceremony concluded with fans joining hands to sing "Imagine." As the somber gathering dispersed, Luis flipped the album over to get a shot of the cover, John and Yoko locked in a kiss frozen for eternity, their matching black shirts blending together as if one. Against that dark background, Brandon had written "Holden was here" in gold metallic marker. He stood next to Luis, hunched over, trying to block any lingering onlookers. Luis filmed a quick take and snatched the album.

They finished shooting across the street at the Dakota, where Lennon had lived and died. Brandon activated the recorder in his pocket and approached a doorman with a passable Liverpudlian accent, the Ruger wedged firmly against the small of his back. He gave the man fifty dollars and asked to be shown the exact location where "John" had been killed. It cost another hundred to get him to autograph a copy of *The Catcher in the Rye* and read the opening paragraph aloud while they stood over the fateful spot. Josh managed two slow passes along the sidewalk. Luis easily blended in as one of the dozens of tourists who visited the Dakota as a sort of pilgrimage.

The provocative and diversionary teaser, cut down to forty-five seconds in three days, was officially posted online for only an hour, but a flood of reposted screen captures ensured an eternal virtual life. It opened, not in the park, but in a 1940s-era subway car in the Brooklyn Transit Museum. Luis had flashed his expired USC ID to convince the facility's manager that he was making a student short. He said he only needed twenty minutes, spoke to her in Puerto Rican slang, and paid $200 in cash. Brandon had accompanied in a spirit-gummed, scraggly hipster beard, a vintage train engineer's hat, and painter's overalls, posing as a production assistant.

A black canvas bag, propped up against the seat bench, "Pencey" embroidered on its side, foil and epee hilts sticking out, the sound of clattering wheels on track getting louder as the camera zooms in. The voiceover: "Sometimes what you leave behind can have unintended consequences." Cut to a close-up with a slow zoom out, a middle-aged woman in a mink coat (Luis's aunt) lying on the floor of the car, unblinking eyes, loose pearls slowly rolling away from her neck, a saber stuck in her chest like a planted flagpole. Cut to Brandon skating through the park to Frank Sinatra's version of "Just One of Those Things," the crowd scenes and the music at Strawberry Fields, close-ups of Brandon, the mosaic, the album cover. Finally, the eerie exchange between Brandon and the doorman brings the teaser to an end as "Happiness Is a Warm Gun" plays in the background.

Like Douglas, Shari had predicted the firestorm of criticism that would follow. Pundits called it "grossly insensitive," "heartless exploitation," and "borderline criminal." A prominent New York film critic, however, lauded the teaser's "haunting, purposefully amateurish pastiche as boldly evocative of the splintered mind of an acolyte turned iconoclast." The Madison Avenue crowd simply deemed it "savvy marketing." Brandon welcomed the praise but liked the venom even more. The fiery outrage created the perfect smokescreen. No one was saying anything about copyright infringement, at least with regard to Salinger. To milk the coverage further, Brandon posted an email Shari had received from counsel for the multimedia conglomerate that controlled licensing for the commercial use of Lennon and Beatles songs. The curt message demanded the "offending and offensive" clip be taken down "forthwith" and threatened legal action. Brandon tweeted in response that he had "no intention of ever showing the teaser again" and announced a $50,000 "goodwill" donation to one of Yoko Ono's favorite charities. Shari reached a quick and quiet resolution with the music cooperative controlling the rights to the Cole Porter song.

On December 14, a Monday, two days after the teaser had aired, Douglas phoned with urgent news. He had received a call from Judge Adebayo's law clerk. She wanted them in her chambers at one p.m. for an *ex parte* conference, Brandon and Douglas only. Her clerk wouldn't reveal the reason for the unusual summons. "I have to assume it's your latest publicity stunt. She'll probably admonish you to tone it down while you're in production and with the case in abeyance."

"So now she's a film critic?"

"She worked a lot of cases with the ATF as a young prosecutor, gun dealers trucking in illegal firearms from Georgia or North Carolina. I'm quite certain she had no appetite for that ending, especially the not-so-subtle last song."

Brandon imagined being hauled away in handcuffs if the judge had known about his Ruger. "I thought she's supposed to appreciate art. You saw what some of the critics said. The big one from Chicago called it 'sad but captivating irony,' the fact that Lennon himself wrote a song about finding peace in busting a cap. Maybe she actually loved it, wants an autograph."

"I think it's safe to leave your Sharpie at home. And don't be late."

19

The clerk ushered them into a conference room and said the judge would be right in. Citations, plaques, and artwork decorated the lone wall not lined with shelves of numbered law books. A medal from the DEA, a bright color photograph of African women, their heads capped with enormous bundles, walking through an open-air market, a print of a bald white judge peering down at two black men standing deep in the well of the court, and a painting—three primitive skulls, scribbled graffiti-like, wild dashes of random colors, soulless eye sockets, jaws almost chattering. The dizzying trio seemed strung out, as if the artist was racing to finish and bolt for the next fix. The anxious heads had awakened the old feelings, the desperate mania, the burning need for poison as antidote. Brandon wanted to check his phone to distract, but it sat in a Marshals Service locker.

"That's got to be a Basquiat," Douglas said, pointing to the disquieting image. "One of Maeve's favorites."

"Who's that?"

"Such a tragedy. Twenty-seven years old. So much talent." Douglas patted Brandon's forearm. "Glad you got help in time."

Brandon felt unexpected relief when the judge entered. Her presence somehow quieted the stirred-up demons. She smiled and apologized for the "cloak and dagger" routine. "I realize this is highly unusual. Mr. Blackburn can explain why hard facts make bad law. There will be no docket entry for this meeting and no transcript. Given your unique celebrity status, this rare accommodation made sense to me. And it's a favor for an old friend. Wait here." She turned to put a hand on the doorknob and looked back over her shoulder. "Understand that while I may have said 'wait here,' it was meant solely as a request. You are free to go at any time, and it will have absolutely no consequence in the matter pending before me. In fact, I have no idea what this is even about."

Seconds after she left, a man and a woman entered. He was tall, mid-thirties, pale with blue eyes, Joseph A. Bank-cut dark brown suit. She looked younger, five feet at most, short blond hair, Duane Reade dye job, navy skirt, beige collared top. Each held a black leather billfold sandwiching an index finger. "I'm Agent Curran," he said. "This is my partner, Agent Severini." They did a synchronized FBI cred flip like the retired agent had taught Brandon for an appearance on *Law & Order*. Curran turned to Douglas. "We'd like to speak with your client about Salvatore Catarrazzo." He felt a sharp chill, as if he'd been disrobed by the mere utterance of a full name never spoken without consequence.

Douglas sprang up and moved in front of his client as if to shield him. "Why didn't you call me? There was absolutely no need to involve the court in this manner. Can we step outside for a moment?"

Curran ignored the requested sidebar. "It was the best way to avoid suspicions. We're in the courthouse all the time, and your world-famous client here happens to have a pending matter before the judge. Nobody would ever suspect a meeting. Besides, Idara owes me one after all those double shifts I pulled sitting her wires. Why don't you have a seat? This is a completely friendly get-together. You and your client can leave at any time." His sly smirk belied the breezy offer of liberty. Brandon didn't feel at all free to go.

"Who exactly is this Salvatore person?" Douglas sat next to his client and whispered in his ear. "Do *not* say a word. We listen and only *I* ask questions."

"'Sallie 'Choo Choo' Catarrazzo is head of the South Brooklyn family. We have reason to believe your client has entered into a business arrangement with him or entities controlled by him. Isn't that right, Mr. Newman?"

Douglas seized Brandon's wrist to reinforce his admonition. "I need five minutes with my client, alone, please. Or we can end this right now."

"Easy does it, counselor," Severini said. "You can scoot, but I think you'd regret not hearing what we have to say. We'll be right outside." She spoke as if to reassure, but her words sounded more like a threat.

Brandon didn't admit to Douglas that he'd met Sallie, said he'd only heard of him. He served up a watered-down version of the story he'd fed Luis, about meeting Rose through "a friend." He disingenuously described the business relationship, omitting their own "relationship" status and any details about the word-for-word *Catcher* scenes he planned to shoot at Catarrazzo properties. He stressed the arrangement was "one hundred percent legit." The paperwork had recently been finalized by La Traviata's in-house counsel.

Douglas reviewed the new scratches on his legal pad. "They must have a source saying something different, or else they're on a fishing expedition." He went out into the hall for more details. He was absent for what seemed like a half hour but had probably been no more than five minutes. When he returned, Douglas complained that the agents were "frustratingly circumspect." They had said only that Brandon was "involved," and had potentially relevant knowledge. They wanted his help. "I'm going to let them back in, but you keep your mouth superglued." Brandon imagined Sallie adding "*capisce*" as an exclamation point.

"You don't remember me, do you?" Curran asked. Brandon remained mute as instructed. "If I had on a shabby hobo coat, couple of grease stains on my cheeks, a mangy wig, might that jog your memory?" Brandon's face must have flashed recognition. "Looks like you might have had one of those 'aha' moments. Or should I say uh-oh?" Agent Curran had been the dumpster-diving bum in the alley behind Handel the night Brandon met Sallie.

Severini took her partner's hand and rubbed shoulders with him. "How about me?" Something about how she sat up, beaming a newlywed's hopeful smile, had given it away. Brandon hadn't recognized her without the long black wig. The agents had been the childless orthodox couple ogling him at the Brooklyn Zoo. Rose had obviously missed it too, which didn't make him feel any better. Luis had unwittingly served as a perfect diversion. Brandon expected to see an array of 8x10s sliding across the conference table any minute. He turned to Douglas. "I need to talk to you." The agents agreed to return to the hallway.

Brandon admitted to a meeting with Sallie and dating Rose. After Douglas unleashed a startling, profanity-laced lecture about honesty and openness in the lawyer-client relationship, Brandon apologized but stressed the location rentals were completely aboveboard. He offered to provide copies of the contracts but still said nothing about the secret recordings of Rose and Maeve, the upcoming Christmas Eve dinner at Sallie's bomb shelter, or his intent to make an authentic *Catcher*. Douglas made Brandon repeat his explanation of the relationship with the Catarrazzos before inviting the agents to return.

Curran claimed to have no interest in using Brandon as a trial witness. "Celebrities are not worth that kind of trouble. You wouldn't believe what a pain in the ass Steven Seagal was the time he testified against the Gambinos. We would never ask you to wear a wire or even introduce a UC. We only want you to be a confidential source, completely passive. You listen, you observe, and you report back, kind of like deep background for a news story. Think of it like a movie part. No case we make would ever be traced back to you. Point us in the right direction, now and then. That's all."

"Why would my client risk his life to do this for you, assuming he even has the relationships you suggest?"

"Axel Jackstone would do it for God and country," Curran said. Severini kept her head down. Brandon assumed she was biting her lip. "Firstly, it involves minimal and manageable risk. We're not asking your client to put himself out there, snoop around, ask a bunch of questions. Treat us like one of those confessional booths you used to go to on *Celebrity Big Brother*." He elbowed Severini as if he had been planning to work that line into his spiel. "Secondly, and I really hate to even get into this, but here's the thing." He stood up and put his foot on a chair to adjust a sock, revealing an empty ankle holster. "The Bureau is way too busy and, Lord knows, too understaffed to chase down all the perjury claims made in civil cases. However, let's just say we might have reason to believe that your client wasn't entirely kosher, as they say, in his recent sworn statement."

"I don't know what you're talking about," Brandon blurted. Douglas kicked his disobedient client under the table.

Severini thrust clasped hands across the table. "Let's say, for argument's sake, Mr. Newman wasn't really going to do some brand-new movie. Maybe he actually intends to infringe the Salinger copyright. That might make his affidavit a little hard to square with the gospel truth now, wouldn't it? I can promise you the last thing we want to do is serve weekly grand jury subpoenas on Mr. Newman's production company to get copies of any and all new footage. Huge waste of our time, but as learned counsel will tell you, we could do that. I can only imagine how burdensome and expensive responding to a series of court orders like that would be. Don't you agree, Mr. Newman?"

"Hold it. He's absolutely not answering any questions today. Give us a few more minutes alone."

Brandon lied to Douglas about the movie, swore his affidavit had been accurate. "But it doesn't make a goddamned bit of difference, Doug. These Feds are gonna harass me no matter what I tell them, then the trust will get the judge involved, and we'll never get any momentum. Matter of fact, that's exactly what they're counting on."

Douglas agreed with Brandon's preliminary assessment of the government's threatened leverage. He recommended, nevertheless, that they take some time, meet with one of his partners who used to prosecute mob cases. He felt confident he could put the agents off until after New

Year's. Brandon asked for a minute to respond to texts from Shari. He wanted to reach out to his father. It was almost eleven p.m. in Riyadh.

"still coming friday?"

"ETA midnight. Leaving Sunday for your brother's."

"reading a new script, mob informant. might need technical advice."

"Don't do it. They always end up dead. I want to see the tree at Rockefeller Center, definitely the Rockettes."

He put his phone down and agreed to Douglas's proposal. Before they left, the agents shook hands with Brandon and thanked him for the meeting, as if he'd had a choice. At the courthouse steps, Douglas instructed his client to say nothing about the FBI to anyone. He'd already given the same stern warning twice in the elevator.

Brandon released his driver, said he wanted to walk home, enjoy the weather, even though he felt naked without a disguise or the gun on his hip. The day was unusually warm, low sixties, sunny skies. He felt seasick from the swirl of alternatives. He needed to decompress, come up with a plan. His mirror sunglasses, barrister pinstripe, and empty leather briefcase would have to be enough to get him back to his building unnoticed. He avoided a route taking him through Foley Square and past 26 Federal Plaza, home to the FBI's New York office. He had no desire to cross that shadow twice in the same day. He opted instead to take Mulberry to Grand. Across the street from the courthouse, Columbus Park sat empty but for a few stooped, elderly Chinese men standing in a circle, cackling and smoking. They held their cigarettes with stiff fingers, looking frail, thin enough to snap in two. Opposite the park's playground stood stores selling funeral services and supplies.

Refusing to cooperate was not an option. The agents would team up with the trust to screw him over and grab headlines in the process. He could dump Rose tomorrow and buy his way out of the contracts with La Traviata, but that wouldn't help. The Bureau would blow up *Catcher* out of spite. How did they know? It didn't even really matter. Even if they were bluffing, they had guessed right. Douglas had said that prosecutors give FBI agents blank check grand jury subpoenas like promoters handing out strip club flyers in Vegas. A few sheets of court paper could bring down a multinational. What chance did he stand?

As he walked through the fringes of Chinatown, he passed cramped storefronts, men sitting on commercial-grade, upside-down buckets, sidewalks lined with fresh fish iced in plastic tubs, and produce displayed in unpacked crates. A tacky knickknack shop openly sold racks of knockoff Gucci and Tory Burch handbags. The solid metal door of a massage parlor called "Enchanted Garden" tempted without teasing. He almost went in, lured by the prospect of a more immediate, reckless danger that might dull the sound of the impending hazards buzzing in his ears.

The only way to move forward was to play along, outmaneuvering the trust and the FBI until he could finish. He remained convinced that once the movie was completed, he could persuade the trust to back down and by then the FBI would cut him loose. How much could he really help them? His standing as an outsider, however, made him fear that the agents would soon go back on their word, begin pushing him to nose around, to pump Rose for details, to get closer to Sallie. He had to make himself less valuable without doing it too quickly. He'd be sorry to lose her, but he knew he could jump-start a Page-Six relationship at a moment's notice. One call from Shari to more than a dozen agents with aspiring female actors would do it. The tabloids could actually provide him with an alibi for once.

As he crossed Canal Street, the offerings changed—pizza, pasta, espresso, gelati. He had entered what was left of Little Italy. For years, Chinatown had been slowly devouring the neighborhood from all sides. Only a two-block stretch remained intact between Canal and Grand. He turned to look south, the soaring federal courthouse still looming in the distance. Opting for the sunny side of the street, he found himself in front of Umberto's Clam House, the spot where, according to Shari, Crazy Joe Gallo had been gunned down on his birthday. Brandon's twenty-fifth was only a few weeks away. He wanted to go inside, see where Gallo had been seated. If he were to mention Sallie Choo Choo, they would probably serve him a heaping platter of *frutti di mare* on the house. He didn't go in because already he knew the answer. Mobsters always sit with their backs against the wall, eyes on the front door. They want to see it coming. Was that how he would have to sit for the rest of his life? Because of the mob? Holden? Both?

The sight of a closed yellow umbrella held high signaled a tour group approaching from the north. Brandon reflexively ducked into the year-round Christmas store next to Umberto's to let them pass. He kept his sunglasses on. With the holidays approaching, the store bustled with tourists buying decorations, ornaments mostly—NYPD, FDNY, checker cabs, State of Liberty, Empire State Building, and local sports teams. The "Never Forget" ornaments with the World Trade Center seemed less than holly jolly, but no less so than a crucifix. Ceiling speakers caroled "Do They Know It's Christmas?" Brandon picked up a Rudolph ornament for Brock's newborn and one from the Rockettes Collection, four dancers in a line, frozen in a precision knee-lift, for his father.

He used a Boston accent at the counter. For low-end retail purchases, he always paid with a credit card in Shari's husband's name. The young woman at the register, straight dark hair, possibly Hispanic, wore a Santa hat and a bulky sweater with a wide Christmas tree and battery-operated flashing lights. "We don't get too many Irving Mishkins in here." Her eyes bounced between the card and Brandon. He told her the gifts were for his paralegal. "You don't look like some Irving Mishkin either."

"I'm half Jewish. Mom's an Irish Catholic from Southie."

"How do you like them apples?" she said, smiling. He signed the merchant receipt and handed it back to her. She studied his scribble. "Oh my God. I knew it." He grabbed the paper out of her hand. He had signed his real name. "Maria, get up here. Look who it is." A woman in the back of the store stopped folding tree skirts and reported to checkout. Several shoppers turned away from displays to watch the scene. "Maria, oh my God, it's Brandon Newman. I knew you weren't no Jew."

"How could you read it?" Brandon's signature, after a gazillion mindless repetitions, had become a prominent "B" followed by a string of lowercase squiggles.

"I know it better than my own name. My brother went to Comic-Con, got you to sign a poster for me." She hunched her shoulders. "I practiced it in geometry sometimes."

The shoppers had morphed into a paparazzi flash mob. Brandon snatched the credit card out of the young woman's hand. He knew a rush to the door would tank on social media. He pocketed the shades, grabbed a snowflake scarf from a rack and wrapped it around his neck with a theatrical flourish. Drawing on a childhood filled with Christmas specials, he pulled out a sure-fire showstopper and delivered it in a lively transatlantic lilt that would have made Katharine Hepburn proud:

> He sprang to his sleigh, to his team gave a whistle,
> And away they all flew like the down of a thistle.
> But I heard him exclaim, ere he drove out of sight—
> Happy Christmas to all, and to all a good night!

169

The store burst into applause, except for a couple of teens who were undoubtedly livestreaming. He gave a grand vaudevillian bow, dashed out the door without paying for the scarf, and sprinted, serpentine, up Mulberry, dodging pedestrians and motorists just as he had in a dozen chase scenes. He dropped the briefcase midflight, hoping to incite a treasure-hunting frenzy, and didn't stop running until he'd cornered Grand. After ducking into the vestibule of an office building, he stood breathless, pressed up against a wall, and dried his face with the stolen scarf. Sunglasses back on, he pretended to be on the phone with a real estate agent for the benefit of passersby while he waited for his heart to stop beating out of his chest. After returning to the sidewalk, he dumped the scarf in a street-corner garbage can and peeked down Mulberry to make certain he'd lost any followers.

Satisfied with a clean escape, Brandon slouched against the building and lit a cigarette. He blew smoke at the Empire State Building, its tall spire piercing a spotless sky. Josh had once told him preppers call clear days like that "September 11th blue." They were always waiting for the next plane to hit.

As he wandered west down Grand Street, the stores got trendier, the clientele thinner, their clothes darker. He passed a Citi Bike station with dozens of sky-blue bikes for day rental. He was tempted to pedal home, but Shari would kill him if someone were to post a picture online. "You know how much Citibank would've paid us for that?" she would say. He also wanted another cigarette. Holden would have never used a rental bike. He'd take a taxi. Brandon had to admit Luis had been right about that too, Holden being a snob. Plus, he was a germaphobe, couldn't stop talking about Ackley's mossy teeth or Stradlater's crumby razor. Caulfield would have never laid a finger on those filthy handlebars. He liked things untouched. So did Salinger. When Brandon reached West Broadway, he turned south. One World Trade Center, the so-called "Freedom Tower," a replacement for the toppled Twin Towers, dominated the skyline. The building stood taller than its neighbors, but somehow going from two down to one didn't feel like a bold statement of freedom.

He hesitated before stepping off the curb, feeling light-headed, the result of his frenetic flight from Mulberry Street and the failure to eat anything but a protein shake for breakfast. He put his hand against a streetlight for balance and took a long, last drag. Walking up Fifth Avenue, the morning after the unnerving Antolini encounter, Holden worries he'll disappear every time he steps off a curb. Brandon knew that on 9/11, Holden would never dip a toe into the street to save any of those nursery school kids. Neither would Salinger.

Guys like Sallie Choo Choo would rush in, like Brandon's father had thirty years ago. Crazy Joe Gallo had risked his own life to save a prison guard during a riot. According to Wikipedia, Gallo's crew had once saved six children from a raging tenement fire in Brooklyn. They weren't men of honor, but they were men of action, constantly in motion. With Holden Caulfield, the swords are always left behind. Brandon still loved him, the longing for authenticity, the hatred of bullies, the rejection of conformity, the capacity for childlike wonder, but the poor kid is so tied in knots he never manages to escape the stuck side of inertia, like a fish frozen stiff in a solid block of midwinter ice.

Would he be any different from Holden or Salinger? Would he keep a safe distance from the falling debris and human rain, behind the lines, shell-shocked, watching the horror unfold, streams of lukewarm urine yellowing his leaden legs? He stepped into the street, his arms at his sides, straight and stiff but slightly spread away from his body, and moved, one foot in front of the other, toe and heel simultaneously touching the ground, along the white stripe border of a crosswalk.

20

Chuck had rejected the offer of a spare bedroom, reminding his son that he would be getting in very late and that his company was putting him up at the Warwick. To avoid a repeat of the awkward meeting in Dubai, Brandon had asked Josh to join them at the Rockefeller Christmas tree and for Alda and Charlotte, home for the holidays, to "run into them" at the outdoor skating rink. A table had been reserved, in Josh's name, for brunch at the adjacent ice rink cafe.

Brandon wore a white mesh ballcap with "USA" in tacky patriotic flair, an orange puffy winter coat, midnight-blue mom jeans, and shoe-box-white Nike high tops. A braided leather belt held the loaded Ruger in place. He hadn't shaved since his meeting with the FBI. On the way to Midtown, he stopped at a street vendor to pick up a pair of thick, black sunglasses with "VERSACE" illegally stamped in shiny gold on the temples. As usual, the purchase had nothing to do with the weather, which blanketed Manhattan with a low ceiling of smoky gray clouds. The tacky shades perfected his former Soviet republic, fresh-off-the-boat look. He hoped the absurd outfit and the size of the bustling crowd would allow him to go unnoticed.

They met at ten thirty a.m. beneath the titanic evergreen on the last Saturday before Christmas. Speakers from the sunken skating oval located directly below the towering spruce filled the air with "Winter Wonderland." Hundreds of visitors snapped selfies in front of the tree and lined the railing above the rink to watch the skaters. Father and son exchanged a firm handshake but no hugs. Chuck Newman stood taller and broader than Brandon. He wore a light gray jacket and a navy hooded sweatshirt. His skin had been tanned to a bronzed leather from years of scorching desert rays and scouring sandstorms. A curvy, black tribal tattoo snaked up one side of his neck. He looked jacked out, like he might have been in the middle of a steroid cycle. He wore the same flattop crew cut—a little more salt than pepper since their last encounter—and had added a diamond stud earring to his general "don't fuck with me" look.

Brandon introduced Josh as a good friend he had met at a moto-cross track in Jersey. He never discussed his addiction with the former DEA agent. The tiniest of small talk followed—international travel, hotel accommodations, dirt bike preferences, crowd size estimates, how many people it took to decorate the tree, and general agreement that the temperature, high thirties, could have been a lot worse. According to an informational display, the seventy-eight-foot, ten-ton Norwegian spruce had been trucked in from Gardiner, New York. Josh hummed a few notes from "Norwegian Wood" and winked at Brandon. "That's a Lennon track."

Josh asked Chuck if he had seen any of the recent videos of his son at the Christmas store. When he said he hadn't, Josh immediately played a clip. Brandon repeated his cover story—that he had to meet Douglas at the courthouse downtown to sign a supplemental affidavit acknowledging the terms of Judge Adebayo's interim ruling.

"New York One did a piece about the scarf," Josh said. "Shops across the country sold out within twenty-four hours. Can't even find them online anymore."

"I got a box delivered yesterday."

"People from here to Timbuktu are doing video copycats of your boy—flipping the scarf, reciting the end of that Old St. Nick poem, and making like Usain Bolt for the door. They been running out of Mickey Ds, Walmarts, high school cafeterias, emergency rooms, you name it. Some base jumper in Cali even did his best Brando before taking a flying leap off El Cap. They call it 'brand-dashing.' It's like planking for the holidays."

Brandon stretched over a rail behind the tree, searching for Alda. "I tried to get tickets for the Rockettes, but they were all sold out. Busiest time of the year." It was a lie, of course. "I did manage to get us reservations for dinner at the hottest new barbecue joint, Bones of Contention, on the Lower East Side. Figured that might be something different. I asked my agent to join us. Shari goes totally nuts for pulled pork. Plus, she can't ever eat pig in front of her husband."

Chuck stared right through his son, as if he knew that nothing was ever sold out for Brandon Newman. "That's too bad about the Rockettes. I'm sure you tried your best, though." He flicked Josh's arm with a back-hand. "They don't grow legs like that in the desert." He eyeballed the tree, bottom to top. "I suppose I wouldn't mind chowing down on some swine. I'd be grinning and sinning like your agent. Good luck finding a pork chop or a slice of bacon inside the Kingdom."

"Here's what I don't get," Josh said. He lit a cigarette and offered the pack. Chuck declined and asked him to stand downwind. "Pigs roll in shit and goats munch on trash. Some ancient, worm-holed piece of paper tells you you're going to hell if you snack on Elmer Fudd, but feel free to snarf on all the Billy Goats Gruff you can eat. Please, that's supposed to be some kind of divinely inspired cookbook?"

"Books can even get you to believe that two plus two equals five," Brandon said. He turned away from the rink. A Chinese bride and groom, dressed like they'd just walked out of church, were trying, with broken English and hand gestures, to clear space in front of the Christmas tree for a guerrilla photo shoot.

"Mr. Newman, you ever seen *Book of Eli*?" Josh had made Brandon watch the film twice. It was a consensus prepper favorite about a man who smuggles a King James Bible to sanctuary in a post-apocalyptic world without books.

"Few months back, overnight in Qatar."

Josh extended an arm to hold the cigarette away from Chuck. "Here's this sadistic warlord, Gary Oldman, willing to kill for a copy of the good book. You know why? Sheep herding made easy, that's why. To the fleecing with a smile." He flashed a full-face grin, eyes squinting like a kindergartener who'd just said "cheese." "That movie got the ending dead right, turning Alcatraz into one big library. Old King James ought to be tossed into solitary confinement for all the trouble he's caused."

Chuck hacked and spit into a dry fountain below. "Had a hold on his mother, that's for damn sure. Didn't take long, though, before she learned how to tame it."

Brandon scanned the ice again. "Sheila would be plotting one helluva prison break if they ever locked up her precious moneymaker."

Josh touched Chuck's shoulder. "You ever get lonely, over there?" He jerked his head toward Fifth Avenue.

"What? Women?" Chuck pulled a toothpick out of his pocket and stuck it in the side of his mouth. "I suppose I get by. They ship in boatloads to work in service, mostly the Filipinos, Malaysians. They love us Americans."

The three men rested forearms over the railing in quiet observation of slapstick slip-and-falls, white-knuckle wall hugging, and the occasional graceful spin near the center of the rink—all accompanied by the original recording of "Wonderful Christmastime."

"McCartney," Josh said. "The lucky one. If you think about it, Chuck, even this spot's not really all that decked out for the Advent. Over here we got this huge tree, pagan symbol from like eons before Mary had her little matzoh in the oven, and then right below us, look who we got." They leaned over farther to get a better view of the statue. "Right there's your golden boy with the sticky fingers, Prometheus, stealing flame from the Greek gods before little Johnny Baptist even got his feet wet. You'd like to think somebody's trying to tell Jesus, 'Hey, buddy, you're a little late to the party.' Know what I mean?"

"I'm surprised your mother hasn't thrown a fit about it on Sirius." Chuck shook his head and let it drop below his shoulders. An orchestral version of "I Wonder as I Wander" began to play.

"She's been too busy trying to tank my career."

"If she hates that book so much, there must be something pretty goddamned good about it. I can't even recognize her anymore, swear to God, she's so stretched and shellacked."

"If you have time tomorrow morning, I was thinking maybe we could visit the 9/11 Memorial."

Chuck glared at his son like he'd made a threat. "You really think I need to be reminded?" He cleared this throat, which made his voice only slightly less croaky. "Doc says I still got like a million little particulates courtesy of Alfred P. Murrah lodged down there in my air sacs. I've been a walking memorial crime scene for the last twenty years. I really don't think I need to see another one."

Brandon reached for his cigarettes but left them in his jacket when Chuck blasted another cough into a fist. "They say half of the contractors over there are really CIA. Suppose you couldn't tell me which half you belong to."

"I could, son, but then I'd have to kill you." He tried to laugh but it sounded like he had something caught in his throat.

"Look." Brandon pointed to the rink. "Alda, hey. Up here." She smiled and waved while tugging at the back of Charlotte's jacket. He explained to Chuck that he had met his lawyer's daughter at a couple of meetings as he led the men down a staircase to rendezvous with the girls near the restaurant entrance. After a round of introductions and Brandon's "impromptu" invitation to lunch, Alda and Charlotte changed out of their skates and joined them at a table with a view of the rink through floor-to-ceiling windows. Brandon had no choice but to sit with his back to the skaters. Even with sunglasses and thick stubble, he wouldn't risk sparking the spontaneous formation of a collage of faces and smartphones pressed up against the plexiglass.

A server took drink orders—black coffee for Chuck, iced cappuccinos for the girls, grapefruit juice for Josh, and a double Bloody Mary for Brandon. He removed his coat to reveal a white sweatshirt with "I LOVE NEW YORK" in rainbow colors. Josh asked if he was auditioning to be grandmaster of the pride parade. Alda suggested he get one of those foam Statue of Liberty crown hats. She started to tell Chuck about brand-dashing, but Brandon cut her off, explaining that the territory had already been covered. She said her AP U.S. History teacher did it after their midterm. Chuck asked Charlotte where "her people" were from. She said Sixth-Ninth and Madison. The server returned with a basket of pastries.

"Dad, that's not okay. We all come from somewhere else if you go back far enough."

"I got plenty of witnesses who can testify I'm no racist." Chuck stared at Brandon as if to say even an adult child should never correct his parent.

"I'm Korean-American. It's fine. I knew what you meant."

The drinks were delivered, and the food orders placed. "We're all really excited for your son's movie about *The Catcher in the Rye*. My mom, she's an English professor, thinks it's going to be totally groundbreaking."

"When are you getting started?" Chuck asked.

"Soon as I can, right after New Year's?"

"So how are you gonna find time to do that other one, about the mob rat?"

"That's nothing. Forget it."

"What mob flick?" Josh asked. His eyebrows pinched, and he held out an open hand toward Brandon as if seeking an explanation for why he hadn't been told.

"Brandon texted me last week, wanting advice about being an informant against the mafia." Chuck elbowed his son. "Is it for somebody good at least, Scorsese?"

"Well, that's some interesting timing," Alda said. She popped her eyebrows at Brandon as if to suggest that no one else would get the inside joke.

Brandon's eyes fired back poison darts. Doug must have said more than he should have at the dinner table. Alda couldn't have known about Josh's connection to the Catarrazzos, which made her oblivious to the danger her reckless comment had posed. His stern look apparently did enough to let her know she needed to backfill the hole she'd dug. "I mean, you know, you've got this big court case going and all. Like, all this *Law & Order* stuff all at once, I mean. It's stupid. I don't know what I mean.

Forget it." She made googly eyes and bounced her head and shoulders from side to side.

Brandon watched Josh as she spoke. "I told Shari to take a pass."

"Hold on, Brand. You been dying to play a gangster for years. Now somebody actually wants to cast you as a hoodlum and you blow it off?"

Had Josh become suspicious or just curious? Brandon needed a cover story. He sipped on his drink to stall. "It's a no-go. I thought about it for a day. Literally, that's it. There's, like, there's this huge deal-breaker . . . they want me to sing again." Brandon put a hand over his face and shook his head in fake frustration while he cobbled together an elevator pitch. "This mafioso takes control of a boy band from Massapequa, Long Island on the brink of making it. The manager is a degenerate gambler. He lets the mafia take over the group because he can't pay his debts. Mob busts them out, starts robbing the kids blind. Concert tickets, concessions, merchandising. I'm supposed to play the lead singer. Wears a wire for the Feds."

"Got a working title?" Josh asked.

"It's so stupid."

"C'mon, what is it?"

Underneath the table, Brandon twisted a cloth napkin in his hand like he was wringing out laundry. He made eye contact with each of his guests, hoping to appear as if he were creating a moment of drama while using the delay to come up with a convincing answer.

"*Miked Up.*"

"Let me guess," Chuck said. "You play Mike."

"Geez, that sounds worse than the third *Godfather*," Alda said.

Josh pinched his nose and waved a hand in front of his face. "No offense, Mr. Newman, but whatever technical help you could give Brando ain't gonna be nearly enough to save that turdzilla."

Josh's playful critique gave Brandon a sense of relief. Any dangerous suspicions had been nipped in the bud. He flashed palms to signal a definitive change of subject. "Trust me, boy band is the last thing I want to do. It's about as stupid as asking me to play, I don't know, what's the dumbest role they could offer me?"

"Barack Obama," Chuck said.

Alda raised her hand. "How about Joan Rivers?"

Brandon pointed at Charlotte. "You've been pretty quiet so far. Who do you think? What's the dumbest part they could possibly offer me?"

Her eyes shifted left, right, and down. She whispered her answer so softly that Brandon couldn't hear it. "What was that? Go on, speak up there, Bambi."

"Timothy McVeigh."

Brandon felt like the air had been sucked out of his lungs. Everyone else froze. He tried to take a deep breath and blinked his eyes as if he'd been rocked by a sucker punch. "Jesus, I wasn't going in that direction, but yeah, that would be one hundred percent certifiably insane."

Nods of agreement circled the table.

"You know," Chuck said, "him and those stalkers, they aren't really so different." He sat back, his chest puffed out, as if he knew that they would need help to understand the depth of his observation.

Brandon felt the blood draining from his face. His stomach tightened. "What are you talking about?" He tossed his sunglasses to the table.

"I read an article in *Newsweek* on the flight over. What with all the stories on TV about the court case and Sheila's latest publicity stunts. Turns out all three of them had a copy of *The Catcher in the Rye* with them when they went to do the deed. Got me thinking." Chuck touched a finger to his temple and kept it there as if to show them the precise spot where that thinking was actually done. "That neo-Nazi sicko McVeigh got collared ninety minutes after with what in his car? A .45 Glock and his all-time favorite novel, *The Turner Diaries*, white-supremacist, anti-government, militia bull crap. It's where he got the idea to blow up a federal building. They should've executed that author too far as I'm concerned. All four of them basically got the same profile: picked on in school, lousy with women, felt like nobody paid them no mind, and hooked on a made-up book that lit a fuse under their asses."

"And that guy and J.D. Salinger were both decorated ex-army," Josh added.

"Makes me sick," Chuck said.

Brandon's pulse throbbed as they spoke. He downed a full glass of water. A leg twitched under the table. He remembered what he had glibly said to Luis, about reading *Catcher* and returning to the scene of the crime. Was that what he had been doing all along? Had his fascination with *Catcher* been about its destructive power? Had he learned about McVeigh's fatal infatuation with *The Turner Diaries*? He must have, at some point in childhood, heard about how a novel had inspired the bombing that massacred his playmates. Was his obsession with making the movie completely unrelated to his survivor's kinship with Holden Caulfield or his quest for transcendence? Did he, subconsciously, want to experience what that kind of combustible rage felt like? Did he want to get inside and defuse the bomb? Did he always know that Holden had the potential to grow into McVeigh? Was that why he hated Salinger?

179

Not because of his perverted lust for teenagers or his greedy hold on the copyright but for the black magic of his words, his demonic ability to fertilize bad seeds? Was that why Brandon felt like he had to rescue Holden?

"Don't tell me that guy had read . . ." Brandon's chest heaved. He kept one hand clamped around the water glass, the other steadying a convulsing knee.

"Please, no way, Brando," Josh said. "An anti-Semite like that wouldn't have been caught dead reading a so-called Jew book like *Catcher*."

Josh was probably right, but it didn't help. If McVeigh *had* read *Catcher* the night before the bombing, it wouldn't have stopped him. He would have felt more justified, more motivated. Inspired. Incited. And Brandon's faithful cinematic reproduction, if released back in 1995, would have had the same disastrous effect. He tried to blink it away, but he couldn't make the mortifying scene-flash disappear.

The committed militia man sits in briefs and a white muscle tee in the middle of a musty bed at a cheap motel on the outskirts of Oklahoma City, inspecting his Glock, studying a hand-drawn getaway route. Music and sex seeping through paper-thin walls. A rental truck packed with fertilizer and explosives parked in the lot. He flips channels until he chances upon Brandon's meticulously authentic *Catcher*. He identifies with Holden, becomes captivated, emboldened in his righteous indignation. He finds courage and motivation in his frustrations, loves him just as much as Chapman and Hinckley and Bardo. McVeigh lets the bitterness, the resentment, and the anger build inside, just like the others. A chorus of slighted voices echoes in Brandon's head as they would have for each of them.

Why do people always ruin things?

Why don't people ever notice anything?

NOTICE ME.

Why don't people ever believe you?

BELIEVE ME.

Why don't people listen?

I WILL BE HEARD.

If McVeigh had kept a copy of *Catcher* next to *The Turner Diaries* in his car when that state trooper pulled him over, nobody would have been the least bit surprised. A *Hollywood Squares* box of FBI profilers would have appeared on cable news networks the next day to proclaim that it made perfect sense.

Was that why Salinger had never wanted the book turned into a movie? Did he understand the danger? Was Dr. Frankenstein trying to strap down his monster? Was that why he had to keep writing to nobody for decades, every day, hour after hour, in that bunker, alone, filling unread pages, blowing out matches, defusing his own bomb? Did *Catcher* belong in its own cell at Alcatraz?

"Don't turn around," Josh said, "but you're starting to draw a crowd." Brandon discreetly picked up his phone, despite shaky hands, to open the photo app. He used the selfie function to peek over his shoulder. Two bubbly skaters had already begun snapping pictures. Alda and Charlotte checked their phones. Somebody from inside the restaurant had posted a shot of their table on social media a minute earlier, right after Brandon had discarded the fake Versaces.

He jumped to his feet. The glass wall bloomed with iPhones and Samsungs. Several diners pretended to check messages with phones at arm's length. "I got to go. Stay, eat your food." He picked up his sunglasses and put a hand on Chuck's shoulder. "Josh'll handle the bill and bring you to my place after." A growing hoard of tourists elbowed each other at the restaurant's entrance, trying to get a clear shot. A host with arms outstretched strained to hold them back.

Brandon ran toward the kitchen. Even as he snaked between an obstacle course of closely set tables and chairs, he couldn't help imagining the awful social media—Brand-dashing II: The Sequel. He didn't care how bad he'd look or how viral it would be. He flung open a swinging door. The dark shades proved a blessing under the blaring overhead fluorescents and gleaming tile walls. Cooks, bussers, and dishwashers stopped working and snapped their heads up in unison like a clan of startled prairie dogs. He grabbed the first person he could, a woman in a food-stained apron carrying a tub of live lobsters. "I need to get out, back exit. Now!"

A huge man, nearly three hundred pounds, wearing a tall toque, separated Brandon from the stunned sous-chef. "I'm sorry, sir. You're gonna have to leave out the front. No patrons allowed. Health regulations."

Brandon couldn't go back to a million cameras poised to shoot. He reached behind his back, stepped away, and pulled out the Ruger, holding it with two hands, arms erect, like he had on set. He fanned his aim from left to right to deter any approach. The sous-chef dropped the lobsters to put her hands up. They spilled onto the floor, scurrying under prep tables and sinks. Big Toque and the rest of the staff stood stock-still.

"Now, is somebody gonna tell me how to get the hell out of here?"

A dishwasher in the back pointed a trembling finger to a door next to the meat locker. "It's an exit, stairs to tunnel, comes out next level."

Brandon ordered them to clear a path, and with his gun pointed to the ceiling and close to his ear, he stutter-stepped and hop-skipped past a row of double ovens and an enormous flattop covered in burning omelets and steaming home fries. His head swiveled from side to side. As he hurried to the door, the ideal camera position popped into his head—a trailing up-close steady-cam like a reverse of the long take at the Copa in *Goodfellas*.

Opening the door set off an alarm. He bounded down the stairs two at a time and found himself in a dimly lit service corridor lined with drainpipes, air ducts, and electrical cables. Glasses off, he raced past a series of exit arrows in a maze of underground passages. Fearing what might await him at the other end, he diverted to a side tunnel with a small hatch at the end marked "Track Maintenance Access Only." It was shut with two large clamps but no lock. He pried them open and climbed onto a catwalk parallel to the subway line. It had to be the B•D•F line somewhere between Forty-Second and Forty-Seventh Streets. Lights to his right signaled a station not more than one hundred yards away. He would have to go onto the tracks to reach it. He shoved the gun in his jeans and waited for the next train to pass. Once it did, he hopped over a railing and dashed toward the platform, keeping an eye on the flickering third rail when he wasn't checking over his shoulder for approaching headlights. He felt like he kept going in reverse—a bizarro Bernie Goetz running to a subway platform with an ice-cold pistol. When he reached the station, the train had just left. He braced himself against the near wall of the tunnel and waited to give departing riders time to clear the exits. A rat scurried across his feet. When he leaped up, the platform was deserted except for a lone musician, little more than a skeleton with gray dreadlocks playing jazz trumpet, an open case with a few singles and some coins at his feet. The busker didn't miss a beat as Brandon walked past and continued playing as passengers trickled into the waiting area. Brandon texted Shari to have a car pick him up in front of the Fox News building across from the subway entrance on Sixth Avenue.

Awaiting his ride, Brandon stood beneath the blaring red news scroll, huddled behind an artificial Christmas tree trimmed in a patriotic palette. After a few frantic miscues off fumbling thumbs, he managed to confirm online what Chuck had said about the similarities shared by McVeigh and the *Catcher*-obsessed assassins. The Oklahoma City bomber had also been a committed prepper and suffered PTSD after the First Gulf War. He had read *The Turner Diaries* religiously and sold copies in gun shows around the country at a loss. The poem "Invictus" had been his final statement before execution. It had also apparently been a favorite of Nelson Mandela. How could those two men love the same poem? How could Holden Caulfield be the patron saint of survivors and murderers?

Trying to make sense of the contradictory attractions had become excruciating, unbearable. Brandon couldn't reconcile the intimate kinship he felt with the inevitable embrace of a terrorist who had shattered his family, murdered innocent children, and nearly killed him. His brain twisted inside out. Was that what cognitive dissonance felt like? He could sense himself falling, accelerating, but couldn't distinguish up from down. He'd lost all focus. Pedestrians strode past in hazy, double vision. Car horns, air brakes, and a mix of garbled voices seemed to scream as if he had accidently clicked headphones to max volume. He was caught, and not the good kind of caught, like being saved by a stranger or a guardian angel from tumbling over a cliff, the bad kind of caught—cornered, checkmated, exposed, arrested, his back against the wall, nowhere left to run.

There was no other choice. He had to do it.

Eject. Abandon ship. Abort the mission. He would relinquish his dream to save himself, to save the future victims of a madman-to-be spurred on to violence by a spot-on portrayal. As Brandon staggered away from the building's facade, he felt faint again, like he had on West Broadway. In the middle of the sidewalk, he propped himself against a massive concrete planter, one of dozens encircling the building. The sickly shrubs on top barely disguised the anti-truck-bomb perimeter. The inside of his mouth felt sandpaper dry, his palms hot and sweaty. He bought a Gatorade from a street vendor and downed it in two gulps. He had been right. Holden was a slow fuse, but he had never followed that spark far enough as it sizzled away toward powder kegs buried beneath the surface and packed with a potent mix of magical thinking, fecklessness, testosterone, and rage.

On the ride home, Brandon got a text from Douglas's assistant confirming a meeting with the FBI on January 6 and a pre-meeting with his partner, the ex-prosecutor, two days earlier. He took small satisfaction in the opportunity to tell those smug agents, face-to-face, that he was shit-canning any and all projects related to *Catcher*, his fantasy and their leverage dissolving in an instant. He tried to think of other collateral benefits to ease his distress.

The about-face would also free him to do what Salinger and McVeigh couldn't. Shari had stacks of scripts about the horrors of Iraq and Afghanistan, the war crimes, the psychological struggles of veterans. Brandon would show and tell exactly what had happened to those soldiers, how it broke them, their families, scarred them forever. He texted Luis. "ur right. jd should have written about the war plain and straight up, not some angry teenage parable"

Luis replied, "exactly why plato banned poets from the republic. pretzeling the truth confuses everything"

As the car passed Madison Square Garden, Josh called. He claimed to have done a better mop-up job than Winston Wolf in *Pulp Fiction*. He had gone into the kitchen right after Brandon had escaped. "I told them who you were. I think they knew already. Said you're this uber-method actor, got special permission from the mayor's office, real-life rehearsal for a chase scene. They were all totally convinced by that realistic studio prop. The clincher was when I made it rain, peeling off hundos like Oprah in her studio audience. Please, it was downpouring men all right, every one of them named Benjamin. Your dad and the girls don't know what happened. I hustled them right out." Brandon expressed concern nonetheless about a potential visit from the police. "Bad for business, bro. And none of the staff got a pic. I made sure. They think it's cool. Case closed."

Brandon thanked him and said they'd settle up later. He felt lucky to have a resourceful friend like Josh, lightning quick on his feet and not afraid to do whatever was necessary to get out of a jam.

"You still got your sidekick, Brando?"

"I'm thinking about taking him for some fresh air along the Hudson before I go home."

"Good idea. I hear he likes to swim. Your pops wants to see the *Intrepid*. I'll bring him over after."

Brandon asked to be dropped off at Greenwich and Christopher and walked to the far edge of Pier 45, which had been repurposed with a long rectangular lawn and a ring of misting stations for summer sunbathing. On that bracing December day, a handful of bundled tourists took photos and video of the Lower Manhattan skyline, the Freedom Tower no doubt anchoring their frames, while a few home-from-college types tossed a football. He sat on the ground in a corner, pretending to talk on the phone, and casually let the Ruger slip into the water. He was about to pocket his iPhone when he noticed a banner notification, a message from Alda.

"u [thumbs up]? char feels so bad"

"IDK"

"having 2nd thoughts?"

"u could tell"
"u looked like [ghost] BEF u saw the fans"
"he would have loved HC. How can I?"
"b/c hc wouldn't love him back. u want to be defined by the lunatic fringe?"
"Idolized is the problem"

He closed the thread. His hands were shaking again. He still had a few of "those" contacts. He could have it delivered in less than thirty minutes. The urge hadn't been so strong since before Elysian Prairies. Despite a bitter breeze blowing off the water, beads of sweat formed a line across his forehead. Heart pounding, he stood up and started walking toward Christopher Street while searching for a source. After a few paces, a football hit him in the back of the neck and knocked the phone out of his hand. "What the hell!"

A young woman wearing a red-and-white snowman ski headband and a powder blue Villanova sweatshirt ran over to retrieve the wobbling pigskin. "I'm so sorry, sir." She held up apologetic hands in a pair of open-finger gloves. "They're like butter." She had no sooner picked up the ball at Brandon's feet than she dropped it again. "Oh my God."

He grabbed her wrist and put a finger to his lips. "Please. It's been an awful day. Just let me go home. Please."

"I know," she said. "I saw." She picked up the ball again and punted it to within reach of the circle of friends waiting to resume the game. "I'm sure you never got my letter."

He shook his head. "You can't imagine—"

"I know you must get thousands. I'm not really a fan, to be honest, not of your movies anyway."

"What then? Amateur critic? Need an operation?"

"It was about my brother, Danny." Her eyes welled. "He totally loves you. Seen all of your movies about a million times. Danny started using his junior year. When you went on *Dr. Phil*, after you got clean, and talked about what it meant, how rehab had changed everything, how taking that one step was the hardest but best thing you had ever done, my brother picked up the phone and called the number on the screen. I bet you saved hundreds of kids that day."

Brandon hadn't thought about helping anyone but himself at the time. His focus had been on the reboot of his career. Tears rolled down the girl's cheeks. "Could I give you a hug, you know, for thanks?" They shared a freed hostage embrace. She said she would lie to her friends. "I'll say you were one of my camp counselors."

He resumed scrolling on the walk home. He had to do it, make the call he hadn't been tempted to make in months.

"Brandon, long time, how you been?"

"I'm not okay."

"At least you're honest. Good place to start."

21

He woke up at one p.m. on Sunday, alone, still in his clothes. Luis had left on Friday for a family wedding in Elizabeth. Brandon's NA sponsor had stayed on the phone with him until Josh and Chuck showed up. He had blamed his brush with relapse on the pressures of fame, the lack of privacy, the constant sneaking around in stupid disguises, the added stress of his father's visit. It was all true but far from a complete confession.

He rubbed his eyes until the room resolved into focus. The hangover had wrapped most of Saturday night in a dense fog. Snapshots of the evening spun out momentarily from the thick haze before plunging back into the clouds—Chuck talking about amputees at Syrian refugee camps, complaining about how there were no movie theaters in Saudi Arabia, asking Brandon which "starlets" he had bedded, and Shari grumbling about right-wing Israeli radicals while she sucked on a charred St. Louis rib. And both of them taking turns making playground-level ass jokes about their colonoscopies. Brandon had signed three, maybe four cocktail napkins. He may have thrown up in a stall. The back of his throat burned, and his mouth tasted like garbage left to bake in the sun. Shari must have hustled him into a car.

He had four texts and two missed calls from Chuck, more than all of last year. They were apparently supposed to meet for breakfast at the St. Regis at ten thirty a.m. Brandon had no recollection. Chuck went alone to the Brooklyn Diner on Fifty-Seventh Street. His last message came at eleven forty-five a.m. "Still out cold? My advice: raw eggs, tabasco, and lime juice. Missed the best Texas French Toast. Heading to JFK. Will call on Xmas."

As expected, social media had blown up the "Rock Center Run." Even the restaurant's official Instagram account spread the virus, liking and reposting clips and memes. "Don't snub free pub." Josh and Shari had both been right. In contrast to his highly contagious brunch sprint, last night's outing had barely left a mark online. Brandon had somehow managed to skulk out of the barbecue restaurant with only a few harmless table snaps before he'd had too many shots. It could've been much worse.

For the next two days, he didn't leave his apartment. He texted his housekeeper to take the week off and ignored the phone, allowing messages from Shari, Rose, and Josh to queue while he set new high scores on a bank of vintage arcade games lining the walls of his rec room. When he did respond, it was with the same message each time: `"can't talk. in the zone."`

By Monday evening, Luis had returned, unaware of the radical break Brandon had made. He found his groggy landlord playing Frogger in a pair of camo boxers and a plush Ritz Paris bathrobe. "Jesus, you look like you walked off the set of *Weekend at Bernie's*."

Brandon picked up a slice of cold pizza from a box he'd left open on his pool table since Sunday night. He had shared most of it with Hendrix. "Want some?"

"Uhh, dude, your breath, it's only six o'clock. I'm guessing the family reunion didn't go as well as mine. I saw the video."

"That's an understatement. You have no fucking idea." Brandon grabbed a half-empty bottle of vodka from a Ms. Pac-Man cocktail table and headed to the kitchen for ice.

Luis pleaded with him to drink some coffee instead and made the innocent mistake of bringing up *Catcher*. He had taken a stack of potential scripts to read on the train and found one that he said he was certain Brandon would love. In response, Brandon stomped into his bedroom and shouted, "You want to talk about scripts. Let's start right here." He took out a first edition from his nightstand and tore the book from its binding.

Luis stopped at the threshold. "What the hell are you doing?"

"What I promised all along. I'm setting Holden free. Fertilizing all those impressionable young minds." Brandon ripped out handfuls of pages and began throwing them from his twenty-third-story window. He yelled "cut, print" after each wild fling without any idea which chapter had just been unleashed on the unsuspecting pedestrians below. The loosed pages spun and fluttered in an unstable spiral like a wobbly dust devil. Once he had shortened the novel by half, he threw the abridged version against a vintage Janis Joplin poster from her October 25, 1969 Oklahoma City concert, cracking the glass and slanting the frame.

"*Joder*. What the hell happened to you?"

"You were right, goddamn it." He grabbed Luis by his sweatshirt and shoved him against the wall. "He's the pied piper for angry white boys.

He's not saving anybody from falling off a cliff. He's the one doing the *pushing*. Jesus Christ, so was my goddamned mother." Brandon collapsed to the ground, cradling his head.

Luis stepped over him and sat on a bench at the foot of the bed. "Dude, *what happened?*"

"Leave me alone. You're fired."

"Again?"

"For real this time. I'm done with it. All of it. You heard me. Now get out."

"You know what, Brando? I'm starting to believe you must actually love remakes because this is about the fifth time I've seen the same identical petulant garbage from you." Luis now stood over Brandon, who avoided eye contact. "If you think I'm gonna babysit you through another temper tantrum, you're more fucked up than you look. Call Shari, call your sponsor, call whoever the hell you want, but don't you dare call me to come running back until your snowflake pity party is over." He picked up the ravaged chunk of book and tossed it in Brandon's lap. "At least Holden had enough guts to put his fist through the glass."

He got up after Luis left the room and let himself fall face first into the middle of his bed where he lay motionless, anticipating the door slam.

On Tuesday, he had finally watched his screener of *The Walk,* the biopic about the Twin Towers tightrope walker. Petit, he realized, was the anti-Caulfield—an optimistic, fearless, passionate risk-taker, a visionary. No terrorist or murderer would ever carry around a copy of his autobiography. The contrast did little to console him. It felt like a realization that had come too late. Lingering envy over the part and a pervasive sense of inescapable haplessness glued Brandon to the couch. His People's Choice Awards looked like stacks of frozen teardrops. He wished they would all melt away. Hoping to fall asleep, he cued a "Spa" playlist over Sonos and rolled toward the cushions. After a restless and hopeless ten-minute effort, he managed to pry himself up to pick the second half of a double feature, the latest screener to arrive, *The Revenant.*

Despite the gruesome, violent scenes, the film had managed to lift his mood. He watched it twice with only one bathroom break. The brutal, bloody story of primitive survival, good versus evil, the enduring strength of the human spirit, had begun to soothe the seas sloshing inside him. It was actually *not* about anything else, not some clever, convoluted metaphor for adolescent anxiety, crooked governments, or hypocritical religions. There were no mixed messages, no possibilities of misinterpretation.

After the second viewing, Brandon texted a rambling apology to Luis including the promise of a new dirt bike and video equipment. He also invited Rose to come over on Wednesday and watch DiCaprio.

For the first time in four days, he was showered, shaved, and sober. She came straight from work and borrowed a pair of sweatpants and a pinstriped Mickey Mantle jersey. Hendrix did figure eights around bar stools as they sat in the breakfast nook scrolling through takeout options, eventually settling on Middle Eastern.

"Mantle was my dad's favorite player," Rose said. "He always used to say bad knees knocked them both out of the game."

"Born right outside of Tulsa," Brandon said.

"How was the visit with your father? The part I didn't see on Facebook."

"You saw the highlights, trust me. He's more like this kooky uncle, like a lifer in the Navy, drops in every few years and ships out again, used to send money and birthday gifts when I was a kid. Neither of us wants to get into it." Brandon sipped from a sports bottle filled with vitamin water. "We're like two boxers dancing around the ring without throwing punches, waiting for the bell to ring so we can just go back to our corners."

"You've really been barricaded in here, the whole time, working on your script?"

He wadded a dish towel and sunk a turnaround jump shot in the sink. "Had to D-N-D the world. Firing on all cylinders like Rain Man."

She tapped his nose and stood up on bare toes to kiss him. "Slow and steady wins the race, you wascally Babbitt."

They ordered falafel platters and lentil soup and sat on the floor to eat in front of his wall-screen. He didn't tell her that he'd already seen it. He expected wincing and tears at least a few times, but she didn't shed a drop, or turn away once, not even for the excruciating grizzly attack. She watched without blinking for two and a half hours, called it one of the best "films" she'd ever seen. "So, which version of *Catcher* are you *really* gonna make?"

"Did you even finish it?" he asked.

She rested her head against his. "Two days ago. I still don't like him too much, but I have to admit I love the way he talks. Sounds exactly like some of my father's friends from the waterfront, the old-timers, from when I was little and they used to have the clubs." She took his hand and held it in her lap. "So, what's it going to be?"

Her warm touch had found a weak spot. He fought back unexpected tears. "Let's not talk about that now." He kissed her cheek and buried his head in her shoulder to hide his eyes and dry their mist. Her fingers slid down his stomach and started to massage his crotch. "I'm sorry, Rosie. It's just—I haven't slept at all this week. I hope you don't mind if we don't—"

She took his face in two hands and lifted it up to kiss him. "It's okay. I've got to get up at the crack of dawn anyway. I couldn't have stayed long."

"What for?"

"Christmas Eve Day. The drive up north takes about three hours from Brooklyn."

"Jesus, I totally forgot.

"Be ready to go four p.m. sharp. My father's probably sending Dominic. Not much of a talker but punctual like a Japanese bullet train."

"How should I dress?"

"Promise you won't laugh." She plucked at his sleeve. "It's an ugly sweater party."

He looked down at his navy blue Loro Piana vicuña. "You cannot be serious."

"We had one a couple years ago for the office. He totally flipped for it. Ever since then it's been the official dress code. You must have something good in that men's warehouse of yours. Speaking of which," she stood and ran a finger up and down her outfit, "mind if I borrow a few more things?" Brandon shooed the question away with a limp backhand, and they went into the bedroom to rummage.

While Rose searched for a pair of athletic slides on a shelf stacked with factory-tagged samples, Brandon dropped an unopened package of multicolor ankle socks at her feet. "I keep imagining your dad's hideout like a cross between Cheyenne Mountain in *War Games* and that underground house on Tatooine where Luke Skywalker grew up."

After finding the right fit, she stuffed her work clothes into an unused Fendi duffel. "Good guess. It's this abandoned mine, dolomite limestone, natural cement they call it. Dad got it for a song about ten years ago. The owners had apparently defaulted on some financial obligations. Bradley used to love to go up there on weekends, hiking, canoeing, camping out. At the time, my father hadn't come up with the idea to start burying nuts for next week's worldwide catastrophe. Brad and I, we used to cook over an open fire right inside the cave. And there were these amazing triple echoes. We would get baked and sing 'Row, Row, Row Your Boat' as a round, loud as we could. Total trip." She tried the first verse, but there was no reverb in the closet, and, fortunately, no fine crystal. "Must be all the clothes, like sponges. Dad's bunker building did the same thing, killed the acoustics. Bradley actually opened his mouth to my father about pouring all that concrete flooring, which, I have to admit, took guts. I think your Holden would have admired Brad for taking a stand, being all brave and honest."

Brandon stood behind his smiling foamboard surfer self, still wearing the orange trapper hat, and shoved the rigid imposter face down to the floor. "Yeah, he probably would've. That's the whole problem. Bravery and honesty got nothing to do with telling right from wrong." He thought about the verse he had read a dozen times since the infamous brunch. "You know that poem, 'Invictus'?" She cocked her head and rolled up her eyes. "You at least know the ending. 'I am the master of my fate, I am the captain of my soul.' Well, guess what? That says zilch about what you believe or why you do what you do."

Rose snatched a red satin cape Brandon had kept from wardrobe and draped it over her shoulders. "You turning into Captain America?"

"I'm nobody's caped crusader." He scooped up the fallen hat and flipped it onto his head. "All these so-called heroes—cowboys, cops, soldiers, athletes, even superheroes—they only end up letting you down once you're up close and get to know them."

"You left out movie stars."

"They're the worst kind of hero," he said. "You can't believe anything they say."

22

By the time they had passed Newburgh, the sky was already pitch black. Dominic, as promised, had little to say, other than asking for his passenger's preferred temperature setting and whether he minded the easy listening holiday classics. Brandon felt confident he'd win best outfit. He had sent his personal shopper out early that morning to purchase the most outrageous Christmas sweater in New York. Her East Village find depicted a reindeer team around an open fire in a wintry woodland scene, Santa's sleigh in the background, a team member skewered on a spit. It was captioned "The Donner Party."

He was determined to focus on the positive, to not let his mind wander into the hall of funhouse mirrors that had been the disorienting, abrupt breakup with *Catcher*. His decision to let the project go had made tonight's dinner much easier. He wouldn't be attending under false pretenses, and he'd never have to run the risk of being caught in the crossfire, real or otherwise, between the mafia and the FBI. And he could continue to date Rose.

Dominic exited the New York State Thruway near Poughkeepsie and drove through a string of small towns. The homes spread farther and farther apart as they headed west. After thirty minutes, only thick forest edged narrow two-lane highways. An overcast sky blocked even a sliver of moonlight from slipping through. Snow flurries danced through high beams.

After turning onto a single-lane dirt road, Dominic pulled over and parked the aging Lincoln Continental. Brandon's pulse quickened. He hadn't told anybody his plans for the night. They wouldn't even know where to look. He wished he still had the gun. It would be too cliché. He was too famous. "What's happening?"

Dominic twisted around and extended an open hand. "I need your phone."

"Already?"

"Open it up first so as I can shut down the GPS. I'll have it right here waiting when youse are leaving." Dominic stored Brandon's iPhone in the center storage compartment and, without warning, cut the lights, inside and out.

"What the hell?" Brandon could hear Dominic's hand fumbling in the glove box. He tried to open a door, but it was locked from the front.

"Easy, kid. I got to wear the night visions rest of the way. Security protocols. So's youse can't see the way in." He adjusted the goggles and shifted into gear. "Hang on to your hat. I'm gonna be taking more lefts and rights than Rocky Balboa." After fifteen more minutes in the dark, they had arrived at a dimly lit driveway with a high metal gate. Dominic entered a code on a keypad, and the gate swung open. He drove a few minutes more with goggles back on before parking. Once the engine was shut off, floodlights illuminated the entrance, a camouflaged loading dock built into a hillside.

"Where are the other cars?"

"Nobody parks here. He's got a shuttle bus from the commuter lot. Merry Christmas and remember to save me some *calamates* for the ride home."

There was a steel door next to the bay. Vincent the Beanpole stood guard holding a metal detector. They exchanged friendly, knowing smiles. He wore a sweater with Santa in hot pursuit of a female elf, his hand pinching her behind. "Christmas Goose," it read. They exchanged compliments. Brandon made himself into a human letter T for a quick wand and frisk. Vincent opened the door and told him to go inside and wait for Josh.

The anteroom had a smooth concrete floor and high-domed ceiling where the limestone had been scraped out. A wall-mounted barrel held thick iron bars, apparently at the ready to be mounted on cleats affixed to the bay's jambs. To the left, there was a locker room draped with hazmat suits, a pair of decontamination showers, and a coiled fire hose. To the right sat a gun safe the size of a bank vault. A heavy wooden slab branded with black letters hung above the truck-wide tunnel leading into the mine:

> Conflagrations were started, famine set in. All things and
> all men were perishing. The plague grew and spread wider
> and wider. In the whole world only a few could save them-
> selves, a chosen handful of the pure, who were destined
> to found a new race of men and a new life, and to renew
> and cleanse the earth; but nobody had ever seen them
> anywhere, nobody had heard their voices or their words.

194

While Brandon stood with his head cocked back reading the passage, Josh rolled in on an electric golf cart. His sweater bore a headshot of "Johnny Mathis" surrounded by snowflakes with the caption "Chestnuts Roasting." "I had that plaque made special for Choo Choo. It's from *Crime and Punishment*, Dostoevsky, the Russian novelist. Ought to be the doomsday prepper's creed. Sallie near pissed himself from laughing when I told him the name of the book. He loves it."

Brandon knew someone else who would have loved that quote. "This place is like out of James Bond, where Goldfinger or Dr. No lives."

"Wait until you see the rest—storerooms, bunks, gym, first aid station, short wave shack, two kitchens, a wine cellar—he's got Barolos and Chiantis you can't even find in Italy—hydroponic greenhouse, composting, and tons of Soviet military surplus. He drilled three wells right here on the inside and dug ventilation shafts poking out all over the mountaintop."

They passed under a row of caged overhead lights as Josh drove deeper into the mine. The tunnel opened into a cavern like a European cathedral. The ceiling must have been twenty-five feet high, the room twice as wide, and half a football field long. Lights had been mounted into the rock walls. Shelves stacked with blue plastic storage barrels lined both sides. At the far end two more tunnel openings.

"Dinner's not ready yet. Rose is in the kitchen. You got to see the home theater. Brand new. Stadium seating and everything." Josh took the tunnel to the left.

"Where is everybody?"

"Other direction to the dining hall. More on the way."

Josh parked at the first door on the right and entered a keycode. The room looked like a compact version of a multiplex cinema. Five rows of cushioned, full-recline seats filled the room. Silver art deco sconces lined burgundy walls. Below them hung vintage opera posters. "Sallie's got like twenty years of Met performances on DVD. I helped Choo Choo put together this 'what to do if' short for survivors who make it here when the shit hits the fan. You gotta check it out."

Brandon plopped in the middle of the front row after Josh left to cue the video. A minute later, Rose entered from a back door. Her hair was clipped up, and she wore a white double-breasted chef's coat, half unbuttoned, and baggy black pajama pants. She brushed fingers across his chest. "Not bad but no venison tonight, Rudolph." She put her arms around his waist, and they started to kiss. "You get enough rest?" She reached for his belt.

"What about Josh? Your dad?"

"I sent Josh back to the kitchen. Dad's giving my cousins from Weehawken a tour of the wine cellar. We've got twenty minutes. Don't worry, I switched the lock code." She had already opened his blue jeans when she pushed him back onto one of the seats and reclined it all the way back. In less than a minute, he was naked from the waist down and ready to go.

"I'll be right back."

"What for?"

"Finishing my period."

She must have flicked a switch on the way out because the room went black. Brandon couldn't see his free hand in front of his face. Two minutes later, he heard the door creak open.

"You don't need the lights?"

"I've got a mental map."

He could hear her bare feet kissing the concrete floor as she walked toward him.

When her approaching footsteps stopped, he said, "You can't see it, but I'm holding a piece of mistletoe right over the old yule log."

Leathery fingers wrapped around his scrotum and twisted his nuts like they were about to be plucked. He let out a high-pitched whelp like an injured dog. Bright overhead lights flooded the room. Sallie Choo Choo stood over Brandon, wearing a "FRANKIE VALLI SAYS RELAX" sweater and holding him by the balls. Night vision goggles clung to his forehead. Josh approached on the right flank, pointing a shotgun, and Rose stood against a wall, next to the light switch, her arms folded.

"I thought I told you to wear a cup whenever you're dealing with my daughter."

"I don't understand." Brandon held up his hands and panted from the pain. "What's going on?"

"As our friends from the government like to say, we're the ones asking the questions."

"What's this about? Josh, what the . . ."

"There you go again." Sallie released him and shook a finger in Brandon's face. "I'm gonna give you one chance to tell the truth."

"Is this about Rose?"

"Buddy, if I was an umpire, you would've just been called out." Sallie stabbed a thumb over his shoulder. "That's strike three. Answers only. Understand? Listen up, 'cause I'm not asking this again. Are you, or are you not, working for the Federal Bureau of Investigation?"

"No. I'm not. No. Really, I'm not. What would—" Brandon stopped mid-question.

"Joshua here says you were talking sideways at brunch. Rambling on about making some movie, being an informant against the so-called mafia, powwowing with that half-a-cop father of yours. Then that lawyer's kid makes some smart remark. What the hell was it she said?"

"'Interesting timing,'" Josh replied, keeping his aim steady on Brandon's chest.

"And then to put a cherry on top, you go and do the classic Mickey Mouse Club disappearing act. Going AWOL for a couple of days right afterwards. Exactly what the Feds do when they're turning a guy rat. Yank him off the streets, pump his stomach, and give him a crash course in rodent boot camp. Snitches always come back with some piece-of-shit alibi—visiting a sick aunt or sneaking out of town with somebody else's girl. Last chance, Brandon. You better come in spic-n-span and *pronto*."

Brandon slowly put down his quivering hands. "They tried to recruit me, all right, but that's all it was, I swear. It was an ambush. I didn't say shit. My lawyer was there. I didn't say anything. I already decided, definitely, I'm not doing it. Swear to God."

"What agents?"

"Curran and—"

"Severini," Sallie interrupted. "Only thing worse than a cocky Irishman is a self-hating guinea with something to prove. What they get on you? You still using?"

"No. Not at all. I don't know how, but they knew I'd lied in court, in my statement, about making a different movie. They threatened to come after me for it."

"How'd they know about us? You been flapping your gums to that agent of yours?"

"No, nobody. Curran was in disguise outside the club first time we met, and the two of them were in the park when I met Rose, dressed up like Jews."

Sallie turned to Josh and Rose, who both nodded as if he had sent them a telepathic assessment. "And now you say you're going to tell them to pound sand?"

"Absolutely, one hundred percent."

"And get your ass prosecuted for perjury?"

"Not anymore." Brandon sat up and realized that he was still half-naked. "Could I get dressed?"

"Put your drawers back on. My advice, kid, you better stick to the family movies. I don't think you're cut out there for the after-hours market." Brandon's erection had long since deflated, leaving little more than a wrinkling mushroom cap. He slipped on his jeans, and Sallie ordered him to sit down.

"I don't want to make *Catcher* anymore. I'm giving it all up. I figured out, after all this time, my obsession with that book, with Holden Caulfield, Jesus, it was all knotted up with that psycho prick McVeigh, the bomber, and what made him blow up the building, what almost blew me up. Turned me upside down, that's why I was MIA. There's no way. I'm through with it. The Feds can't make me do shit now."

"You got the good cordless, Rosie?" She passed a phone to her father and put a hand on Brandon's shoulder. "Sorry, honey, but we got to make sure. It's nothing personal. This'll all be over soon. Just do what he says."

"Same here," Josh said. "I'm the one who brought you to them. You gotta understand I had no choice. Story checks out it's straight to the crab dip and shrimp scampi, like none of this ever happened."

Sallie wanted to hear from the lawyer. He instructed Brandon to call the law firm's main number on speaker, get patched through to Douglas, and make him confirm Brandon's account without revealing their presence. He wouldn't allow a direct call to Douglas's mobile. "You could be code-wording anybody that way." An overnight operator transferred Brandon to Sag Harbor.

"Blackburn residence." It was Alda. Holiday music and overlapping conversations droned in the background.

"It's Brandon. Sorry to call on Christmas Eve. I need to speak to your dad. It's important."

"Are you okay?"

Brandon stared down the twin shotgun barrels. "Totally."

"Oh my God, we should have invited you. I'm so sorry." She was slurring her words. "We're having this grand fête. Don't you just hate the word 'grand.' It's so phony baloney. Isn't it so phony to be on the phone-ee? Get it? Tell Luis I hate him. Our trees are already all decorated, but you can come over tomorrow if you like. Chase is home. He's dying to meet you. He thinks that *Top Gun* remake was simply marvelous."

"Are you drunk?"

"No. Stop it. I merely appointed myself official secret double eggnog taster. A very serious responsibility. A little more nutmeg, or maybe rum, and it'll be perfect."

Rose squeezed her cheeks to keep from laughing. Josh bit his lower lip. Sallie whispered, "Get the fucking lawyer."

"Alda, I really need to speak to your dad. I'm in a hurry."

"Okay, okay. I'll get him. Meanwhile, here's your number one fan."

"Hello."

"Hi, Charlotte."

"I'm so sorry about the McVeigh thing."

"It's ok. I needed to hear it. You're not drunk too, are you?"

"My face turns into a beet if I drink."

"Where's Doug?"

"He's in the kitchen making milled wine or something. I hope you don't mind me asking. This is so embarrassing." She giggled nervously. "But my parents, well, they want me to see if I could, possibly, you know, some way, do a summer internship with you, even for only a couple of weeks. If you say no, it's totally fine, obviously. The thing is they won't leave me alone about it since I told them I met you."

Sallie covered the microphone. "Give the kid a break. Let her walk your dog or something, that is, assuming, of course, you . . ."

"Yeah, sure. I owe you one. We'll talk."

"Really? Oh my God! Thank you. Here's Mr. Blackburn. Merry Christmas."

"Brandon, good wassail to you and yours. What can I do for you?"

"Sorry to bother, Doug. I need to clear my head about a couple of things. Did you tell those agents anything, ever, that I said in our client-lawyer conversations?"

"Of course not. That would constitute a serious breach of the code of ethics. I could be disbarred. Plus, it would be a downright rotten thing to do."

"That's what I thought. Did I say anything wrong when we met them?"

"What are you talking about? I didn't let you open your mouth. What's the problem? Something happened?"

"No, nothing. I keep thinking about that meeting. How did they know to do the surveillance?"

"Could be lots of ways. Somebody in the family gabbed, or they got a wiretap or a bug somewhere, or good old-fashioned tails."

"Right. I wanted to let you know I've decided for sure I don't want to help them."

"It's your decision, of course. I think their threats were pure bluff. They don't want to go after a celebrity on a wafer-thin perjury case, even if they had that much. But let's meet with my partner, the ex-prosecutor, to go over it all once more. Abundance of caution." Brandon held up open palms toward Sallie, who extended his lower lip toward his nose, his head bobbing like Bobby De Niro.

"That's fine, Doug, but I'm not changing my mind."

"Client's prerogative, Brandon. I hope you have a very Merry Christmas wherever you are."

"Same to you. Give my best to your wife and keep Alda away from the punch bowl."

Josh lowered the shotgun, and Rose planted a wet kiss on Brandon's lips. Sallie took the phone from him to make sure it was disconnected. "Sorry to make you go through that, kid. Tell you the truth, we thought the chances were pretty slim, but you know what they say about an ounce of prevention." He took Brandon's hand and pulled him out of the seat. "Hope you still got your appetite."

Josh slapped him on the back. "You just saved two birds with one phone, buddy boy."

"And one more thing," Sallie said. "Don't give up."

"Give up what?"

"Let's take a walk while they get back to the kitchen." Sallie led Brandon farther down the tunnel. "I want to show you my latest additions."

Sallie opened a door labeled "Food Processing." A long utility table topped with vacuum sealers and plastic bags of various sizes sat perpendicular to two massive units that looked like they belonged in a laundromat. "These new freeze dryers, they can each do over a ton of fruits and vegetables a year." Sallie opened a dryer porthole to show Brandon a rack of shiny stainless-steel food trays. "I already contracted with a produce guy upstate for next year's harvest. Gonna need a helluva lot more than an apple a day once the grid goes down." He gestured for Brandon to sit on a metal platform hand-truck. "The movie, Brandon. The original. Don't give up on making it. I gotta admit it's a pretty damn good book."

Brandon leaned back, bracing himself with straight arms. "But it's like a flamethrower in an oil refinery." He let his head drop and swivel.

"Bookstores are still selling thousands every year, aren't they? Hasn't exactly been outlawed?"

Brandon sat up to rub his temples. "I can't stop seeing McVeigh whenever I think of Holden Caulfield. You understand why it's so personal?"

Sallie sat next to him and patted his knee. "Sure I do. I'm not exactly unfamiliar with the malcontents. I also know, according to Wikipedia,

The Catcher in the Rye has sold sixty-five million copies. That means you got all kinds of types who love it—your priests, your junkies, boy scouts, perverts, probation officers, soldiers, your schoolteachers, tech billionaires, maybe even some goddamned FBI agents, if they actually read. From my point of view, two or three bad apples against sixty-five mill is as close to a sure thing as you're gonna get. Put it to you this way: Did it make you want to kill anybody?"

"No, of course not."

"Straightened you out. The complete opposite, correct?"

"That's right."

"You think you're the only one? Must've been thousands by now. Maybe more. You understand what I'm saying to you?"

"But, Sallie, nobody ever got killed over *The Grapes of Wrath* or *Huck Finn*."

"But maybe nobody ever got saved over them either. Not gonna find any stats for that one in your online databases. Feds sure as hell don't keep track of all the beefs I squashed with handshakes instead of black-jacks. Only thing they care about is the demerits. Problem is you got your wires all crossed up here. *The Catcher in the Rye*, it ain't like a detonator; it's the other way around. It's like antidote, or some kind of vaccine. You gonna stop making penicillin because a couple of kids once in a blue moon got an allergy for what's good for them? Forget about it." He elbowed Brandon's rib cage. "And you want to know why this particular cure works? I'm gonna let you in on a little secret and tell you why." He palmed the top of Brandon's head. "Brain surgery." Sallie shook Brandon's skull and stood up, pressing against him for leverage. "You got three pounds here of Grade-A veal between a couple of *orecchiette*." He pulled on his own lobes. "Which gives us what? The Holocaust, the A-bomb, *Don Giovanni*, the Sistine Chapel, and Joltin' Joe DiMaggio. What the fuck are we supposed to do with something capable of all that? It ain't no kidney bean. Most people feel better knowing they aren't the only ones confused, their noodles twisting with all kind of mixed-up thoughts, trying to make sense of what makes people tick. And another thing. Don't forget the kid's only sixteen. You're expecting a lot from him."

Brandon recalled Alda's insight. *". . . massively flawed, like all of us. He's nobody's hero. Heroic is the last thing anybody should call him."*

"The point is this kid got help and told his story, opened himself right the fuck up without hurting a flea. And I got more news for you. Think about it like this for a minute why don't you. Say a kid like Holden hits the used car lot for his first set of wheels. You imagine he's the type who's gonna buy his ride off of Mickey Hair Gel, some greasy shark with cuffs shot out of a shiny three-piece suit? Please, he'd want to bash that slickster's head in with a tire iron." Sallie snatched a broom from a corner and choked it up mid-shaft for a vigorous demonstration. "This kid, I guarantee it, buys his jalopy—some hunk of junk he doesn't even really want—off a stuttering slob with a clip-on and soaking wet armpit stains, some broken-down valise who keeps apologizing for screwing up all the facts and figures. You see where I'm going here?" Sallie stared at Brandon and hunched over to perch his chin atop the broom handle.

"Underdogs."

"Give the man a box of Cracker Jack." Sallie mimed a stadium vendor's overhand toss. "When you stop and actually think about what's coming down the pike, sooner or later, and I for one say sooner, we're all bucking the long odds. You found the upside in him, the hope, the compassion. So do most people." With a swift sweep forward, Sallie jabbed the broom brush against Brandon's shins. "My advice, keep driving toward the goal line. Like they taught me in economics class, inaction has got a lot more hidden costs."

"But what about the FBI?"

"They can only get you for lying, correct?"

"Right."

"So, what if you're not lying?"

"But I am."

"Not so fast." Sallie flipped the broom up to hold it horizontal in front of his chest, arms extended, like a martial arts stick fighter. "What if you make both pictures at the same time? That other one with the three nutjobs—Josh filled me in on what the papers left out—sounds pretty good if you ask me. Matter of fact, my opinion, you want a surefire blockbuster, find a way to get that Jodie Foster involved." He tossed the broom to Brandon.

"Jesus, I could make her the professor. She'd be perfect."

"That's what I'm talking about. Same places, same actors. It wouldn't cost you that much more to do both, and then Cagney and Lacey got no axe to grind."

"But once the trust finds out I'm making a classic." Brandon put the broomstick against the back of his neck and wrapped his arms over it to pillory himself.

Sallie slapped a hand on top of one of the freeze dryers. "I should've known better than to give a prop to an actor. Listen to what I'm trying to tell you. It's what they always say, 'Timing is everything.' You know why I bought these two? Dehydrating foods, that's a completely different process, it's only good for ten, fifteen years tops. But if you freeze dry, factory guarantees freshness for twenty-five. Matter of fact the installer told me truth is fruit like fresh strawberries is still gonna spill your spit glands even after a cool fifty."

"They'd taste the same?"

"Like you picked them yesterday. You following what I'm talking about?"

Brandon rose to his feet, now clutching the broom like Axel Jackstone might hold an M16 at inspection arms, shoulders back, chest out. "Not letting the strawberries go bad," he said, "but eating them later."

"Bull's-eye, soldier. I think you're noticing where I'm aiming. You know what they say. 'Strawberry fields forever.'"

23

The courtroom barely contained the standing-room-only crowd. Douglas, Ernest, and Brandon huddled at counsel table. Shari, Josh, Luis, Maeve, Alda, and Charlotte filled the row behind them. Agents Curran and Severini crouched in a back corner. The Catarrazzos stayed away, having expressed no interest in running into a swarm of microphones, or their friends from the Bureau. The pack of reporters brimmed with anticipation over the surprise status conference requested by the defendant to make a "major announcement that could lead to a disposition of the matter."

Douglas rose to speak first. "Your Honor, we are truly appreciative of the speedy accommodation."

"You should see my docket, Mr. Blackburn. It's more stuffed than a corned beef sandwich from Katz's. Anytime I've got the chance to trim the fat I throw on this frock and hit the bench."

"I would also like to thank the trust's counsel for making herself available on short notice."

"Duly noted, counselor. Ms. Ricciardi has the Court's appreciation as well." The judge lowered her glasses and surveyed the room. "Looks like we've all got our Raisinets and popcorn ready, Mr. Blackburn. The stage is yours."

"Your Honor, Mr. Newman would like to read a prepared statement, which will be filed with the court following the conclusion of this appearance."

"Please proceed."

Brandon wore a navy suit and a bright red tie. He could have been announcing his candidacy for political office. "Your Honor, opposing counsel, ladies and gentlemen." He looked over his shoulder to acknowledge the gallery. "I'm not used to having my back to the house, but rules are rules. As the Court is aware, it has long been my desire to produce and star in a faithful version of *The Catcher in the Rye*. I believe that it is a story worth telling and that Holden Caulfield, for all his faults and contradictions, is a character worth knowing. I feel, moreover, that I can bring unique insight into his charms and his weaknesses, his pain and his longing, and, most of all, his humanity, even more so than I had originally imagined. At present, the owner of the copyright, the Cornish Perpetual Literary Trust, forbids a movie based on the novel. My lawyer has advised me,' and I've got the best," he patted Douglas's back, "'that there is no way to break or circumvent that prohibition until the copyright runs out in 2046.

"'Ninety-five years seems too long to hold a monopoly on a creation that has been shared with the world since 1951. Parents have to let go of their children after only eighteen. Aristotle, Shakespeare, and Mozart, to name but a few, never had the benefit of a copyright, and their legacies are none the worse for wear. I've come to understand, however, that this court is in the wrong branch of government from which to seek reform of the intellectual property laws.

"'Despite the many advances in anti-aging medicine, I cannot credibly play the lead role at the age of fifty-six.'" Brandon couldn't resist playing to the crowd with a brief ad-lib. "Even Tom Cruise would be too old by then. Talk about your mission impossible." The gallery giggled politely. Douglas looked poised to stand. "I'm sorry, Your Honor, occupational reflex. Back to the script. 'I wish the trustees would relent and allow me to share my rendition of the novel with millions around the world, but I understand that their hands are tied by a legal rope kinked with lots of knots and not one loophole.

"'For this reason, I will shoot the movie outlined in my affidavit and detailed in the treatment submitted *ex parte* and under seal, a film which will be, I believe, an artistic critique of the novel, its enigmatic and frustrating author, and the tragic but few incidents of misinterpretation at the hands of the mentally ill. We hope to release the movie by Christmas of next year. Pursuant to that goal, we are, today, prepared to enter into the nondisclosure stipulation proposed by the trust and provide them with access to the treatment. It is defendant's position that this plot summary leaves no doubt whatsoever that the project rests solidly within the essential protections of both the fair use doctrine and the First Amendment.' My lawyer wrote that part. I'm always reading other people's lines." He glanced at the sketch artists, whose heads stayed down.

"'At the same time, in many of the same locations, and with some of the same actors, I also intend to film a classic version of *The Catcher in the Rye*. For this second movie, there will be no publicity whatsoever during production, and the cast and crew will be contractually prohibited from discussing the project. Perhaps most importantly, I am today announcing the creation of the Newman Cinematic Trust. This classic version, once completed, will be transferred to the trust's sole and irrevocable ownership. I will be its only trustee with my agent, Shari Mishkin, initially serving as my successor. Upon reaching the age of twenty-five, my lawyer's brilliant daughter and budding Salinger scholar, Esmeralda Blackburn, will replace Ms. Mishkin as my successor and serve as trustee in the event of my death or incapacity.

"'All copies of my *Catcher*, including outtakes, will be preserved in a special vault at the Museum of Television and Radio right here in New York City until the year 2046, when the late Mr. Salinger's monopoly expires. Then, and only then, will that film and a companion "making of" documentary be released in theaters nationwide.'" Brandon put down his statement. "Thank you, Your Honor." Douglas stood to shake his hand, and both men took their seats.

"Your Honor, on behalf of the trust, I can state that we are pleased Mr. Newman recognizes the validity and extent of the Salinger copyright, and we are relieved to finally have an opportunity to review the treatment of the film described, albeit sparsely, in the defendant's affidavit. Frankly, however, I don't see how this will lead to a disposition, even assuming the movie is as has been vaguely sketched. And, of course, we will be requesting additional time to submit a supplemental memorandum, once I've had the chance to confer with my clients regarding the filming of a classic version while the novel's copyright undisputedly remains in full force and effect."

"I think, Ms. Ricciardi, you might do well to take your winnings and leave the table while you're ahead. As you'll no doubt recall, this Court has had an opportunity to review the proposed contemporary production. I cannot see, in all candor, how you will succeed under the prevailing state of copyright and free speech law. What's more, after the last appearance, I don't have to remind you of the serious lack of justiciability, ripeness in particular, regarding a film not yet made, and *a fortiori*, as to a film not to be released for thirty years. In fact, if you were to continue to seek judicial relief given the current state of the case, I would have a serious obligation, under Rule 11 of the Federal Rules of Civil Procedure, to, *sua sponte,* consider whether sanctions against you and/or your firm for the maintenance of frivolous litigation might be in order. If, however, you sincerely believe your client wishes to challenge the present outcome, I'll grant you a very brief leave to submit your supplement; nonetheless, I strongly urge a candid chat with the corporate trustees about the wisdom of overplaying a hand. As I recall, your partner, Mr. Shapiro, is about as good at poker as he is at golf. You might want to seek his counsel as well."

"Of course, Your Honor, we will revisit the matter as you propose and advise the Court forthwith."

"I knew I liked you, Ms. Ricciardi. This matter is adjourned."

24

A week after the hearing, the trust withdrew its case against Brandon without prejudice to its ability to file a new complaint "should Mr. Newman deviate materially from the position taken in his last court filing." Shortly thereafter, Douglas, a life trustee at Darlingbrooke Hall, presented Brandon's request to film on campus. The school agreed immediately. Its administration welcomed the publicity surrounding Brandon's project in the wake of the recent, scandalous dismissal of the firearms instructor. An anonymous source had reported Monty's storage of an assault rifle on school property.

With the backing of a major Hollywood studio, Brandon had opted for a big-budget crew. In early February, he sat in the director's chair on the first day of filming while Luis, the director of photography, set up the next shot. They had moved one of the cannons from outside the ReFire shooting range to a hill overlooking the football field. A drone was to dive in from high behind Holden, standing alone, and then slowly execute a 360-degree sweep. With Brandon staring off into the distance—the script called for a "wistful and bemused gaze"—the audience was to hear the book's opening internal monologue, a voice-over explaining the ground rules for how he would tell his story.

"Here you are, Brandon. Two sugars and almond milk." Charlotte handed him the coffee and asked if he needed anything else. Rudy Dunbar, wearing a neon yellow jacket with "SECURITY" in black letters across the back, stood nearby, clutching a walkie-talkie and reading the *New York Post*.

"Let me see that," Brandon said. He had been craning his neck to skim articles in Rudy's paper. A bold headline caught his attention. "Mob Muscle Makes Bad Bet." Below it a crime scene photo showed a corpse covered with a white sheet under a pier. He thought about James Castle, the boy who died after falling from a window at Elkton Hills. After lunch, a stuntman wearing Holden's sweater would be tumbling out of Alda's dorm room.

"The body of Vincent 'Skinny Vinny' DiBiasi, 24, of Gravesend, was found early yesterday morning by a jogger on Brighton Beach. He was shot twice in the back of the head. Law enforcement sources say DiBiasi had been an associate of the South Brooklyn family and served as personal protection for its reputed boss, Salvatore 'Sallie Choo Choo' Catarrazzo. Those same sources told the *Post* that DiBiasi had run up a debt to Russian bookmakers in the hundreds of thousands of dollars. Mafia watchers speculate the Russian mob wouldn't have killed DiBiasi without first getting permission from Catarrazzo. 'It would be seen as highly disrespectful to take out a boss's bodyguard without his blessing,' said one retired NYPD detective. 'The Russians wouldn't risk starting a war over a bookmaking debt.' The investigation is being conducted by a joint NYPD/FBI organized crime task force."

Brandon flashed back to the look Sallie had given Josh and Rose in the bunker's home theater on Christmas Eve, right after he told them Agent Curran had been waiting in the alley that night outside Josh's bar. It was an "I smell a rat" look. The newspaper pages began to flutter as his hands shook with comprehension. Sallie must have planted that gambling debt cover story on the streets. Brandon turned away from Alda, who had taken over camera duties for the documentary, and told her to stop filming. He wanted to text Josh, or Rose, hoping to clear his conscience, but he knew from the movies, and from recent experience, to stay off the phones. Even if he were to ask in person, his questions had the potential to end a close friendship, imperil a promising relationship, or worse. Don't ask, don't tell.

Brandon's stomach churned. His eyes misted. He'd said more than he had to on Christmas Eve. He had to admit the FBI's approach, but did he have to mention their surveillance? And in such detail? The panicked, self-serving confession, though honest and accurate, had likely gotten Vincent murdered, whether or not he had really been a turncoat.

Brandon knew exactly what Salinger would be thinking at that moment—words, even when you're only trying to tell the truth, can still get somebody killed.

He would remember Vincent joking about *The Godfather* and smirking in that goofy "Christmas Goose" sweater. He might even cry, thinking about all the empty chairs at the wake, the rent-a-priest giving a plain vanilla eulogy for a kid he didn't know, recycling worn-out lines about the tragedy of dying young. He would drive to the cemetery, staying in his car for the burial. But, on another day, a sunny morning with nobody around, he might lay flowers at Vincent's grave.

"We're ready for you, Brandon."

"Who?"

"You, we're ready for you."

He stood up from his chair. The crew, the equipment, the extras, everything was in place, waiting. He wiped coffee from his lips, slapped the rolled-up newspaper into Rudy's stomach, and took his place beside the cannon.

"Action."

ACKNOWLEDGMENTS

I am deeply indebted to so many for their interest, support, suggestions, corrections, and patience. Pride of authorship has, in my experience, little to do with the real work of telling a story, and it is vastly less important than the story itself and the sharing of that story with others. Ecclesiastes long ago taught us that we are at best filters for what flows downstream. I have been influenced profoundly by voices big and small, distant and near, from the works of Shakespeare to the fragments of teenaged conversations overheard on the subway.

I am particularly grateful to Woodhall Press for, once again, choosing to publish one of my books. I especially want to thank Chris Madden, my wise, kind, and careful editor, for believing in this book and what it could be.

I must also thank two professors from my MFA program for their invaluable assistance. Hollis Seamon, my mentor and friend, gave me encouraging and indispensable comments on the early drafts. In the later stages, the poet (and novelist) Baron Wormser helped to shape the final version of the novel.

I also had the benefit of honest critiques from several early readers: Jeffrey von Kohorn, Ph.D., Nathaniel Basch-Gould, Nicolas Bourtin, Hayley Battaglia, and Paull Goodchild.

Thanks also to Alan J. Kaufman, Esq. for his careful legal review.

My final and deepest thanks go to my wife and daughters for their love and encouragement. It simply means everything.

About the Author

Before earning an MFA in fiction writing, Tom Seigel was Chief of the Justice Department's Organized Crime Strike Force in Brooklyn. He's prosecuted mob bosses, corrupt cops, murderers, and even an NBA referee. His first novel, The Astronaut's Son, was a medalist in the 2018 *Foreword Reviews* Book of the Year Awards and a finalist for the 2019 Connecticut Book of the Year. About his debut, *Publishers Weekly* praised: "Equally strong on plotting and characterization, Seigel does better than many other thriller writers in making his lead's pain and uncertainty about the past palpable." *Mensa Bulletin* raved the book would "keep you on the edge of your seat all the way through." Tom lives with his family in Connecticut.